No $imple LIE

A
MCQUAID BROTHERS
NOVEL

samantha christy

Saint Johns, FL 32259

Cover designed by Coverluv

Cover model photo by WANDER AGUIAR

Cover model – Matheus R.

No $imple
LIE
A
MCQUAID BROTHERS
NOVEL

Samantha Christy

Chapter One

Hudson

Depositing my gift on the table at the front of the restaurant, I walk over to Mom, lean in, and plant a kiss on her cheek. "Happy birthday."

"Thanks, sweetie." She smiles brightly. "I'm so happy all my kids could be here tonight."

I raise a brow and look around the restaurant. "Holland is here?"

"In the back with Addy."

"You mean Holland's drillmaster boss actually let her leave the city for the night?"

"I hear her boss isn't the only one who runs a tight ship." Mom gives me a hard look. "Nurses talk, Hudson. You should go easy on them. You don't want to go getting a bad reputation as someone who's hard to work with. Especially when you're already known as a man who's hard to…" She goes quiet and shakes her head.

"Hard to what, Mom?"

"You're not actually going to make me say it, are you?"

"One: I'm not a hardass boss. I *just* became an attending. I have to prove myself, especially given my age. I like things done right, is all. If that's wrong then sue me. And two: just because I don't want to settle down with one woman and have a gaggle of snotty-nosed kids doesn't make me a deplorable person."

"Tell that to the three women in the booth over there who've been staring daggers at you for the last five minutes."

I turn to see Lynda Graves, Elsa Truman, and—I have to think hard on it—Krista or Kristin something or other, all watching me like I kidnapped their children and sold them for parts. I roll my eyes. "I thought this was a private party."

"I didn't want them to turn away any paying customers just for little old me."

I watch Cooper Calloway, one of the managers here at Donovan's Pub, deliver drinks to the brooding trio. He stops to wish my mother a happy birthday on his way back. Then he holds his hand out to me. I chuckle as I shake, knowing that not even a year ago, Cooper and his brothers, Tag and Jaxon, were the archenemies of my brothers and me. We grew up hating each other for sport because of a bet made by our ancestors. "Hey, man, what's up?"

He tosses a look over his shoulder. "Might want to steer clear of that side of the room."

"Noted," I say as he hurries off to another table.

A hand claps my shoulder. I turn to see Hunter holding his two-month-old son, Myles—the baby I personally delivered. And although I never plan to have children of my own, I'm happy being an uncle to his. Next to Hunter is our oldest brother, Hawk, holding twenty-month-old Rivi.

Mom fawns over their kids as she does all the children here. Being a grandmother, aunt, mom, and stepmom is her entire life. The baby starts fussing, and Mom takes him just as her husband, Jonah Calloway—the man she left our father for (enter another reason we hated the Calloways)—comes up next to us.

"Heather, my love, what do you think?" he says, his eyes bouncing between both kids. "Do you think we should have another one of these?"

She giggles. "I'm flattered you still see me as someone young enough to do that."

He kisses her cheek. "You look twenty-nine to me."

"Get a room," Hawk says jokingly.

Jonah laughs. "We might just do that."

Dani, my fourteen-year-old half-sister, butts in, saving us all from the rest of that conversation. "Mom, have you seen the pile of presents? It's huge."

Mom doesn't bother looking at the gift table, but her eyes sweep the rest of the room. "I'm very fortunate to have a lot of family and friends, aren't I? Speaking of that, I'd better go make the rounds." She hands Myles off to me. Not back to Hunter. *Me.*

I'm so tired of this shit. I get it. I'm the third and youngest McQuaid brother. The only one who hasn't been broken, bribed, and manipulated by our rich-as-shit grandfather, Tucker. What nobody seems to get is that I won't be. I can't be. I'm different. I have a career I love and no desire to end up pussy-whipped like my brothers.

"Well, would you look at this," a stilted feminine voice sneers behind me. "Hudson McQuaid holding a baby, looking like a perfect little family man when we all know he's nothing more than a lying, cheating, pig."

I turn to see Krista, or Kristin, or whoever, glaring at me. Her two friends stand in solidarity behind her, arms crossed as if going to battle. I hand Myles off to his dad. "Listen, Krista."

Lynda steps forward. "It's Krystal, you bastard. How easily you forget the name of the woman you cheated on me with."

"You're kidding, right? First off, we weren't in a relationship, Lynda. We fucked. And secondly, if you're so pissed about it, what are you doing here with her? She was obviously a willing participant."

"We didn't know each other very well until it happened," Krystal says. She locks arms with the other two. "We're all friends now. Along with Julianne Hubbard, Olivia Madsen, Linney Granger—"

"What the hell?" I say, hearing her run off a list of the women I've slept with. "Have you formed a club or something?"

"Or something," Elsa says, getting in my face.

Elsa is gorgeous with a banging hot body that's difficult to forget. She's a former patient of mine, as are some of the others mentioned. Which means I know her very well, inside and out. Okay, so yeah, technically I shouldn't go around screwing former patients. But being one of about six OB/GYNs in Calloway Creek, I'd have to rule out a shit ton of women if I didn't. I'm not stupid. I've never propositioned a patient. And I don't actively seek them out. But there's nothing wrong with me hooking up with them if they've moved on to another doctor. Which, okay, I may have suggested they do once or twice before boning them so I wouldn't get brought up on charges after.

Elsa smells like oranges. She did back then, too. Must be something she washes her hair with. My dick twitches when I close my eyes and remember that smell as she sucked me off. Oh, that mouth. It's one for the books.

My eyes fly open when she slaps my face, the sting of it turning a happy memory to exasperation.

"What the hell did you do that for?" I yell.

I don't miss the fact that my brothers have taken the children across the room, and that the place has gone silent.

"We're boycotting you, Hudson McQuaid."

"Boycotting me? So you really have started a club." I laugh and rub my cheek. "What's it called, the *I fucked Hudson and now I'm sad he won't marry me and give me all his money* club?"

Another slap heats up my face.

"Jesus." I step back, out of range. "It's not like I led any of you on. You knew the score. I don't do relationships. Get over yourselves already."

Lynda sidles up next to Elsa. "You're going to be hard pressed to find a woman in this town who will fall for your misplaced charm, Hudson. It's a small town. By the time we're done, your balls will be so blue, the only thing you'll be fucking is your right hand."

"Now, see—that's where you're wrong. I'm left-handed."

Chuckles come from behind me. Probably from my brothers.

The three women turn in unison and walk out of the restaurant. Who do they think they are, butting in on Mom's birthday and laying into me like that? They're the ones with the problem, not me. Every chick in this town knows I'm not looking for a wife, a girlfriend, or even a long-term lover. And they may think they come off as high and mighty, but everyone knows all they really want is a meal ticket. They know who I am, what I come from, and how much money sits in my trust fund. And they're just pissed their name isn't on it too.

I, for one, know the numbers in said fund are enough to lure a lot of girls away from their so-called 'club' and into my arms, even if only for a night. Because sooner or later, they all think they could be the one to land me. Especially since my brothers, who were also certified bachelors, have both recently been 'landed.'

Finally, the silence is broken when Hawk's fiancée, Addy, and my sister, Holland, come out from the back holding a cake with a crap ton of candles aflame on top. The whole place breaks out in an off-key version of 'Happy Birthday.' Everyone in the entire restaurant is singing. Everyone but me and one other person.

Pappy stares me down from across the room, his eighty-six-year-old eyes boring into me. I curse the three girls who left, knowing they're the reason he's not going to leave until he opens a can of whoop ass and pours it all over my goddamn head.

~ ~ ~

Mom thanks everyone for their presence and their generosity and people start filing out the door. My brothers and I are carrying her gifts to the car when a sound coming from the shadows makes me physically gag. It's the distinct phlegmy sound only a really old man can make when clearing his throat. And I know I'm being watched, scrutinized, and judged by my older-than-dirt grandfather.

"Here it goes," Hunter says, standing back and leaning against Jonah's SUV.

Hawk settles next to him, an amused look on his face.

I put the last of the gifts in the trunk and shake my head at them. "Both of you can fuck off."

Hunter holds up his hands. "Hey, I'm just here for the show."

"There isn't going to be any *show*," I huff. "I'm not like you sorry saps. I won't be manipulated into doing shit for that fossil."

Both of them just stare as footsteps approach me from behind.

"Hudson," Pappy says. "A word?"

I thumb to my car. My sleek red Maserati parked at the end of the row so it doesn't get dinged by any of the cut-rate used cars in this sleepy little town. "Actually, I've got to get going."

"Someone waiting on you?" he asks. "A date perhaps."

I don't bother answering. We both know he's posturing. My grandfather is old and well past his prime, yet he can somehow command all the attention in every room. Some would say he earned respect by building his empire from the ashes left by his father. I say it's because he's richer than God and people bow to money like it's a deity.

"Why don't we head back inside," he says. "I'll buy you a scotch."

"I'm on call tonight."

"Well, then, I'll buy you a club soda."

"I need to go home and get in a few hours of sleep."

"In the morning then. I'll come by your house. I'll bring breakfast."

"Like I said, Pappy, I'm on call. I'll most likely not even be there. Whatever you have to say, say it now."

He looks over my shoulder at my brothers. I just know they're holding in laughter waiting to hear what ultimatum I'm about to be given. A threat of disinheritance. A bribe maybe. Something to make me fall in line and become a better person.

Our grandfather is a hypocrite. He was a lying, cheating husband until well into his seventies. Yet now he stands here and pretends like none of that meant anything because he's somehow been reformed. And he thinks all of his descendants need to be like him. Well, maybe not all. I never see him wasting time on my father. Could be he thinks he's a lost cause. Or maybe it's because Dad already has a good share of Pappy's money. Maybe he thinks since he still controls my trust fund he controls me too. Well, think again, old timer.

"I was just thinking what an embarrassment it must have been for Heather when those women confronted you."

"Mom didn't even notice."

"Oh, she noticed, boy. And the look on her face said everything. You claim you want to be a highly respected physician, yet you treat women the way you do. The two can't go hand in hand, Hudson."

"What I do in my private life is not your concern."

He steps closer, the white whiskers of his wiry beard poke at my ear. "Everything you do concerns me, boy," he grumbles.

"What are you going to do, Pappy? Cut me off? Blackmail me like you did my brothers? It isn't going to work. You can't banish me to the city with a few thousand dollars—I have a job. You can't force me to raise a kid—because, oh, wait… I don't have one. You can threaten to take away my trust fund, but we all know when it comes down to it you won't really do it. And, come on, I'm your only grandson who's even done something worthwhile with my life. I graduated from college early. Got through med school on an accelerated program. I'm twenty-eight fucking years old and am an attending physician. I'm like the golden child. So I like women. In the overall scheme of things, is it really that bad that I only choose to like them for an hour or two at a time?"

He gathers the material on the front of my shirt with his fist. "Watch your tone around me, boy. I may be old, but I'm not above giving you a whoopin'."

My pager goes off. Pappy releases my shirt, and I smooth it down before fishing my pager out of my pocket. I smirk as I hold it up to him. "I guess you could say I'm saved by the bell. Duty calls."

"We're not done," he says with a curl of his lip. "We're not nearly done."

"Let me save you the trouble, Pappy. We *are* done. I am who I am, and if that's not good enough for you, then take your damn trust fund back. I'm making good money. I've got the house, my car, my family, my investments. I'll be rich enough without you or your money."

As I start to walk away, I see the fire in his eyes simmer. It's a look I rarely see from the great Tucker McQuaid. It reeks of defeat.

And I know I've won.

Chapter Two

Dakota

The judge looks directly at me when he delivers his decision. That must be good, right?

"I hereby approve the petition for guardianship of Travis Daniels to Wayne and Patricia Daniels. As for you, Ms. Daniels, I'm granting you visitation rights with the lad every other Saturday, though they will be supervised by one of the appointed guardians or someone designated as their representative."

When his gavel comes down onto the wooden desk, it may as well be smashing my heart. Because as I sit here, stunned at how my son has just been taken away from me, I'm in pieces.

The courtroom is abuzz as I turn and look at my lawyer, Larry Silverton, through pools of tears. "How is this possible? You said it was unlikely. How can they do this?"

An empathetic hand lands on my arm. "Unlikely but not impossible. We can appeal, Dakota."

"When? When can we appeal?"

"We have thirty days. I'll appeal on the grounds of the judge abusing his discretion. He clearly never should have been on this case. He went to law school with your father-in-law. He should have recused himself. I believe we can win the appeal on that alone."

"Thirty days?" My heart sinks into the pit of my stomach. "I have to go thirty days without having custody of my son?"

Larry looks green around the gills. "That's just how long we have to file the appeal. Dakota, you have to understand, appealing a family law case is a marathon, not a sprint. It could take up to a year to go before the court."

My knees go weak, and I want to vomit. My whole body shakes. "A year? He's only four. He'll f-forget me," I stutter. "He needs me, Larry. This is w-wrong. How is this happening? How can they take him away from me?" I look over at Wayne and Patty. Through blurred vision, I see Patty glance my way. She can't even look me in the eye. She knows this is bullshit. I stand and plow over. "How can you do this? You know I'm a good mother. You *know* it! Brian never would have wanted this. He loved Travis. He loved me. You saw us together. How can you be so cruel?" I swallow and say the words I swore I never would. "He's not even your grandson."

Wayne looks at me in disgust. "You'll say anything, won't you?" He snaps his fingers at the bailiff. "Can we get security in here?"

Larry pulls me away. "This is not how you want to start the appeal process. Being held for disorderly conduct in a courtroom will not bode well."

"It's true," I plead. "Travis isn't theirs."

He takes my elbow, leading me away from the bailiff who's getting closer. "Walk away, Dakota. We'll talk outside."

He guides me out the door of the courtroom as dozens of eyes watch. Only one set of eyes shows any hint of sympathy. Benji, my dead husband's brother, is shaking his head. He knows this is wrong.

"Benji!" I call out. "Talk to them. Please. Help me get Travis back. I'm begging you—"

The doors to the courtroom close behind me after Larry bulldozes me through. He takes me by the shoulders. "You have to stop with the emotional outbursts. Every one of them can be held against you."

I laugh maniacally. "You want me to stop begging for my son's life? You expect me to sit back and accept the fact that my son—the baby I carried for nine months, fed from my breast for eighteen more, bandaged every cut, kissed away every tear, and read to sleep every night—has just been ripped away from the one person left who loves him." I point behind me. *They* don't love him. All they want is a piece of Brian, which isn't even what they're getting. What I said is true. Travis isn't their grandchild. He's just someone they want to manipulate into being another twisted version of themselves. Hurting me in the process is just a bonus. They didn't like me from day one. It was all a lie, Larry. They lied about me to get custody. How can they get away with that?"

"The hope is they won't. Not in the long run. But you have to trust the process. And first, you have to tell me everything about Travis. If you're being honest about his lineage, why on earth didn't you tell me this before? It would have saved you this heartache."

I look at the ground, feeling like I'm betraying Brian in the worst way. "I promised Brian I'd never tell anyone. He was ashamed he couldn't get me pregnant. He felt he would come off as less of a man. And he was sure his parents would never welcome me into the family if I was pregnant with a child that wasn't his." I wipe a tear and look up. "But Larry, you all but guaranteed me no judge would take a child away from a loving mother."

Oh, God. Why didn't I tell him sooner? Why did I put so much blind faith in my belief in the system? Why didn't I foresee this? It's *them*. They'll stop at nothing to ruin me—the person who took their son away.

"Still, you should have told me, Dakota. I can only do my absolute best for you if I have all of the relevant information. We have our work cut out for us now. Even with this new information, it doesn't change the fact that they've been awarded guardianship. It just means we have more grounds for appeal. But you'll have to prove it. I assume you can get the evidence?"

I shrug. "Brian made all the arrangements. Knowing him, he burned the records. He never wanted anyone to know Travis wasn't his biological son."

He sighs. "Well, then, we'll focus on getting a court order for Travis, Wayne, and Patty to submit to a paternity test. If they are blood relatives, it will show. But, Dakota, I'm warning you, they have the best attorneys in the city working for them. They'll think you're bluffing. They'll delay as long as they can. Throw up every roadblock imaginable. And it may become extremely personal and even more hostile before the end." He looks down at his phone and reads a text. "We're to wait out front on the steps. They'll get Travis from the social worker and bring him out where you can say goodbye."

I slump against the wall. "How do I do that? How do I say goodbye to him? He won't understand. He'll think I'm abandoning him. How do I explain to a four-year-old that his corrupt grandparents manipulated the system and now he has to go and live with them?" My chin quivers. "He doesn't even have Charlie."

"Charlie?"

"His frog. It's the last thing Brian ever gave him. He loves that stupid overstuffed bullfrog. He can't sleep without it."

"We'll figure out a way to get it to him. He'll need his clothes and other things."

I shake my head and look at the ground. "They won't want them. They won't want him to have anything I got for him. What they want is to erase me." I clutch my heaving stomach and look out the window. "How can I say goodbye?"

"Come on. Let's get you some fresh air."

Out on the steps, I attempt to make myself presentable. Surely I must look hideous. Puffy face, streaked mascara. I get out my compact, wet a finger and run it under my eyes. Then I powder my cheeks and apply a light coat of my favorite pink lipstick. But my efforts are wasted. I still look like death warmed over.

The Daniels emerge from the courthouse with their team of three lawyers. They spot me and walk in the other direction, standing as far away from me as they can get. Brian's siblings, Bethany and Benji, dutifully stand behind them, though Benji is clearly distraught by the judgment. He was always on my side. Brian's side. The problem is, he's never had the guts to stand up for us. While the rest of them avoid eye contact, Benji looks at me with a sad smile. He mouths *I'm sorry.*

I turn away, not able to look at someone who could have possibly made a difference, but chose not to speak up for fear of repercussions. That makes him as bad as they are in my book.

Larry nods to the door. "Here he comes."

My heart stops as I figure out what I'm going to say to him. Will I even be allowed to speak to him privately? *Oh my God—how is this my life now?*

"Travis, sweetie, we're over here," Patty says.

My son looks at Patty, her arms outstretched as if he's supposed to lovingly skip into them, then he scans the steps at the front of the courthouse until he sees me. "Mommy!"

He runs over to me as I fall to his level, my knees hitting the unforgiving concrete as I sweep him into my arms. "Baby."

I pull him close, wondering if I hold him tightly enough they won't be able to get him away. I smell him, wanting to remember his sweet boy scent. I run a hand across his dark floppy hair, needing to chronicle every bit of him for the time we're apart.

"Mommy, you're squishing me."

"I'm sorry, baby. I just love you so much I don't ever want to let you go."

"I love you too, Mommy."

I close my eyes and let those words etch themselves into my memory.

Footsteps fall behind Travis. Then a traitorous voice bellows, "We must be going. We have lunch plans."

I look up into the cold, hard, steely eyes of Brian's father. "Give me a minute, Wayne."

He melodramatically checks his fifty-thousand-dollar watch. "You've got two, then we're leaving." His eyes follow a tear that's running down my cheek. He scoffs. "It's not like you won't see him again. Next Saturday is only ten days away. Stop disgracing yourself."

"Do you mind?" I say through gritted teeth.

"You heard the judge. I have the right to supervise your interactions with the boy."

"*The boy* has a name." I turn my back to Wayne and gather Travis in my arms again. "Travis, baby." I start to choke up but know I need to say these important words. Because what I say right now might stay with him forever.

I was stupid not to prepare him for this possibility. But I never really thought it would happen. Through all my research, and from everything Larry told me, I found that the court likes to keep children with their parents when at all possible. I was sure they would see right through the Daniels' false claims. I was sure they would see the bond Travis and I have when we met with the judge privately. I was sure they would see I'm a good person and not who the enemy made me out to be.

I was so sure that I did nothing. I said nothing. And now I have two minutes to explain to a four-year-old that he won't be sleeping in his own bed tonight. And that his mother, who has sat on that bed reading his favorite story for the thousandth time, because he loves "The Frog Prince" almost as much as he loves Charlie, won't be there. And that tomorrow morning he won't have waffles with meticulously placed blueberries in each crevice, whip cream hair, and syrup drizzled over the top in a smiley face.

"Mommy, why are you sad?"

I can't tell him what I really want to tell him. That he's going to be a prisoner in a castle. That he's going to be raised by servants and pretentious grandparents, who not only aren't his blood relatives, but who think the world should cater to their every whim. That the people who've been appointed to raise him are monsters. I can't tell him any of it because of who's standing five feet away.

I swallow the huge lump in my throat and pray I have the courage to get through this. "Travis, you're going to go on an adventure."

"What kind of adventure?"

"Well, you're going to live in a mansion. Do you know what that is? It's a very big house. Maybe even fifty times the size of our apartment. You went there a few times when you were a baby, but

I doubt you'll remember it. It's so big you might even get lost. So be careful."

"But you'll find me. Right, Mommy?"

"Oh, baby. I'd like to go with you, but I can't."

He frowns. "Why not?"

"There is a man called a judge who wants you to live with Grandma and Grandpa for a while."

"Are you going away?"

"No, baby. I'll be right here. In fact, I'll come visit you every other Saturday. So I'll see you in ten days. Do you remember how many that is?"

He holds up his hands and counts his fingers.

"That's right, my smart smart boy."

Wayne clears his throat behind me, a reminder that I'm no longer in control. Of Travis. Of my life. Of my emotions. He's about to take everything from me.

I pull Travis in close. "I love you. I love you more than the moon and the stars. I love you more than any mommy has ever loved any son—do you know that?"

"I know, Mommy. You tell me every day."

"And I still will." I crane my head around. "I can talk to him, right? You'll let me call and say goodnight?"

Wayne shrugs one shoulder. "If it fits into our schedule."

My chest heaves. I know exactly what that means. I lean in and whisper in Travis's ear. "I love you, baby. Remember those words. Remember them even if you can't hear me say them. Remember this hug. Because even if I'm not there to tuck you in, I'll be hugging you. I'll be in bed at our apartment, and I'll hug my pillow. And you'll be in bed at Grandma and Grandpa's, and you'll hug your pillow, and it'll be like we're hugging each other. Promise me, Travis. Promise me we'll hug every night."

"What about Charlie?"

I turn to Wayne. "He wants his stuffed frog. It means a lot to him."

"I'll send someone to pick it up. *Just* the frog. He won't be needing anything else."

"See?" I say to Travis, conjuring up the best smile I can. "Charlie will be with you. So hug him and hug your pillow, and you'll be hugging me. And I'll be hugging you, baby. I promise."

"It's time," Wayne says. "Come, Travis." He holds out his hand and Travis takes it.

Wayne and Patty aren't strangers to him. I've allowed them to see him often, just not in their territory. I allowed it even when I knew they were trying to take him away. It wasn't fair to Travis to keep him from Brian's family, especially since I have none. I was hoping eventually they'd come around and see how good we are for each other. It's a mistake I'd like to regret but can't. If I'd kept them from him, he'd be going with a stranger. At least he knows them. But that doesn't keep my heart from breaking as they walk away.

Travis turns as he's being pulled along. "Mommy, aren't you coming?"

The tears I've held inside start flowing. He's only four. He doesn't fully understand what's happening. That we won't see each other every day.

"No, baby, I can't. You have to go with them. I'll see you in ten days. I promise. And I promise we'll be together again soon. Don't forget I love you."

He rips his hand away from Wayne's and runs back to me. I welcome one last hug as we both cry into each other. "Mommy, come with me."

"I wish I could. You have no idea how much I wish I could." I don't let him go as I turn to Wayne. "Maybe I could come too. Live in the guest quarters, just to make the transition easier."

His head shakes slowly back and forth. "That's just not possible. Come, Travis."

Travis holds onto me for dear life. "I don't want to go, Mommy. I want to stay here with you."

"I want that too, baby. But it's not my decision."

Wayne forcibly removes my arms from around Travis. "Time's up. Do I need to fetch the judge?"

A hand lands on my shoulder. "Dakota, it has to be this way," Larry says.

Travis is pulled away, kicking and screaming. "Mommy! Mommy, I don't want to go!"

I stand and try to follow, but Larry holds me back.

"Travis!" I yell. "I will never stop fighting to be with you every day. Do you hear me? I'll never stop fighting."

"Oh, stop creating a scene," Patty scoffs from the other side of the steps. "Have some dignity."

"Mommy!"

Travis tries to escape Wayne's grip. I can only imagine Wayne is holding his hand so hard it probably hurts. And that makes my heart break even further, knowing my son is going with a man who doesn't care who gets hurt as long as he gets his way.

"Travis! I love you!" I fall back to my knees, hoping, praying with every last shred of my soul that Wayne and Patty will see what this is doing to us and reconsider. "I love you, baby."

"Mommy!" His shouts become strained and weaker the farther away he gets. He's picked up by Wayne, and he looks at me over the monster's shoulder. "Mommy! Don't go."

"Travis! I love you. I love you. I love you." I chant the words until they disappear around the corner. Then I crumble into a ball on the steps of the largest courthouse in the city and let out a guttural scream. It's a scream of utter devastation. Of complete ruin. Of absolute, indescribable pain.

I'm broken.

They've broken me.

And I want to die.

But the only reason I won't go home and slit my wrists is the forty-pound piece of my heart that was just dragged away. And I know right here, right now, that I would sell my soul to get him back.

When I finally look around, people are staring. I wasn't aware a crowd had gathered. But that's the least of my worries. I wipe my face of tears and snot and look up at Larry. "Today. I want to file the appeal today. I don't want to be away from him for a second longer than necessary."

"Those take time, Dakota. I can't just march in there and say you want to appeal. There are steps to be taken, a brief needs to be filed. And…"

His hesitation tells me I'm not going to like what I hear next. "And what? Just tell me. It's not like it'll be any worse than what just happened."

"And there's the matter of settling the bill."

Right. I close my eyes. I'm on a payment plan. My credit cards are maxed out. I have zero savings. And Larry was the only lawyer I could afford.

"I've made every payment, Larry. You know I'm good for it."

"My firm won't take on the appeal until the previous bill is paid in full."

"But that's, oh my God, Larry, that's almost ten thousand. I can't come up with that today, let alone in thirty days."

"I'm sorry. My hands are tied. See what you can do. Maybe you can sell something."

"Short of selling my body, there's nothing I have of any value."

"Maybe you can take out a loan."

My eyes meet the ground. "Yeah, sure. I'll look into it." But I know I can't. I already tried. I have too much debt as it is. "Larry, please, if there is anything…"

He nods in the direction my in-laws went. "There are a lot of people just like them, Dakota. People who don't care about others, only about what's in it for them. And unfortunately, that's exactly the kind of people I work for." He glances at his watch. "I'm sorry. I have a hearing to get to. Call me if you figure things out."

"Larry, please," I beg as he walks away.

He turns. "I'm sorry, Dakota. I wish you the best of luck. I really do."

Then he's gone. And I'm alone. Alone and crying and pathetic, unsure of what I do next. Do I just go home to my empty apartment? Do I try to find another lawyer who will take pity on me and work for free going up against the Daniels' high-priced lawyers? Do I sit here until I wither away?

"Miss?" someone says in a gruff, grumbly voice.

I look up into the wrinkled face of an old, distinguished-looking man wearing a suit.

He holds out his hand. "It looks like you could use a cup of coffee."

"Are you a lawyer trolling for cases? Because if you are, I'm the last person you should be talking to. I can't afford a cup of coffee at this point, let alone the bill to file an appeal to get my son back."

"Well then, it looks like the coffee will be on me."

"Why would you do that? You don't even know me."

"Because if I'm not mistaken, I believe I may have just witnessed the worst moment of your life. And because it really looks like you could use a friend."

He's right. And I have a friend. Heidi. My one and only friend who tried her very best to get back from California for today's hearing but got delayed in Denver due to snow. It highlights even more how pathetic I am, having no family and one friend who couldn't even be here. And this man is right. It's the worst day of my life. Even worse than the day Brian died. Because at least back then, I still had a part of Brian. I had his son. Now I have nothing.

"But you're—"

"Three times your age and a complete stranger?"

"Well… yes."

He offers me his hand again. "Tucker McQuaid. I'm from Calloway Creek. I live with the world's finest woman who makes me a better man every time I look at her. I have four grandchildren about your age. And it kills me to think if any of them were ever in a situation like yours, that nobody would be so kind as to stop and help. And I take my coffee with a splash of cream."

I try to smile but can't. Still, I let him help me up. He's old. In his eighties most likely, but handsome nonetheless. And strong. "Dakota Daniels. I'm from right here in New York City. My husband died two years ago, and his parents have wanted custody of my son ever since. Today…" I hiccup and swallow. "Today they finally got it."

"I can see that. So about that coffee?" He nods to a guy ten feet behind him. "Benny will take us wherever you want to go."

"Uh, yeah, Mr… McQuaid is it?" I snatch my hand away from his. "No offense, but you could be a human trafficker preying on a poor, defenseless woman. My day is bad enough without being kidnapped and sold into slavery. I think I'll pass."

He chuckles. "Ms. Daniels, I'm an eighty-six-year-old man. I'm no threat to you. Believe me. But I understand your hesitation. We'll walk then. There must be a coffee place around here."

There are four of them. Unfortunately I know this because of all my visits here. "There's one a block that way." I point. "But, really, I'm fine. There's no need."

"Oh, I'd say there's a need alright. No one in your shoes should have to be alone right now. You're down on your luck and in need of a friend. Perhaps I can help on both accounts."

"You can't help. No one can. Not unless you're some kind of fairy godfather."

He cackles. "You never know, it could be your lucky day."

"Nothing about this day is lucky."

"My apologies. Poor choice of words. How about you tell me how unlucky you are over coffee and a sandwich?"

As if on cue, my stomach grumbles. I was far too anxious to eat this morning, or even last night. I'm so hungry I feel faint. And this man is right. I really don't want to be alone. Or shouldn't. Either way, part of me is grateful for the kindness of a stranger. And for a lack of other possibilities, I decide to accept his invitation. I nod. "Okay."

"Splendid." He holds his elbow out for me.

It feels awkward and old school, but I take it. Something about him makes him seem like a protector. And even though I don't know him, I feel a sense of safety. Then again, I could be way off, and he really is a human trafficker. I thought there was no way in hell I'd lose custody of Travis. I obviously misjudge many things in my life. I hope I'm not misjudging him. Because I really could use a friend, even a geriatric one.

The man behind him walks over. "Where to, Mr. McQuaid?"

"The lovely Ms. Daniels and I will be walking, Benny. I'll call you when we're finished."

"As you wish, sir."

"Dakota," I say. "Call me Dakota."

"And you may call me Tucker."

~ ~ ~

Fifteen minutes later, we're being served turkey subs with a side of kettle chips. Tucker sips his coffee, studying me over the rim. "So tell me why that young boy was so barbarically pulled away from his mother."

Sadness overtakes me. "It's a long story, Tucker. And one I'm not sure you'd believe."

"Why wouldn't I believe you?"

"Even a judge didn't believe me, that's why. He thought I was unfit to raise Travis." I choke up and my eyes drown in tears. "I love my son more than anything in this world. I may not be able to afford a nice apartment, private school, or designer clothes, but he didn't want for anything. What he needed, I gave him. Love. Attention. Bedtime stories. Memories."

"Anyone who witnessed what I did on those courthouse steps could see that. Those were not the tears and screams of a child being taken from an unfit mother."

Over the next hour, this old man, this stranger, this bleeding-heart grandfather who is the complete opposite of the man who just stole my child, sits and listens as I tell him my entire life story.

By one-thirty in the afternoon, I have nothing left in me. I'm talked out, cried out, and utterly numb.

Tucker pays our bill and hands me my leftover container. "You look tired. Please let me drop you back home."

Too exhausted to argue—because all I really want to do is crawl into Travis's bed, curl up, and breathe in the scent of happier days lingering on his pillow—I agree.

On our way to his car, I spot a homeless man perched on a stoop and give him my container. "It's not much. Half a sandwich. But it's yours."

The man locks eyes with me. "God bless you, child."

I feel Tucker's stare as I get into the backseat of the car. He walks around the other side and slides in next to me, then Benny shuts the door.

Tucker cocks his head. "Why would someone who claims to have nothing give her next meal to a stranger?"

I shrug and look out the window. "Because no matter how bad things get, there's always someone worse off."

We ride in silence. He only speaks when we pull up to my dilapidated building. "May I see your phone?"

I don't even have the energy to be embarrassed when I hand over my old phone with a cracked screen to a man in a car that's most likely worth more than my apartment building.

He taps around on it. "Now you have my number. And if you ever need coffee, or just a friend, call me."

I nod even though I know I won't. It's ridiculous to think a twenty-seven-year-old single mom could be friends with an eighty-six-year-old man who gets driven around by a guy wearing an actual chauffeur's hat. I kiss him on the cheek and then Benny lets me out. I poke my head back in. "It was nice to meet you, Tucker. Thank you for everything."

"No, Dakota. Thank *you.*"

"For what?"

"Maybe for… things I didn't even know I needed."

The car pulls away. I fish out my key, not wanting to go into the apartment that will be littered with Travis's toys, but I literally have nowhere else to go. I put my key in the lock hoping it doesn't break off with as hard as it is to turn it. Then I throw down my purse, strip off my thrift-store pants suit, and fling myself onto my son's bed, praying to go to sleep and not wake up for ten days.

Chapter Three

Hudson

I hand off beers to Hawk and Hunter and settle onto the couch, flipping the channel to the season opener for the Nighthawks. "How much do you have riding on this?" I ask Hunt.

"Let's see." His mouth twitches from side to side. "If I remember correctly, if Marco Rivington doesn't get a home run I have to read Izzy two books at bedtime every night for a week. If he does, she has to help Willow and me paint the interior of the new apartment building we just bought."

Hawk stops mid-drink. "Are you fucking serious?"

Hunter shrugs.

"Wait," I say. "You mean to tell me you have no money on this game?"

"I told you I don't gamble anymore."

"At all?" My eyebrows touch my hairline. "Dude, it's opening day. Not to mention April is the best month for sports. I mean MLB, NBA, NHL, not to mention the NFL draft and The Masters. You're telling us you aren't going to bet a single dime on any of it?"

He takes a slow drink. "That's what I'm telling you."

I shake my head. "Damn. If fatherhood turns all men into pussy-whipped robots, count me the fuck out."

Hawk's lips curve up into a goofy grin. "Never say never, Hud."

I look him in the eye. "Never."

My brothers laugh as the first pitch is thrown.

It never ceases to amaze me how different they are from just two years ago. Back then, we'd be sitting here with a bottle of five-hundred-dollar whiskey, a wad of money—betting with our bookies and each other—and reminiscing about our recent sexual conquests, trying to one-up each other for the title of king of the world.

Now it's a case of beer, phones being passed around with pictures of fiancées, wives, and kids, and stories of spit-up, potty training, and family vacations.

Damn, I miss the old days.

"Oh, shit. I almost forgot," Hawk says. "Clear your schedules in eight months. December 20th to be exact."

Hunter cracks a smile. "You finally set a date to take your vows?" He pats our oldest brother's shoulder. "Congrats, man. Not sure why you waited this long to do it."

"Just enjoying the engagement," he says with a wink.

"Are you saying Willow and I rushed into it? Because I promise you, being married has done nothing to settle us down in the bedroom. If anything, it's expanded the menu."

I roll my eyes. "Would you two shut up already?"

"What's your problem, Hud?" Hawk grumbles. "You never took issue with our sex lives *before* we were only doing it with one other person."

"Maybe that's the problem." I point the neck of my bottle at both of them. "It's boring. *You're* boring. It's always the same shit regurgitated over and over again. Don't you miss the variety? The spice? The adventure."

"If you don't think we can have all that being in a committed relationship, *you're* the one with the problem, not us."

"I know what's going on here," Hunter says, laughing. "He's been boycotted by every female in this town." He turns to Hawk. "Haven't you heard? Hell, there's practically a picket line on the sidewalk in front of his house."

"Not *every* female," I assert.

"But enough that your dance card is pretty damn empty this week, eh?"

I toss a nearby pillow at his head. "Fuck you."

"Seriously though, I didn't think they'd really pull it off. I heard what Lynda and the others said at Mom's party. Thought it was a bunch of hyperbole. But I guess when you get a bunch of scorned women together, they're a force of nature."

I get up, toss my bottle in the trash, and get a fresh beer. "Nobody was scorned," I yell back at them. "Never once did I give any of them hope at getting with me for more than a memorable romp."

Hawk turns and talks to me over the back of the couch. "Yeah, but when one romp turns into five and five turns into ten, chicks count that as a relationship."

"Well, that's their problem."

Hunter nods to my crotch as I sit. "No, bro—it's yours."

"Speaking of problems…" Hawk crosses his ankles on the coffee table. "How far up your ass is Pappy?"

"Not far enough to see the color of my shit like he was the two of you."

"So he hasn't threatened you?"

"He can't. The money doesn't mean as much to me. I won't be his little puppet."

Hunter sputters his beer. "I'm calling bullshit. Look at your clothes, Hudson. You wear hundred-dollar T-shirts and designer skivvies. Hell, your car alone reeks of opulence."

"Like the two of you don't drive badass cars." I glance around. "What about my house? This isn't over the top. Four bedrooms. Three baths. No fancy pool like the two of you fuckers."

"Only because you live at work and don't spend much time here," Hunter says.

"Not true anymore now that I'm an attending. No more covering shifts. No scut. No kowtowing."

"Then why stay in a two-thousand-square-foot house when you could live in a mansion?"

"Because unlike you money trolls, I'm saving my money. Investing my allowances wisely. Planning for the future. I have quite the portfolio. And I don't need Pap's millions."

"I know doctors are paid well," Hawk says. "But no way will you ever make forty mil in your lifetime."

"It doesn't matter," I say dismissively. "Because he won't take away my trust fund."

"I think you underestimate our grandfather. He went to great lengths to manipulate the two of us. I wouldn't count him out yet."

"Speaking of your house," Hunt says. "You got a new neighbor yet?"

"No, but I'm sure it'll be some mid-level exec Uncle Paul hires to manage something or other at McQuaid Enterprises. If history repeats itself, probably a forty-year-old brown-noser with two loud-as-shit kids who keep me awake when I'm trying to sleep after being on call for twenty-four hours."

"And yet you still don't move."

"Who's to say if I did, there wouldn't be more loud kids next door to my new place?"

"My old penthouse is still available," Hunter says.

"You haven't sold it yet?"

"It's only been on the market for a few months. Not a whole lot of people in this town can afford it."

"And live next to Lucas Montana—no thank you."

"Lucas isn't so bad, you know."

I lift my brow.

"Hudson, you don't have to have a vendetta against everyone in this town who isn't a McQuaid."

"What's the fun in that?" I point at Hawk. "Besides, since you're marrying a Calloway, I can hardly hate *them* anymore. Thanks for ruining that, by the way."

Hawk tips his beer at me. "My pleasure."

"What are Lucas's brothers up to? Dallas squeeze out a kid yet?"

"Have you been living under a rock? He and Phoebe had a boy a few months before Myles was born."

"Sorry. I don't keep track of who has what babies unless I deliver them myself. What about Blake?"

"Working for the winery like his brothers, but only in the summer. And sleeping his way through college, I hear. Word has it he'll graduate with his master's degree soon."

"Why bother when he'll work for the winery?"

Hawk raises a brow. "Why did you bother going to med school?"

"Why do you think? So I don't have to kiss Pappy's ass until I'm forty to gain control of my trust fund."

"So we're back to that?" Hunter asks.

"No, we're not back to that. Can we talk about something else please, or just watch the damn game?"

"You have any interesting cases at work?" Hunter asks. "Propositions from patients?"

"They don't outright proposition me, you know. They mostly have secret crushes. But, I mean, can you blame them? And they send all their friends to me." I roll my eyes. "Or they did until this week."

"What's the grossest thing you've seen?" he asks. "As in shit you pulled out of a patient."

I turn my nose up thinking of the stories I could tell. "Can I enjoy my beer please?"

"Oh, come on, there must be something entertaining you could spill."

Taking a sip of beer, I think on it. "There was this dude who came in with his girlfriend. He wanted me to perform a vaginoplasty because he said she wasn't tight enough for him. She was twenty-two and hadn't had kids yet. Not to mention she wasn't too keen on the idea. And trust me, she's plenty tight down there. I've done her annuals for years."

"What did you do?"

"I suggested the fucker have penis enlargement surgery because his microdick is what seems to be the issue."

Hunter spits beer. "You did not."

I nod. "I think those might have been my exact words."

"Can't he report you or something?"

"He's not my patient. She is. And she sent me a basket of homemade muffins the next day."

"No shit?"

"It's not the first gift I've gotten from patients."

The doorbell rings. I ignore it.

"You're not going to answer?" Hawk asks.

"I'm not expecting anyone."

He shakes his head, sets his drink down, and disappears. A minute later, Pappy walks in behind him. He's holding a gallon of paint and a brush. He sets both on the coffee table in front of me. Oh, this should be good. Whatever it is, though, he's not going to win.

"The Nighthawks are playing." I nod to the TV. "I'm not in the mood for any of your games, Pappy."

He swipes the remote and turns it off. His punishing stare is enough to tell me I've got a lecture coming.

"Jesus, just get on with it. What did I do now? I promise it wasn't anyone in this town. Not this week anyway. Seems I'll have to start spending my days off in the city."

"Yes, it does seem that way," Pap says. "Now pick up the can and go paint your garage door."

"Mind telling me why?"

"Just do what I say, boy."

"Hudson," Hawk says. "You should do it."

I look at both of them as they stare back with serious eyes. Then, curiosity getting the better of me, I bolt out the front door and look. There, painted on my previously pristine white garage door are the words CHEATING PIG.

My jaw drops. I turn around to Pappy who's holding out the can of paint.

Fuck. I roll up my sleeves and take it.

Chapter Four

Dakota

When I open the door and see Heidi, I collapse into her arms and sob. After twenty-four hours of crying, I'm exhausted and dehydrated. I didn't think I had any tears left. I was wrong.

"Shhh." She runs a soothing hand down my back. "It's all going to work out."

Heidi is ever the optimist. Then again, she's never had anything go wrong in her life. She grew up in a loving family with five siblings who support each other. She's married to her childhood best friend. She has a great job in management at the CPA firm where I work. A wide circle of friends. And she doesn't have to worry about money.

She's been an amazing boss and friend. But she just can't understand.

She's never lost a parent. A husband. She's never wondered if she'd be able to afford groceries because she has to pay a lawyer instead.

And she's never had a child ripped out of her arms and sent to live with people who don't even love him.

But I love her to death.

I pull away. "How, Heidi? How is it going to work out?"

She pulls her suitcase over my threshold.

"You came straight from the airport?"

She reaches into her bag and pulls out a bottle of wine. "Well, not *straight* from JFK. I made one stop. Thought you could use a friend."

"I love you, Heidi Morris."

After wine gets poured and we settle on my couch, I savor the first sip. I don't drink much. Alcohol is not a luxury I can afford. Hell, electricity is barely a luxury I can afford. Not when I owe ten thousand dollars to the lawyer who couldn't even keep my son with me.

How could I have been so naïve? I should have told everyone from the start that Travis isn't Brian's biological child. But Larry, and the stupid internet, had me convinced I'd never lose custody. I close my eyes. And I promised Brian.

Heidi puts a hand on my arm. "How are you holding up?"

"How do you think?"

"You'll get him back, sweetie."

"Possibly. But not until I pay off the lawyer and jump through a whole bunch of hoops."

She takes a sip and raises a brow. "Well, it looks like you have a plan in place. Why have you been holding out on me? Did you think I'd be mad?"

I cock my head. "What are you talking about? I don't have a plan. I haven't the first clue about how I'm going to pay the lawyer, let alone do it in the thirty days I have to file an appeal."

"I'm talking about the phone call I got earlier. The job reference? Listen, I get it. We're a small-time firm doing the taxes for run of the mill clients. You'll never get rich working where we do."

"Did the airplane lose pressure, Heidi? You're making absolutely no sense."

"I'm your friend, Dakota. You should have told me you were looking for another job. Of course I'm going to give you a good reference. I *did* give you one. And, wow, girl, you're really moving up in the world."

I set down my glass, utterly confused. "Please tell me what the hell is going on here. I haven't been looking for another job. I've barely been able to hold onto *this* one with all the shit going on in my life." My breath catches. "Oh my God. Do you think someone stole my identity?"

"Stole your identity and applied for a job as the CPA for one of the largest corporations outside of the city?" She laughs it off. "So you really didn't want a job at McQuaid Motor Corporation? Because in my opinion, you damn well should."

I swallow hard. "Wait. Did you just say McQuaid?"

"McQuaid Motor Corporation."

"Who called you exactly?"

"The owner. Tucker McQuaid." She squints at me. "Dakota, are you feeling okay? I mean other than being devastated that Travis isn't here?"

"I just... I don't understand what's going on. Yesterday outside the courthouse I was approached by an older man who saw Travis being taken away from me. He was very sympathetic and grandfatherly. He took me for lunch." I pinch my brow, still not understanding what's going on. "Heidi, the man's name was Tucker McQuaid. But I never asked him for a job."

A smile overtakes her face. "This just got super interesting. So tell me about this 'older man'."

I scoff. "Heidi, the guy is eighty-six years old. It's not like that. He wasn't looking for anything… sexual." I shudder thinking of it. "He was just a nice guy helping out a distraught woman."

She taps around on her phone and holds it up. "Is this him?"

"Yes." I take the phone from her and scroll down to read the article from *Fortune* magazine. My jaw drops when I get to the part about his massive auto empire and extreme wealth. I look up at Heidi. "Why would someone like that offer me a job?"

"What did you tell him when you were at lunch?"

"I told him about Brian dying. About how the Daniels hate me and are lawyers themselves and knew the judge on the case. About Travis. About my financial problems. And yes, I told him I'm a CPA."

"Well, there you have it. He's a bleeding heart. A philanthropist."

"Still. It doesn't make sense. I'd just been deemed an unfit mother. Why would anyone want to give me access to their company financials? Especially knowing I need money."

She crosses the room, gets my phone, and hands it to me. "I guess there's only one way to find out. Do you know how to contact him?"

"As a matter of fact, he put his number into my phone."

"Well, what are you waiting for?"

I stare at it. "I just don't get it. He's a billionaire."

"Dakota," she whines. "Call him."

I nod reluctantly, find his contact, and make the call.

He answers on the second ring. "Tucker here."

"Hi. Um… Mr. McQuaid. This is um…"

"Dakota Daniels. Is that you?"

"Yes, this is Dakota."

"I've been expecting your call."

Heidi nudges me and tells me to put him on speaker.

I balance the phone on the armrest. "Mr. McQuaid, I don't understand—"

"It's Tucker."

"Tucker. I didn't ask you for a job. I have a job."

"And you're in need of a new one since the one you have isn't paying your bills. The one you have can't get your son back. And the one you have is a dead end. You've been working as a CPA for five years at the same small firm. It's time to stretch your legs and see what you can do."

"I appreciate the vote of confidence, Tucker. But I can't leave my job. I have to be able to work from home. I need a flexible schedule for"—I close my eyes—"court appearances and such. And for my son when I get him back."

"You're turning down the offer you haven't even heard?"

"I—"

Heidi taps the mute button. "Are you crazy? At least hear the man out. Come on, do it for me."

I roll my eyes at this unbelievable situation and unmute the call. "Okay, what's the offer?"

My eyes go wide when he rattles off a number that's three times my current salary. My heart pounds excitedly when he goes over the vast list of benefits. It truly sounds like a dream job. And surely not a job for the likes of me.

"Tucker, I don't think you've thought this through. I do the taxes for small business owners. Not multi-million-dollar corporations."

He laughs. "It's not much different, Dakota. The rules are all the same. What do you say we give it a trial run? Say a few months?

I get the idea your boss would hire you back in an instant if it didn't work out. Wouldn't you, Ms. Morris?"

Heidi and I look at each other knowing we've been caught. Heidi clears her throat. "I sure would, Mr. McQuaid. I think this is an incredible opportunity for her, and I know she won't disappoint you."

"How?" I ask. "With me in the city and you in Calloway Creek. I just don't see how it will work."

"One of the benefits of the job is you get to live in one of the homes we keep for executives. It comes fully furnished with three bedrooms. You'd only be a short train ride from the city. You'd work out of your home with occasional trips to the dealerships as necessary. I assure you, it's all very flexible. If you want to work at six am, work at six am. If you want to work at midnight, no one is going to stop you. Aside from quarterly meetings and the burdens of tax season, which luckily, we've just passed, your working hours will be entirely up to you. As long as the work gets done, you are free to do it whenever you like."

I blink over and over, looking at the phone.

"Dakota? Ms. Daniels?"

"Yes. I'm here. This is all so… unbelievable. Why would you do this? You don't even know me."

"I know the woman who was broken and left in pieces on those courthouse steps. I know the mother who was so distraught she fell to her knees. And I saw the son who loves that mother as much as his next breath. If you agree, I'll get you moved right away at the company's expense. And I'll issue you an advance on your salary that'll be enough to pay off the lawyer. Then I'll help you find a new one. One who will win your case and reunite you with Travis."

"I… this is all so overwhelming."

Heidi mutes the phone again. "You have to do this. You have to do it for Travis."

"Dakota," Tucker says in that commanding yet altruistic voice. "Say yes. Say yes and take the first step in taking control of your life."

I unmute and nod, talking past the lump in my throat. "Yes."

"Splendid. I'll have the contract emailed to you. As soon as you sign, the advance will be issued. The movers will come Saturday. You'll only need your personal belongings and any furniture that is sentimental. The rest can be put in storage if you wish as you won't be needing it. Everything you'll need will be at the house. You'll start on Monday. We'll spend the first few weeks making introductions at the dealerships and getting you acquainted with the books."

"I have a question."

"You may ask anything."

"Who's your CPA now, and what will happen to them?"

"Percy Thatcher is almost as old as I am. He's been ready to retire for years but agreed to stay on until I found the right person to replace him."

"What makes you think I'm the right person, Tucker?"

"Let's just say I'm the kind of man who knows things, Dakota. Check your email this afternoon. Get packing. And I'll see you Monday."

The line goes dead.

I stare at Heidi, wondering if the last twenty minutes actually happened, or if this is all a dream.

She tackles me into the sofa. "I'm so happy for you!"

Tears coat my lashes. I'm still not even sure this is real. I vaguely remember telling Tucker yesterday he couldn't help unless he was a fairy godfather.

Apparently, that is exactly what he is.

Chapter Five

Hudson

"Can't a guy get some fuckin' sleep?" I mumble when I hear men talking outside my window.

I roll over, pull the pillow over my head and hope to catch a few more zzz's. I was on call yesterday. And as often happens when one is on call, I wasn't needed until ten o'clock at night. After Melanie Hanson pushed a ten-pound linebacker out of her vagina at four in the morning in a delivery that required third degree stitches, I was finally able to come home and get some sleep. But, Christ, it's only eight o'clock in the morning. There should be a law against noise this early.

"Not that, Bo!" a deep voice bellows. "That goes to storage."

I sit up in bed, suddenly hating Bo and whoever shouted at him for ruining my lazy Saturday morning. I meander to my blackout curtains and peek out. But what I see is definitely not someone who's named Bo, and it sure as shit isn't someone with a deep voice. It's a woman who looks my age. She's carrying a box, but I doubt she's part of 'Konner Brothers Moving and Storage' as the truck so clearly states.

She must be the new occupant. I look behind her to see if there's a gaggle of kids—that'd be just my fucking luck—but I don't see any. I watch the attractive brunette for a few minutes. And despite the three big dudes carrying stuff from the truck, this woman seems intent on doing her share. She disappears into the house, returning a minute later with water bottles she hands to the three men. She presses a fourth against her neck, unscrews the top, takes a long drink, then gathers her long hair and ties it back with something from her wrist.

Her blue University of Florida shirt, complete with their alligator mascot on it, rides up as she fixes her hair, and I get a peek at the sliver of skin around her belly button. Why that makes my dick swell when I'm sleep-deprived is beyond me. I do not need to have a hard on for the wife of some McQuaid exec who is only staying on company property until they can build their mansion in the hills. One who organizes tea parties and playdates as a career goal.

I shut the drapes and plop back down on my bed.

"Ma'am?" one of the inconsiderate dickheads yells. "Where do you want the bike?"

"You can leave it out. I'm going to explore the town later."

I go back to the window, part the curtains a few inches, and watch the big guy lean her bike against the outside of the garage. I expect more bikes to follow, but they don't. I feel my brows arch. She's single?

I watch Gator Girl interact with the moving guys like they're her brothers. If she's a McQuaid exec, she sure doesn't act like one. No way. She seems far too young to be working in a high-level position for my grandfather or his brother.

"Looks like you've got a flat," the shorter guy says.

"Oh, shoot." She plops down on the driveway and pushes in on the rear tire. "I don't have a repair kit. A friend gave me this. I'm not sure I—" She stops talking when she looks up and catches me watching from my window.

I don't pretend like I wasn't eavesdropping, I just give a sailor's salute and back away. Then I make a bagel, having completely given up on sleep.

Twenty minutes later, I hear the truck pull away. She must not have a lot of stuff. Maybe she's not staying long. I don't usually give much thought to my neighbors, but the thought of her not staying long doesn't settle well with me. Maybe it's because she's alone and there won't be kids yelling and screaming all hours of the day.

Or maybe it's because she's hot.

And single.

And new to town—which makes her fair game.

My phone pings with a text. It's from my grandfather. My lucky day.

Pappy: A new hire is moving in next door today. I'm warning you right now. Stay away. Just keep to yourself. Got it?

Stay away? What the hell? Like he can control who I see and what I do. And even more, he thinks he can dictate what his employees do when they aren't at work. So typical of my domineering grandfather.

Me: Whatever.

Pappy: Hudson, it would do you good to learn some goddamn respect.

Me: Work calls. Gotta go.

Pappy: Work does not call. You worked last night.

I really hate the way he knows every fucking thing about every fucking person.

Me: Which is why I have to go back to sleep. Goodbye.

He doesn't text back. So it's Tucker Gator Girl is working for. Not his brother, Paul. McQuaid Enterprises owns the property next door, along with a shit ton of other properties in the tri-state area, but McQuaid Motor Corp sometimes leases it for their own use.

It makes me curious what the bike-riding beauty does for him.

After breakfast, I catch up on some email and check how my investments did this last week. Then I head out to my garage, open the door, and get my bike. Calloway Creek has miles and miles of trails and I ride three times a week.

I use the keypad to close the garage door and head out. But before I turn out of my driveway, I see the backside of Gator Girl walking down the street toward McQuaid Circle. It's not far, a half mile from here, but she said she wanted to explore the town. It would have been so much easier on her bike.

I glance over and see it still leaning against the house. I have four bikes myself. A ten speed, a cruiser, a hybrid, and a mountain bike. Surely I have the right size tube to fit her tire. I go back inside my garage and gather all my different sizes, along with my repair kit, and walk over, glancing back down the street to make sure my neighbor hasn't doubled back. It's stupid, I know. But I've never been seen as a particularly helpful or even friendly neighbor. I don't need to go ruining that rep now.

Her tire fixed and inflated, and both of her brakes correctly adjusted, I'm finally on my way.

And damn my grandfather for texting me. I'm fairly sure that once I found out she was working for him and not my uncle, I'd have stayed away anyway. I don't need to go messing in McQuaid Motor Corp shit. I like to stay as far away from Tucker McQuaid's business as I can.

But now… now she's the proverbial forbidden fruit.

And I'm the guy who likes to break all the fucking rules.

Chapter Six

Dakota

I have a hard time controlling my emotions as I stroll through town. Kids are everywhere. They're racing by me in groups on skateboards. Walking hand-in-hand with their moms or dads. Playing in the huge park.

Travis would love it here.

Living in the city is not conducive to having outdoors like this. Fresh air. Green grass. Wide open spaces.

I grew up in a place like this, a small town in western Florida. I sit on a bench, watching the world go by as I reminisce about my own childhood. It was just me and Mom and Gran. Then it was just me and Mom. Then, after my second year at UF, it was just me.

Brian and I met at UF. He was pre-law, and I was majoring in accounting. It was like one of those romance movies where two star-crossed lovers see each other from opposite sides of a huge room, and they just know they're going to end up together.

Even though we had almost nothing in common but our love of horror movies and sushi, we hit it off immediately. His parents—whom he went all the way to UF to get away from—hated me, which somehow made him like me even more. I knew from the very beginning he wasn't like the rest of his family. I even thought that maybe he was using me to get back at them somehow. But I was in love, so I didn't care.

After graduation he proposed and took me back to New York City. His parents didn't waste any time trying to come between us, blackmailing him and refusing to let him marry a former financial aid student from an undesirable zip code. He convinced me to get pregnant, saying it was the only way they'd accept me. That they would never turn their backs on a blood relative. But when we couldn't get pregnant, Brian's plan imploded. We thought all was lost until he had the idea to have me artificially inseminated.

Travis was conceived on the first try.

Brian swore me to secrecy. He was ashamed he couldn't perform. We both suspected it was because of his drug use—something else his parents drove him to with all their rules, restrictions, and demands. But he was what people would call a functional addict. His habit never interfered with our happiness; if anything, it enhanced it. When he was high, he was more like himself and less like the person his parents were trying to make him become. He was carefree. He was at peace. Well, until…

A ball hits my foot, pulling me from my thoughts. I reach down and pick it up as an adorable girl with blonde ringlets in her hair approaches.

I smile and hold out the ball. "This must be yours."

"Yes. Thank you."

Her parents, I presume, come up behind her. The woman is pushing a stroller. I peek in to see a tiny, pudgy-faced baby. "He's a cutie," I say.

"Thank you," the woman says. "His name is Myles." She nods to the girl. "And that's Izzy." She holds out her hand. "I'm Willow and this is my husband, Hunter. You're new around here."

I nod. "As of this morning. I just moved in. I was sitting here checking out the town." I shake her hand. "I'm Dakota."

"Ooooo," Izzy says. "I like your name. Were you named after a state? I'm learning the states in school."

"I'll bet you're really good at it. What grade are you in?"

"Second. My teacher is Mr. Kinley. He's a boy teacher. Cool, huh?"

"That *is* cool."

"Do you have a girl I could play with?"

I try to control my sadness. "No, sorry."

"That's okay. There are a lot of girls here."

"So what brings you to town, Dakota?" Hunter asks.

"New job. I'm a CPA."

"Where did you move from?" his wife asks.

"The city."

"Ah, same. I haven't quite been here for a year, but I love it. I'm sure you will too." Her eyes train in on my left hand. "Married?"

I shake my head.

"Significant other?"

"Nope. And quite content to keep it that way."

She chuckles. "That might be a good thing. There are a few good catches left in this town, but pickings might be slim." She pulls a pen out of her purse, fishes out a gum wrapper and writes something down. "Here's my number. If you need anyone to show you around, or if you just need a girls' night, let me know."

I open the wrapper and read her name. "Your name is Willow McQuaid?"

She takes Hunter's elbow. "For about six months now. I'm still not used to hearing people say it."

I look at her husband. "Are you related to Tucker?"

"He's my grandfather." His eyes narrow. "Why do you ask?"

"Because he's the one who hired me."

His brows shoot up and meet his hairline. "Tucker hired you to be his CPA?"

"He hired me to be the CPA for McQuaid Motor Corporation."

"Even more impressive. I wasn't even aware Percy Thatcher was leaving."

"He's retiring soon. He's going to show me the ropes over the next few weeks before making it official."

"Well, congrats. I'm sure a thousand people applied for the job. Some might even kill for it. You must be really good at what you do."

Once again, nerves take hold of my insides, because I'm terrified. Over the past few days, I've done a lot of research into MMC. It's a multi-million-dollar corporation. What if I screw this up?

The baby fusses and Willow vibrates the stroller back and forth. "We'd better get this guy home before he starts screaming for his next meal. It was nice meeting you. Good luck with the new job, and please call me."

I hold up the gum wrapper. "I will. Thanks." I wink at her daughter. "Bye, Izzy. Have fun in second grade."

As they walk off, I don't miss how Hunter turns around and stares. He's probably thinking what everyone else will think: that I'm too young to have been hired for this job. I look down at my clothes— stretchy yoga pants and one of my old UF T-shirts—and remember I'm not wearing makeup. I must look a sight. A very unprofessional one. What if he goes back and talks to Tucker and convinces him he made a mistake?

Then again, Tucker saw me at my worst. Crumpled and broken. And he still offered me the job. It's something I'm having a hard time getting my head around even after I signed the contract. Even after the moving company showed up this morning. Even as I sit here and wonder what's to become of my life, my son's life.

But then I remember what Gran would say. "Never look a gift horse in the mouth."

I took the advice to heart, even when I was ten and didn't know what she meant. And I remembered those words when I met Brian and thought I'd died and gone to heaven. And again when Travis was born. Because he was the ultimate gift. The cherished treasure I never expected. And the one thing Brian gave me that reminds me every day of his amazing spirit.

Seven days. I have to wait seven more days to see my son. It's the purest form of torture. I've never gone that long without seeing Travis. Is he missing me as much as I'm missing him? Crying himself to sleep every night? Calling out for me when he's sad or hurt? Or is he too young to miss me? Out of sight, out of mind and all that. I swallow a tearful lump, imagining what his days are like. Is he being mistreated or brainwashed? Knowing the stories Brian told me about him growing up, the possibilities scare me.

My stomach growls, reminding me I haven't eaten a thing today, unless you call coffee food. I stand and glance up and down the street, still mystified that my employer's family has an entire part of the town named after them. I spot Truman's Grocery across the street and make my way over, picking out just enough food to get me through a few days.

Walking back to the house, I pass by a restaurant bustling with lunchtime activity. The sign reads: **Donovan's Pub**. I make note of it. Maybe I'll come for dinner. But not until I get my first paycheck. Until then, I'll be living off ramen and boxed mac and cheese. I pull out my phone and check my bank account. I've been waiting for Tucker's advance to clear so I can pay Larry. It still shows ten thousand dollars pending. *Ten. Thousand.* A man who doesn't even know me gave me a ten-thousand-dollar advance. Who does that?

"Yes, I know, Gran. You don't have to say it."

I roll my eyes at myself and continue home. *Home.* It's strange to even think of this town as home. I look behind me as I walk away from McQuaid Circle thinking how no place could ever truly be home unless Travis was with me.

My two grocery bags get heavier and heavier along the way. I shift them from arm to arm wishing I'd had the bike. It has a basket on the front that would be perfect. Sadly, though, biking will have to wait until the lawyer is paid, I've been properly fed and clothed, and—

Wait.

I look down at the pavement in realization.

I need to be properly clothed. On Monday, I'll be walking into the main headquarters of McQuaid Motor Corporation to meet with Tucker, Percy, and who knows what other executives. The one good pants suit I have now has ripped knees thanks to the unforgiving concrete at the courthouse. I have to get some new clothes. Power outfits. If this is going to work, I need to fit in.

I vaguely remember passing a second-hand clothing boutique on my way out of Truman's. I'll visit tomorrow and hope they have something, anything, to get me through the first day. Then I'll just take it one day at a time.

When I'm one house away from mine, I hear cursing. I look over and see a man standing in his driveway, bike on the ground behind him, shaking his head as he looks at his garage door. It's the guy who was in the window earlier.

Oh my gosh. When I look at what he's staring at, my hand covers my mouth. In large black letters painted across his white garage door are the words: TEENIE WEENIE JELLYBEANIE. Then on another part of the garage in bright red: JERKWAD.

I hurry my steps and make it to my own yard without him seeing me. I'm sure he doesn't want to explain this to his new neighbor. Kind of a bad way to meet if you ask me. Then again, if he really is what the painted red word says, I might not want to meet him at all.

I'm amused that this town might not be the sleepy little town I envisioned.

Then, as I approach the house, something catches my eye. The bike. The one Heidi gave me. The one with the flat tire. The tire isn't flat anymore. I walk up to it and press down on the rear tire. It's fully inflated. But… how?

I turn my head in the direction of my neighbor's yard, unable to see him through the garage that separates us. There was a bike in his driveway. *Did he…?*

Huh. Maybe Jellybean Jerkwad isn't so much of a jerkwad after all.

Not that I care. I have one goal and one goal only. I don't need entanglements. Or complications. Or handsome neighbors all up in my business.

On my way inside, I look over at the window he was in earlier. I remember the feeling I had when I glanced up and saw him watching me. When he saluted me, bare chest and all. When a bolt of electricity zinged through my body.

When I realized it was the first zing I'd felt in two long years.

Chapter Seven

Hudson

Lynda fucking Graves. I know it was her. Again. I should put up security cameras and then sue her ass for trespassing and destruction of property.

Two times in one week. The chick is off her rocker.

I finish up the second coat of paint and step back, making sure the black and red paint is completely unnoticeable. Out further in the driveway, I have a clear view of Gator Girl's house. I immediately notice the bike is gone. I look up and down the street then back at my garage as I wonder if she saw Lynda's graffiti.

Not that I care in the least.

I glance at my paint-spattered hands and figure I might as well keep doing shit I've been putting off. Like re-staining the back fence. While I'm perfectly aware that hiring someone to do it would be a drop in the bucket, doing mundane tasks like painting and yard work keeps me busy on my days off. I'm not the kind of guy who likes to sit still. I have to be moving. Working. Biking. Running. Anything but sitting around doing nothing.

Maybe it's because I grew up watching my father. When Robert McQuaid wasn't working at MMC, he'd be doing one of two things: a woman, or absolutely nothing. As in he'd sit in his recliner with a beer and takeout food staring at the TV as his cholesterol continued to climb. It wouldn't surprise me if my old man upped and died from clogged arteries before he reaches sixty.

What does surprise me, however, are the gaggle of women who claim to find his ever-growing beer belly attractive. Then again, maybe it's easy to overlook such things when underneath it all is the wealthy son of the richest man this side of New York City.

Watching my father sit around was one of the reasons I decided to go to med school. I wasn't about to follow in his footsteps and sell cars. It started out as a joke, telling him I was going to be a doctor when I was fifteen. He laughed in my face, probably while holding a beer and eating a Big Mac. I never forgot that laugh. That moment was when I realized Mom was right to leave him. He'd never amount to anything but a warm body to fill a seat in Pappy's business. Hell, even Pappy has given up on him.

Pappy. He seems intent on figuring out how to manipulate me like my older brothers. I smile deviously knowing it's never going to happen.

I open the garage and swap the white garage paint for the fence stain then head out back to finish the left side of the interior fence. It won't take long, an hour at most. The daunting task will be re-staining the entire outside. Neither of my neighbors have a fence that connects to this one. I'm solely responsible for its upkeep. I could leave it as it is. I mean, I'm not the one who has to look at it.

Clancy Barker is. He lives to my right. He's an old widower who keeps to himself. He never complains about anything. And Gator Girl on the left would have no reason to put up a stink. It's not even her house, and, if past occupants are any indication, she's only there temporarily anyway.

I decide to leave the outside of the fence the way it is and concentrate on improving things *I* can see. Then I roll my eyes because I can practically hear my grandfather call me selfish.

As I finish up the left fence, I catch a glimpse of movement through a slat. My brush stroke stops as I stare through. Gator Girl is walking around her back yard. She's wearing the same shirt but has swapped her long pants for a pair of shorts. Her jaw is slack as she takes it in, as if she's never seen a back yard. And this one's not even all that special. There's a deck off the kitchen and living room. A flowerbed lines either end. And the yard, though not particularly large, is plush and green, especially for late April.

She wanders the back of the property as if in awe. Which is strange. If she's working for MMC, surely she's lived in better places than this. Unless maybe she's from the city. That makes sense. She's used to high rise apartments without outdoor spaces.

Then she stops, lies on the grass right smack in the middle of the yard, and looks up at the sky, closing her eyes as the spring sun shines down on her. But the strange thing is, she doesn't exactly look happy. Her chest heaves with a sigh and my suspicion is confirmed. Happy people don't sigh like that. I should know, I've done it myself on many occasions.

Her hands rake through the grass on either side of her. Her legs move. She looks like a kid making a snow angel. Only it's late April and there's no snow.

I continue to peek through the slats like a creepy voyeur as she stands, brushes off her backside, walks back to the deck, settles onto the lounger, and—holy shit—takes off her shirt. Tingles zap my junk in anticipation, but they're short lived. She's got a tank top underneath. Still, I can see the outline of her breasts. Her inviting cleavage. The curve of her thighs.

Apparently my dick thinks it's Christmas even though my gorgeous neighbor is halfway clothed.

I think of Pappy's text earlier. The warning. The veiled threat. It has me stepping away from the view and gathering up my supplies. I glance back for a brief second. The old man might have told me to stay away from her, but I'm going to guess he never issued such a warning to Gator Girl. I feel my face crack a smile as I take off my shirt, grab the bucket of stain, and make my way to the other side of the fence.

Pretending not to notice her, I clear out some twigs, set down the bucket and get started. I don't turn to see if she's watching. No self-respecting man would. But I swear I can feel her doing it. I just know she's staring at my back, admiring how my muscles contract as I swipe the brush up and down. Surely her gaze is following the trickle of sweat running down my spine.

I finish a whole six-foot section without a single glance over my shoulder. That's right, she can just sit back and enjoy the view of the unattainable doctor next door. A satisfied grin creeps up my face as I wipe my brow with the back of my hand.

Another six-foot section gets completed. It's getting harder and harder not to turn around, and I can't help but steal a glance her way when I dip my brush in the bucket.

Surprised, I stand straight, turn fully, and crane my neck.

She's gone.

Not only is she gone, but the drapes of her sliding door have been shut.

When did she leave, I wonder. Well, shit. I guess all this was for nothing. My eyes wander over the rest of the fence. There are five more sections. I crouch down and dip in my brush. I might as well finish what I started. There's nothing better to do since the town's female population has boycotted me. I put in my earbuds, turn on some music, and decide not to think of the elusive woman next door.

I glance back once more, at the middle of the yard where she was laying, imagining her there on her back. Imagining myself hovering over her. Imagining myself doing a lot more than hovering.

Damn you, Pappy.
Damn you.

Chapter Eight

I sift through the clothes at the secondhand shop, but I'm not really paying attention. Even after a day, my mind is still occupied with the sweaty back of my fence-painting neighbor. He never looked at me. Never even acknowledged me. He just went about completing his task.

Part of me is relieved. I didn't come to Calloway Creek to make friends. And I especially didn't come here to meet a man. I have one goal and need to stick to it.

I get out my phone and check my account, knowing it's silly to think the advance would clear on a Sunday. But every day wasted is one less I have with Travis. If what Larry said is true, it could be many months until we go before a judge again. Six more days before I see him. It might as well be six years with as slow as time seems to be going.

I stave off tears by looking around the store. It's interesting, this place. It's half bookstore, half boutique. It even has a small coffee counter and a lounge area. I've never seen anything like it.

"Can I help you find anything?" a woman says, coming in from the back room.

"I need *a lot* of help. In fact, if you can find me a killer executive outfit, I'll buy you a cup of coffee."

She extends her hand. "I'm Regan Lucas."

I shake. "Dakota Daniels."

"You're new here."

"You are the second person in two days to notice. Just how small is this town?"

"Well, Dakota, let's find you an outfit and then we'll have that coffee and I'll tell you all about it."

Regan has a contagiously positive aura about her. Here she is working on a Sunday when she'd probably rather be at home with a husband or maybe her kids, yet she's bubbly and bright-eyed. Maybe she thinks I'm going to buy an expensive dress. I should probably say something before she gets her hopes up.

"Um… If you have a sale rack or something, we might want to start there."

She turns and smiles. "You got it. I have just the thing." Walking over to the far wall, she sifts through hangers and pulls out a pretty lavender pants suit. "I'm thinking if you pair this with a black blouse, you'll really stand out and make a statement."

I cock my head. "What statement is that?"

She eyes me up and down. "I'm thinking… oh, yeah, how about the one that says there is no glass ceiling for us. That we can do any job a man can do. Maybe even better. And that just because we possess ovaries doesn't mean we're the 'fairer' sex. It means we're all that more badass because we can do any job we set our minds to *and* populate the world."

I haven't smiled much in the past week. But Regan Lucas just made me break out in a huge grin. I decide I like her.

"Do you think it will fit?"

She looks at the size and back at me. "I do. And it will look lovely with your complexion and hair color."

I take it from her and try not to be too obvious when I look at the price tag. Disappointment overtakes me when I realize I won't be able to afford it. I hand it back, embarrassed. "Maybe something else?"

"Nope," she says confidently, leading me to a dressing room. "This is definitely the one. Sundays are half price, by the way." She holds the curtain of the sole dressing room open. "I'll go find you a blouse."

A few minutes later, I'm admiring myself in the mirror. Regan was right. This is amazing. I even have a pair of low heels that will go with it. If I wear my hair up in a bun, I might even be able to pass for the corporate executive I'm pretending to be. Then again, it might be better if I'm just myself. I've never worn my hair in a bun in my entire life.

A knot forms in my stomach as I once again feel like everyone I'll meet tomorrow will know I'm a fraud.

"Well?" I hear from the other side of the curtain. "You're killing me, does it fit?"

I step through and twirl around.

She squeals like we're friends and I just found my dress for the prom. "I knew it. You're going to knock 'em dead."

I smooth down the material of the jacket. "You have no idea how much I need that to be true."

"Now, none of that. If you start to doubt yourself, look in the mirror. You look stunning, Dakota. Now take it off. I'll go get the coffee."

When I'm dressed back in my jeans and T-shirt, I stare in the mirror noting just how different I look from a moment ago. I hang everything up and go out to find Regan.

She's already sitting in the lounge area with two cups. She nods to the empty clothes rack by the counter. "Just hang them there and join me."

I do what she asks, glancing around behind her at the wall of books. "Tell me about this place. It's so eclectic."

"Creamer?" she asks as she also pushes a packet of sugar across the round coffee table in the middle of the seating area.

I shake my head.

She takes a sip. "There's not much to tell. I've owned this place for about ten years. It used to be my parents' shop. They retired to Florida. It was a full-on bookstore until the pandemic hit and everyone started getting everything online. I realized I needed to keep up with the changing world, so I asked myself what McQuaid Circle needed. And here we are. It turned out to be one hell of a business decision. My intention was to work on consignment, but so many women just started donating their clothes." She shakes her head. "You really lucked out, Dakota, because this town is amazing. One of a kind."

"People just give you their old clothes?"

She nods. "They do. Even knowing I'll profit from them. I do end up taking about half of what gets donated to the store on the other side of town that raises money for a women and children's shelter. I only keep the designer stuff that can pretty much pass for new. Oh, and I donate ten percent of my profits to local charities as a way to give back to the community."

"You run this place all by yourself? Are you married?"

"Not married. I'm single and loving it. Although I've pretty much tapped out the guys in this town." She points to the ceiling.

"And I live upstairs with my cat, Joey. Most of the buildings along the circle have apartments above. It's super convenient." She takes a drink. "Enough about me. What brings you to Calloway Creek?"

I glance over at the lavender suit. "A job. I'm so nervous. It's way above my pay grade and I'm probably totally in over my head. But… I had to take it."

"What do you do?"

"I'm a CPA."

"Wow. Well, I'm sure you'll do fine. The first few weeks at any new job are bound to suck. Just hang in there. And if you need more clothes, just let me know. I'm happy to let you take some and try them for a week before you decide to buy."

Translation: she gets that I'm broke and won't get paid for a while.

I think of the other woman I met yesterday, Willow, and wonder if everyone in this town is as nice as these two.

"Thanks. I think I'll just take it one day at a time. I'll mostly be working from home, but I'll need to shadow the current CPA for a few weeks to learn the ropes. After that, I won't need much of a wardrobe."

"Okay, give me the good stuff now. Husband? Kids? Super-cute boyfriend? Ooooo, do you have an older brother?"

"I…" I swore I wouldn't get into my predicament with anyone. I mean, not only would they think I'm a horrible mother since my kid got taken away, I just don't see the need to air my dirty laundry to strangers. "It's just me."

"Ahhh, then you've come to the right place. I can pretty much tell you everything about every eligible bachelor in this town. We've got some good ones. Some not so good ones." She laughs. "And even one who's being boycotted by the town's single female population."

I shake my head. "I'm really not looking for a guy. I need to focus on my job. It's all I have room for right now."

She stands, gets the carafe, and tops off my cup. "I get it. Establish yourself as a power woman first." She narrows her eyes. "I could tell that about you the second I saw you. You're a woman on a mission. You're determined. And you won't let anything stand in your way."

Regan Lucas has no idea how right she is. Nothing will stand in my way of getting Travis back.

"Can you tell me a little about Calloway Creek? I just love McQuaid Circle. I can walk here. It seems to have everything I need. Which is good. Because I moved from the city and don't have a car."

Suddenly I'm struck by a touch of reality. I'm supposed to meet with Tucker and Percy Thatcher, the retiring CPA, tomorrow. We're meeting at the MMC headquarters, which is at one of the dealerships on the other side of town. I glance at the pants suit, imagining myself wearing it while riding the bike. It's a ridiculous notion. I'll have to Uber. Oh my gosh, does this town even have Uber drivers or cabs? My anxiety level has just increased tenfold.

"Dakota? Are you okay?"

I nod. "Just feeling anxious about tomorrow."

She cocks her head. "Want me to make that coffee Irish?"

"No, I…" I can't think of an excuse why not. "Actually, that'd be great. But only if you join me."

She laughs and fetches a bottle of whiskey from behind the counter. "As I'm the proprietor, I make the rules."

As we sip our coffee, she tells me all about the town.

"Let's see, Calloway Creek has a population of just over twenty thousand. That population goes up by about seven thousand during the school year thanks to CCU—Calloway Creek

University. There are four lakes here and a fantastic park that's just at the end of the circle. One of our claims to fame is the high school football team. They are very good. They've won state a few times thanks to my friend Nikki's husband, Jaxon, who coaches the Cavaliers." She regards the pants suit. "In fact, I believe that may have been hers. Maybe you've heard of her. Nicole Forbes. She's the weather anchor for XTN."

My jaw drops. "I'm buying something worn by Nicole Forbes?"

"I have a lot of her stuff here."

She goes on to tell me about Donovan's Pub across the street. I remember it from yesterday. The circle has a bowling alley, a movie theater, and several small eateries.

"Oh, and every Tuesday evening, me and a few others meet in the small park behind the ice-cream shop for coffee." She nods to the left wall. "Ava Criss owns the coffee shop next door." She holds up her cup. "Her liquid gold puts this stuff to shame. You should join us. Seven o'clock. Consider it a standing invitation."

"That's very nice of you."

The front door chimes and two women walk inside. "Excuse me for a second," Regan says.

She walks over to the women, who are looking at the bookshelves. Nobody speaks. They all do sign language. Even Regan. A minute later, she comes back and sits.

I raise a brow. "You know ASL?"

"There's a school for the deaf and blind around the corner. We get a lot of teachers and students in the shops in and around the circle. I've picked up a lot over the years and even took a free course online once."

I drink my coffee, fascinated as I watch the two women peruse books and sign to each other. It's a beautiful language.

When another customer comes through the door, I figure I've taken up enough of Regan's time. I stand and deposit my empty cup in the trash, my stomach warmed not only from the coffee, but the shot of whiskey. "Thank you so much for everything, Regan."

She goes behind the counter and pulls out a business card, handing it to me. "You need anything. More clothes, a smutty book, a tour of the town, someone to talk to about your amazing first day, or even a shoulder to cry on if it's overwhelming. Or maybe just another cup of coffee, even if we forget the coffee and just go with whiskey. Whatever you need, call me."

I think of my pathetic life and my one friend—who is probably only my friend because she's my boss. Or she was. All those years I spent in the city. Just another anonymous face on another busy street. An empty shell since Brian died.

In two days, I've already met a few women who are so incredibly kind. If I had Travis with me I'd be in heaven. I think I'd love it here if he were with me. I *know* he'd love it. We could build a life here. It's the perfect place to start over. I'd have a job. I'd have my son. And eventually, after everything else, I even think I'd be ready to open up my heart to a man.

Regan hugs me like we're already friends. I get the feeling she thinks we are. I hug her back, because if there's one thing in this world I need, it's friends.

She rings me up and covers my purchase in plastic.

"Thank you so much."

"Tuesday at seven," she calls out after me. "Behind the ice-cream shop. Don't forget!"

I wave and walk out of the shop.

I go straight to the house, not wanting to wrinkle my purchase. As I turn the corner onto my street, I see Jellybean Jerkwad mounting his bike. He puts earbuds in, stuffs a water bottle into the clip on his frame, and takes off in the opposite direction.

Before I know what's hit me, I'm lost in a fantasy. One that has him shirtless and painting his fence. He sees me on the back deck, throws down his paintbrush, and strides over, his eyes full of heat, determination, and power. He sweeps me up and into his arms, carries me into the house—no, scratch that, he leaves me on the lounger, leaning over me as sweat from his brow falls onto my thin top. He bends over, getting closer. He smells of cinnamon—no, wait, I don't like cinnamon. He smells of spearmint. And paint. He definitely smells like paint. And man sweat—but his kind of sweat is sweet, an aphrodisiac even. It has me reeling. He doesn't even talk; he just kisses me. Passionately. Possessively. The world is lost to me and it's just him and me in this perfect little bubble. And then he stands. I'm flushed, speechless, and languid, having been kissed stupid by a stranger. He still hasn't said a word. Neither of us has. He just strolls away and goes back to painting his fence. And I go back to watching him. But we keep staring at each other like we just know we'll end up together. That even without speaking a single word, we're connected. Cosmically. Spiritually. Eternally. And then—

"Excuse me," someone says from behind.

I turn, about to be run over by a woman pushing a twin stroller. I'm totally blocking the sidewalk. I hop off into the grass. "I'm sorry."

As she walks away, I think of how silly I must have looked standing here gazing down the street in a stupid trance. Because of him. Teenie Weenie Jerkwad. My neighbor I know nothing about but am somehow intensely drawn to.

~ ~ ~

At seven thirty, I pick up the phone and dial the house number. Wayne and Patty never wanted me to have their cell numbers, only the house number. Probably because they are never the ones to answer the house phone.

"Daniels residence," Janet, their live-in housekeeper, answers.

"Hi, Janet. It's Dakota. Is Travis there?"

Janet sighs into the phone. "I'm sorry, Miss, he's gone off to bed already."

"He has? But I called a half-hour early specifically to get to talk to him."

"I'm sorry, Miss."

One time I've gotten to talk to Travis since he was ripped away from me on Wednesday. *One. Time.* They are keeping him from me, and it kills me.

"Janet, are they forbidding you from letting me talk to him?"

"No, ma'am, of course not."

Her voice is not very convincing.

"May I speak to Patty then?"

"Mr. and Mrs. Daniels are out."

"They're out a lot, aren't they? Who watches Travis?"

"That would be Ms. Laura."

My insides crumble yet again. "Who is Laura?"

"The nanny."

"They hired a nanny? Who is she? What's she like? Does she take good care of him? Does he… like her?"

"You'd have to ask Mr. or Mrs. Daniels about that. Ms. Laura seems nice enough."

"Janet, please. If they're out, they won't know if you let me talk to him. I know he won't mind if you wake him."

"I can't do that, Miss."

"Janet, you have children of your own, yes? I know they're grown, but put yourself in my shoes. Please. Mother to mother."

"I sympathize with you, child. I do. But it'll be my job if I disobey them. My husband is on disability. I need this paycheck."

"Can you please tell Patty I'd like to speak to her tomorrow?"

"I'll get her the message."

"Janet. Is he… is he okay?"

"He's got plenty of toys. And the back yard. And he's taken to the dog—they've become quite the duo those two."

"But is he okay?"

She's a mother. She understands what I'm asking.

"It is my opinion that children are better suited being with their parents, Miss. I really must go. I'll pass on your message. Goodbye."

Children are better suited being with their parents.

So he's not okay.

I plug in my phone, turn off the light, and hug my pillow so tightly he may actually be able to feel me hugging him all the way from here.

And I cry.

76

Chapter Nine

Hudson

Usually, I'm up at six and in the hospital by seven for a morning surgery before heading to the office. Today, however, the scheduled hysterectomy was postponed due to the patient's infection, so I'm able to lie in bed a few more hours. I *lie* in bed—not *sleep*—because this morning, just like the last few, sleep is elusive as my mind wanders to the woman next door.

She didn't think I saw her yesterday when she was coming down the sidewalk carrying a dress or something, looking all casual in snug jeans and another gator T-shirt. She must have gone to the University of Florida. And if so, she's smart. That's a top-five public university. I should know; Pappy always chastised me for enrolling in a number twenty-five school—even though NYU is a top-twenty-five school, is private, and is much more like an Ivy League school.

Before I can stop myself, my left hand slides beneath the band of my skivvies and strokes my morning wood. Pictures of Gator Girl flash through my mind. Her wearing the T-shirt and *only* the

T-shirt. Her milky-white thighs and a hint of the globes of her perfect ass peek beneath the hem.

My hand works faster and my breathing accelerates as I imagine her straddling me. She's not wearing panties, and she's soaked, her juices coating my stiff cock.

She likes the way I stroke myself. Her shirt is discarded and tossed aside. Her breasts are bare, perky, and inviting. She palms them and throws her head back. My dick enjoys the show, becoming more engorged with every stroke of her hands across her perfectly puckered nipples. She traces a hand down her taut belly, through the tiny patch of manicured hair where two fingers separate her labia, allowing me to see her glistening pussy.

Pre-cum oozes out of me. My impending orgasm is coming imminently and hard, especially when she looks me in the eye and inserts a finger inside herself.

My balls tighten, my jaw tenses, my world stills, then I gloriously spurt jizz all over her fabulous chest as I shout her—

My head falls heavily back onto the pillow when I realize I don't know Gator Girl's name. I'm shucking the goddamn corn, fantasizing about the sexy neighbor I don't know a fucking thing about.

Maybe it's better that way, I surmise, as I clean up and get ready for work.

After breakfast, I'm backing out of my driveway and almost slam the Maserati into my mailbox when I see her. Gator Girl is coming out of her house looking… well… amazing. The light purple suit she's wearing stands out against the black blouse underneath, and her hair—no more ponytail—flows across her shoulders in soft brunette waves. And she's wearing heels. Man, what I wouldn't give to see how those heels make her bare legs look. She innocently tucks a piece of hair behind an ear and my insides shudder like a kid in a porn store.

Ho-lee shit she's gorgeous.

Then I remind myself that I'd probably think that about anyone Pappy forbade me from touching. Everyone wants what they can't have. Why should the off-limits girl next door be any different?

She looks up and catches me staring. She doesn't become self-conscious and slink back into the house. She doesn't become defensive and put her hands on her hips at my blatant ogling. She doesn't turn up her nose at my pretentious car. She just stares back. She stares as if we know each other. As if we've met and are friendly neighbors sharing a morning greeting. Hell, she stares at me as if she's having a goddamn fantasy akin to the one I had not an hour ago.

Her alluring eyes do nothing to tamp down the tightening of my pants.

I swear to God it feels like we'll do this forever. Are we both wondering who will break the stare first?

My answer comes when a car pulls up to her curb and she finally shifts her gaze.

Benny, my grandfather's driver, appears from within and invites her to sit in the back.

Gator Girl looks surprised. It's her first day of work and apparently Pappy sent a ride, something it looks to me was unexpected. Did she think she was going to walk to the dealership? Or bike? In *those* heels?

There are so many questions flying around in my head right now, I don't even know where to start. Where is she from? How did she land a job at MMC? What color are her eyes? *Who* is she?

I've never been so interested in learning such details.

Why now?

Benny honks and waves as the car passes behind my driveway. The back windows are tinted, but I'd bet my trust fund Gator Girl is still looking at me. And suddenly, I can't wait for my day to be over so I can get home and find out some answers to my questions.

~ ~ ~

"Morning, Dr. McQuaid," Kelly says flatly as if speaking to a cockroach she just squished with her shoe.

She's a lab tech and the first person I run into after entering through the back of the medical building. Kelly, and the rest of the female medical staff, have all joined in on the boycott, giving me nothing but disapproving looks.

I don't get this shit. I didn't do anything to deserve this. There are thousands of guys like me. Certified bachelors. Fun-seekers. Men who don't want to settle down. Is it my fault the ladies get attached to me after seeing what my tongue and cock can do to them? Never have I given any one of them hope for a relationship. Yet somehow I'm the bad guy.

When I'm at my desk, going through my schedule for the day, Lyle Richards plops down in one of the chairs in my office. He's one of the senior physicians I was working under when I was doing my residency. Now, he's just a fellow attending. But he's still got one thing on me: he's a partner in this practice, along with Vance Peterman.

"Trouble in paradise?" He pops a granola cluster into his mouth and nods to the door behind him. "Your name has been whispered no less than a dozen times this morning—and not in a good way."

I roll my eyes. "Just some vendetta started by a few girls who thought they should be the ones to settle me down."

"Ahhh." He nods. "Well, you're doing a fine job here, Hudson. Try not to let your personal life affect your professional one. The last thing this practice needs is to be blacklisted by the women of Calloway Creek. They do have other options, and Ken Warrington would laugh all the way to the bank if a flood of our patients went over to Cal South OB/GYN."

Lyle is nice enough about it, but I get the underlying meaning. Yes, I'm an attending now, but that doesn't exactly give me tenure. There are only three places I can work in this town. Here, Cal South, or the hospital. And this is a small town. If bridges are burned, everyone will know about it.

"I get what you're saying, Lyle. I do. But—"

My phone buzzes. "Dr. McQuaid, room eight is ready for you."

Lyle stands. "All I'm saying is lie low for a while. And perhaps go to the city for any… urges."

Jesus. So not only am I being boycotted by the ladies, a senior partner is telling me to keep my dick in my pants. And my grandfather has made my neighbor off limits. There are far too many goddamn rules flying around here.

I enter the patient room and wash my hands, looking down on them as I remember this morning, thinking how my left hand may be the most action I'm going to get in the foreseeable future.

What a depressing fucking thought.

Chapter Ten

Dakota

Benny lets me out of the back of the car and I try not to wince when I stand. My feet are killing me after a long day of wearing heels.

I gather up my purse and all the papers I accumulated today. "Thank you, Benny."

"Same time tomorrow, ma'am?"

"You really don't have to."

"Mr. McQuaid insisted. It's my understanding that you don't own a vehicle yet. And after next week you'll be primarily working from the house. So you see it's really no trouble."

"Okay then, I appreciate it. I'll be waiting."

He hands over a business card. "Anything you need, feel free to call."

"Thanks, Benny."

"My pleasure."

As soon as he pulls away, I remove my shoes and walk barefoot up to the house. I can feel the blisters already. Thankfully,

I don't have to wear heels again anytime soon. I learned a lot today, and not just things about my job.

One: every day is casual Friday at McQuaid Motor Corp.

Two: Tucker's son, Robert, is a creep who came on to me no less than four times in our half-hour meeting.

Three: Tucker is a kind and generous boss, but is mostly hands-off as his son basically runs the company.

Four: Lloyd's Restaurant is heaven on earth to a girl who only eats what's on sale at the local grocers.

And five: I think I'm going to like this town.

Oh, and six: Percy Thatcher is amazing. He's really taken me under his wing. He didn't even bat an eyelash at my greenness when he started talking complicated corporate tax codes that I hadn't heard of since college.

The rest of this week and next has been scheduled so I'm meeting with the bookkeepers of each dealership in the mornings and going over past tax returns with Percy in the afternoons. It's going to be backbreaking work.

But it's exactly the kind of work I need to keep my mind off the fact that when I return home every day, no one is waiting. No husband to ask how my day went—that ship sailed two years ago. No son to jump into my arms, plant kisses on my cheek, ask what's for dinner, and cuddle up with before bed.

I go inside and strip out of my power outfit, glad that I made a good first impression, but even happier I don't have to buy more of them. I pour myself a glass of wine, take my phone to the couch and say a little prayer as I dial.

"Daniels residence," Janet answers.

"Hi, Janet. It's Dakota. I'd like to speak to Travis."

"Please hold ma'am."

I sip my wine, my heart hoping beyond hope that I'll get to hear his precious voice. God, I love that little boy more than my own life. I'd give anything for him. *Do* anything for him.

Oh, gosh. It occurs to me I was so nervous I never checked my bank account today. I put the phone on speaker and navigate to my banking app. My eyes bug out when I see the check has cleared and the balance is more than I've ever seen.

Even when Brian and I were married, we had separate accounts. His parents refused to give him an allowance if we had a joint one. His account was always fat. Mine was never bad, because back then, he paid all the bills allowing me to save all my money. He even paid for my last year in college, the extra courses I needed to earn my CPA, and the expensive CPA exam.

Suddenly, I'm elated. It's a feeling I haven't had since before Travis was taken away. With this huge advance, I can pay off Larry and have enough to put down a retainer on a new lawyer. Tucker was kind enough to ask the MMC corporate lawyer to provide some recommendations for good family lawyers. Finally I feel things may start happening.

"Dakota," snarls a hoity voice I recognize as Patty's. "Now's not a good time. Travis is eating supper."

"Patty, you have to let me speak to him. The judge said I was allowed phone calls."

"Well, maybe you should take it up with him then."

"Wait. Please. I'll be quick. Just two minutes." I try not to sound like I'm a beggar, although at this point that's exactly what I am. Patty already sees me as weak and pathetic. If I want to talk to my son, I need to come across as confident and reasonable. "Patty, I know you love Travis like he's your own. And I appreciate that. So you'll understand as a mother how important it is to keep a good relationship with our children. I'm sure you did the same with yours when they were at boarding school. It's more for Travis than it is for me. Surely you don't want him to feel abandoned. He could act out and that wouldn't be good for anyone."

Silence. For a moment, I'm wondering if she's still there. I look at the phone and see we're still connected. When I hear her huff, I know I've won even before she says it.

"Fine. Two minutes."

I smile and sink back into the comfortable leather couch with excited anticipation.

"Mommy, is it you?"

My heart soars, my throat swells with emotion, and I almost can't speak. "Y-yes, baby. It's me. Oh, I've missed you so much."

"I miss you too, Mommy. I hugged my pillow. I did it just like you told me."

A tear slips down my cheek. "I hug mine too. Every night I hug it. I hug you, baby. Did you get Charlie?"

"Charlie's here. But I only get him at night. Laura said those are Grammy's rules."

Right. Laura. The nanny.

"How do you like Laura?"

"She plays soccer with me. Do you know how far I can run now?"

"How far?" I ask, excitedly.

"Way far. Really super big far. There's a lot of grass and it goes forever."

"I'll bet you are fast."

"Laura says I'm the fastest."

I check the timer I set for two minutes knowing Patty won't dare give me a second more. "What else do you do? Do you get waffles for breakfast?"

"Yucky oatmeal," he says in a whisper which tells me Patty is listening. "But sometimes I get grilled cheese for lunch and Laura cuts off the crust. Where are you, Mommy? When are you coming back?"

"Well, baby, I started a new job today. And you'll never believe where I get to live. Travis, you'd love it here. There is a swing set in the back yard and lots of grass to play in."

"Can I see it?"

I sigh, not knowing when that could happen. "Maybe. But for now, I'm going to come to Grammy and Grandpa's to see you. Today is Monday and we get to see each other on Saturday, that's only five more days."

"Will you play soccer with me?"

"We can do whatever you want."

"Say goodbye, Travis," Patty demands in the background.

"Grammy says I have to go."

"I love you, sweet boy. Don't ever forget it. I'm going to hug my pillow extra tight tonight."

"I'll hug mine, too."

"I can't wai—"

"Goodbye, Dakota," Patty says, and then the line goes dead.

I put down the phone, a rush of emotions hitting me all at once. I'm sad, happy, pissed, determined, exhausted.

The doorbell rings. I sit up straight and wipe a tear. My first thought is that it's the jerkwad. He's finally come over to welcome the new neighbor. I look down at my wrinkled lounge pants knowing there's no time to change. But I do pull my hair out from the ponytail. Then I chastise myself for it. What do I care about the guy next door when I'm *so* not up for dating. And I'm definitely not up for dating a guy who gets derogatory epithets graffitied on his garage door.

Looking through the peephole, however, the person on the other side is about as opposite as you can get from the gorgeous guy next door.

I open the door to an older woman carrying a large basket. She smiles brightly when she sees me.

"You must be Dakota," she says jubilantly.

"Yes."

"I'm Rose Gianogi."

Cycling through everything I've learned about this town over the past few days, I remember who she is.

"Oh, you're Tucker's Rose."

I could swear I see her cheeks turn the same color as her name. "That I am. Although I like to think of it as he is Rose's Tucker."

I chuckle. "I rather like it that way myself." I motion to the hallway. "Please, come in."

"I wanted to drop off a care package. I know moving can be stressful." She hands the large basket to me.

"That is so generous of you. Would you like coffee? Or something stronger? I just opened a bottle of wine."

"Thank you for the offer, but I can't stay long. I just wanted to see how you're settling in."

I set the basket down. "This house is… well, it's more than I ever dreamed of. And it's almost perfect."

"Almost?" She gives me a sympathetic look. "I'm sure it will be as soon as your son is here to fill it with love and laughter."

When I look at her with fear in my eyes, she puts a gentle hand on my shoulder. "Not to worry, your secret is safe with me."

My gaze meets the floor. "I just don't want anyone to think I'm a terrible mother."

"Oh, sweet child. With what Tucker told me of your circumstances, I think everyone would believe quite the opposite."

"Still, I'd rather nobody know I have a son until this is worked out."

"As you wish. I do hope you're making friends. Have you met any of your neighbors yet?"

Her eyebrows go up with her last words and it has me wondering if she knows something I don't.

"I haven't met any neighbors. And I'm not sure I've made friends, but I met some very nice women. Do you know Regan Lucas? Oh, and I met Willow. I guess she's Tucker's granddaughter-in-law."

"I consider her mine as well." Her smile is a mile wide. "Willow and that adorable Izzy have been such a lovely addition to this town. Regan is quite charming as well. You'd be hard pressed to find better friends."

"I'm glad to hear it."

She checks the time. "I really must go. My love is taking me out for dinner. I hope we can sit for a longer chat very soon."

"I'd like that."

She nods to the basket. "My phone number is attached. Please call me anytime."

"Thank you so much for the housewarming gift." I don't tell her it's most likely the only one I'll get.

"I'll let myself out. You enjoy your wine. I'm betting you need it after today." She winks, turns, and heads for the door.

I take the basket to the table and go through it as I drink. There are muffins, two bottles of wine that are far more expensive than what's in my glass, scented candles, a bath bomb, some cheeses, nuts, and crackers, a gift certificate to a spa, and a small sign that reads **Welcome Home.**

I stare at the painted engraved wood, wanting so badly to consider this home, but knowing the only real home I could have is one that includes Travis.

Setting all that aside, I send off three emails. One is to Larry letting him know to expect a check within the week and also that I won't be needing his services any longer. The other two are addressed to the family lawyers recommended by Tucker's guy. I looked them up. One of them has won over eighty-five percent of his cases. I'm hoping my ties to Tucker McQuaid, along with my hopefully compelling story, will get a quick response from one of them.

When I peek outside, I notice what a clear night it is. I want to take my bottle of wine out back and look up at the stars.

It's only May first, and it still gets chilly at night, so I grab a blanket on my way out. Then I shut off all the lights so it's as dark as possible, and I pull a lounger to the middle of the yard.

I love looking up at the stars. I did it often as a child. But living in the city it's just not possible. There is too much light pollution. But here… it's fabulous. It's quiet. It's serene. It's dark enough to make out a few constellations. It's—

I can't help my scream when something crawls across my foot. Wine spills on my shirt and my blanket falls onto the ground as I bolt out of the chair and shake off my leg, still screaming at whatever it was that was slithering across my skin. But knowing it could still be in the grass, I hop back up and stand on the lounger.

"Jesus, are you okay?" a male voice booms.

I'm mortified that I'm wine-stained and disheveled. But I'm glad it's dark enough that maybe he can't see it. I calm myself enough to respond. "I… I'm fine. I just really really don't like bugs."

"Then maybe don't sit out here in the pitch black."

There is light coming from his back porch. It was dark a moment ago so he must have flipped it on before running over. I can't make out his face, or anything about him really since the light is behind him, but what I can see is that he's wearing a towel. And *only* a towel.

"I was, um, looking at the stars."

He laughs. "So I don't need to call 911? You're not dying?"

"Not unless it was a black widow crawling across my leg."

"So I can go finish my shower now?"

"Yeah. Uh, sorry."

I may be a little preoccupied wondering what he looks like up close and wishing my deck light was on. But then something occurs to me. Is he really going to leave without introducing himself?

As he's walking away, I step off the lounger and race up to the deck. But before I go inside, I turn back and shout. "See you around… Itty Bitty Jellybean."

He stops and spins. "So you saw that, did you? And it was Teenie Weenie."

I almost laugh. "I figured it wasn't the best time to make introductions."

He *does* laugh and then continues on his way. Just as he reaches the gate of his fence, he looks back over his shoulder. I can see him more clearly now as he's illuminated by his security lights. His eyes practically smolder when he says, "See you around, Gator Girl."

And then he's gone.

Chapter Eleven

Hudson

After lunch, I'm sitting at my desk trying to keep my eyes open. I didn't get much sleep last night. And not because I was on call either.

The girl. My neighbor. The forbidden woman next door. She's even more gorgeous up close. Her hair falls beyond her shoulders in glossy waves. Her nose is small and turns up ever so slightly at the tip. And her eyes seemed as dark as the night sky—a deep dark chocolate brown.

That she was bouncing from foot to foot atop a lounger with a wine-stained shirt somehow made her even more appealing. And I'm not even going to try and unpack that bit of a revelation.

Shit. She saw the graffiti. Does she think I'm a douche?

Kara comes through the door and hands me a cup of coffee. "It looks like you could use this. You seem to have been dragging all morning."

I have been. And my morning coffee wore off long ago. Thankfully the surgery I had this morning was routine.

I don't have trouble sleeping. Back in med school, and especially as an intern, I learned how to fall asleep quickly. Most of the time I was so exhausted I was out before my head hit the pillow. There was no time to think about anything, let alone a pretty girl.

Back then, if I wanted to get my rocks off, there was always another over-tired, stressed-out intern willing to work out her anxiety between the sheets for five minutes. Those were the days. No attachments. No expectations. No graffiti painted across my garage. No distracting girl next door.

I look up at Kara. "Being nice to me now?"

"Just being human, doctor. You falling asleep at a patient's bedside, or worse, messing up somehow, will not look good for anyone here."

I take the cup and put it on my desk so hard a bit sloshes out. "I don't mess up, Kara." I wipe up the spill and toss the napkin in the trash, noticing the way she's standing and staring. "Was there something else?"

She takes a step closer and lowers her voice. "I'm not with them." She nods behind her. "You know, all the others who blame you for being a guy who doesn't want to settle down." She shifts her weight from leg to leg. "I pretend to be because, well, women band together. But I wanted you to know, I'm…" She glances over her shoulder. "I'm available. For… whatever."

My brows go up as I take her in. She's young. Pretty. And she's new here, a recent grad from CCU. I knew there would be some who weren't drinking the poisonous swill spread by Lynda and her cronies. Ordinarily, I'd jump at the opportunity to bed someone like her. Hell, my dick would've been hard five minutes ago. The fact that it's not is, well… fucking strange.

Then again I have been giving my left hand quite a workout lately. It could be that. It could also be Lyle and his passive-aggressive warning

Or it could be the forbidden reptile next door.

My speaker goes off. "Exam three is ready for you, doctor."

I take a long drink, then raise my cup. "Thanks for this, Kara." I put my lab coat on and walk by her without one hint of a seducing glance.

~ ~ ~

When I finally pull into my garage, it's well after seven. People don't realize just how much time is required for this job. They think we deliver babies, do pelvic exams, and dole out advice. In reality, we do one twenty-four hour day of on-call per week and then spend three to four days in the office, waking up before dawn to make it to our 7:30 a.m. surgery, getting to the office by nine if that surgery goes as planned, and then seeing patients all day. Not to mention the occasional on-call weekends. And even though we schedule our last patients at three thirty, we're always so far behind, we're not done seeing them until after five. Then we spend a few hours jotting notes, charting, and making calls. We're always rushing. And we're always behind. And those are the good days. On days when one of the attendings has an emergency surgery or a patient goes into labor, we have to pick up the slack.

I walk to my mailbox, unbuttoning the top buttons of my shirt as I go and scrubbing a hand across my tired eyes. I might skip dinner tonight and go straight to bed. If I ever needed sleep, tonight is the night. I'll be the lead surgeon in a twin c-section tomorrow morning. Twins are rare in this small town and this will be my first set as an attending. It has to go well.

I blink twice when I see Gator Girl walking toward me. She's barefoot, wearing a men's shirt over a tank top, unbuttoned at the top and rolled up at the sleeves. The shirt is so long you can't see her shorts underneath. Maybe she's not wearing any. *Damn.* Her attire is doing nothing to squelch my attraction. A quick fantasy plays in my head like the reel of a movie, cut short by the realization that our mailboxes are only a foot apart. She's not walking toward me. She's going for her mail.

"Hey," she says.

My mind scrambles to figure out if it's a shy greeting—as if still embarrassed by the yard incident—or a casual one—as if I'm nothing more than any other neighbor retrieving his mail.

"Hello, Gator Girl."

"Why would you call me that?" She looks at me strangely. "My name is Dakota."

"It was your shirt."

She glances down.

"Not *that* shirt. The day you moved in. You were wearing a UF shirt."

It looks like she wants to smile, but she doesn't. I get the idea her smile would make her even more gorgeous, but somehow she won't do it. Or can't. It makes me wonder what her story is.

She holds out her hand. "I suppose we should formally meet then. I'm ordinarily not that squeamish about bugs, given I'm the one who has to kill them. But it was dark, and I was taken off guard."

I shake her hand. "Good to know."

She looks inside her mailbox. It's empty. She seems disappointed, which is strange considering she's only lived here a few days.

"Expecting something?" I ask.

She shrugs. "More like hoping for something." She turns and starts up her driveway. But then she stops and looks over her shoulder. "You know I'm happy to keep thinking of you as Jerkwad if that's how you want it."

I chuckle and shake my head. "It's Hudson. And I can explain," I say, nodding to my pristine white garage door.

"No need. Nice to meet you Hudson."

She's almost to her house. She didn't ask anything about me. It's as if she couldn't care less who she lives next to. "So, Gator Girl…"

She turns and gives me the stink eye.

I shrug. "Sorry, old habits die hard."

"Old habits? I just moved in four days ago. What is it?"

"I was wondering how the job was going."

Her eyes narrow. "What do you know about my job?"

I shrug. "It's a small town. CPA for McQuaid Motor Corporation. Impressive."

"I suppose. I kind of lucked into it."

Luck. The look on her face as she says it tells me she feels anything but lucky. And it only intrigues me more.

"So it's going okay?"

"As okay as you'd expect for a new job that has me being thrown in with sharks."

"Sharks?" I tuck my mail under an arm and walk up my driveway so we don't have to keep raising our voices.

"Well, one shark. The owner's son keeps hitting on me. It's creepy." A look of disgust crosses her face. "And I'm supposed to have lunch with him at his office on Friday."

It's apparent she has no clue who I am. And I'm not about to tell her now, especially since the shark she's referring to is my own father.

"Maybe you should tell him to fuck off."

"Maybe you didn't hear me say he's the owner's son."

"That doesn't mean he can hit on you."

"I won't have to deal with him much after this week. He doesn't have a lot to do with the financials. Besides, there are worse things to have to deal with."

Why do I feel the need to invite her over and hear her life story? Because the 'worse things' scenarios are flying through my head.

"Anyway," she says, looking at her phone with urgency. "I'd better go. I have to make a call."

"Okay." I wave my mail in the air. "Same time tomorrow?"

I hear the words come out of my mouth and I want to kick myself in it. I sound like a stupid adolescent.

She cocks her head.

I nod to the mailbox. "You know, for the mail."

"Oh." She doesn't laugh at my joke. "Being as we live next door, there is that possibility."

And then Gator Girl disappears inside.

Chapter Twelve

Dakota

I don't meet him at the mailbox—the gorgeous jerkwad next door. But I do gaze at him from my window. I observe as he walks slowly down his driveway, shuffling his feet. Is he tired after work, or is he stalling for some reason?

And I watch him tinker with his bikes, something he does a lot. And I look at him when he rides off down the street. Sometimes I wish I were riding off with him.

I'm… over Brian… right? The tingles I get when I look at Hudson is all the answer I need. But the empty bedroom down the hall is what's important now. Not starting a relationship with the guy next door, who may or may not be a jerkwad with a small penis.

I swallow. Now I'm thinking about his penis.

I'm retreating from the window when I see his car back out of the driveway. I really like his car. It seems to suit him. It's sleek and gorgeous and… dangerous—all the things I believe him to be.

It's early. Six-thirty in the morning to be exact. It's not the first time I've seen him leave this early. It's the third, but who's counting. His car comes to a stop in the road. His window is rolled down and I can see him clearly. He looks at my mailbox and then up at my house. Before I can step away, he catches me watching him and salutes me like he did that first day from his window.

I sip my coffee and pretend I wasn't standing at the window specifically to see him. Then I nonchalantly raise my cup to him before I turn and walk away.

~ ~ ~

There are a lot of things that are good about today. First, it's Friday, and who doesn't love Fridays? It's the last day of a long week; one I actually survived. And not only did I survive, I think I've done a pretty good job learning the ins and outs of MMC's financials. Second, I got an email back from Karl Wheeler, the lawyer who has agreed to file my appeal. And third, and by far the most important, I get to see Travis tomorrow.

Yes, there are a lot of good things about today. But being dropped off to have lunch with Robert McQuaid is definitely not one of them.

"What time shall I fetch you, Ms. Daniels?" Benny asks as he opens my door.

I want to ask him to stay close in case I need to make a quick getaway. Tucker's son gives me the creeps. When we met on Monday, I got the idea he thinks every woman at the dealership works for him in any way he asks them to.

He reminds me of Brian's parents. Entitled. The type of people who think that because they have money they are somehow superior to those of us who don't. And we should automatically give them whatever they demand. Because they also never feel like they need to ask for things they want.

"I'm not sure. It's a working lunch, so maybe a few hours."

He checks his watch. "Two o'clock then. Perhaps I'll make it one-thirty just in case."

The way he's looking at me confirms every suspicion I have about Tucker's son. At least I'm comforted knowing we won't be alone. The office manager and the bookkeeper will be joining us. That reminder gives me the confidence I need to hold my head high and go inside the dealership.

I pass by hundred-thousand-dollar cars in the showroom wondering why anyone would choose to spend so much money on transportation. It makes me wonder what Hudson does to be able to afford his flashy, ostentatious ride.

I shake the thought out of my head and scold myself for not being able to go mere hours without a man I hardly know invading my thoughts. Again.

This is only one of twelve car dealerships Tucker McQuaid owns. I've been to seven of them this week, and this one is the largest. I get the idea that's why his son works here instead of one of the others. While Tucker is the owner and CEO, Robert is the GM, overseeing all dozen of them. The GM. Not the CPA. Not the CFO. Not even a bookkeeper. So why he insisted on this lunch is beyond me.

I stop at the reception desk, recognizing Carmen from Monday. "Hi, Carmen. Nice to see you again. I'm here for a lunch meeting."

"Of course, Ms. Daniels. Follow me please."

She escorts me down a hallway and *past* the large glass-walled conference room Percy and I used on Monday. Perhaps there's a lunchroom?

"Right in here." Carmen opens a door to a room much smaller than the conference room, and much more private.

There's a table for six and a long console table on one side that's been set up with food warmers and ice trays. It smells divine. I'm wondering if they had it catered from Lloyd's.

"Mr. McQuaid will be in shortly. Help yourself to a drink if you like."

"Thanks, Carmen."

The way she looks at me when she leaves the room is… strange. Like she feels sorry for me having to be around her creepy flirtatious boss.

The door opens moments later. Robert walks through. Only Robert. Then he closes it.

He strides over to me, a huge smile on his face. "Dakota, how lovely to see you again."

I hold out my hand. He doesn't shake it. He hugs me instead. *Hugs me.*

I'm already getting cringy vibes and he's been here all of five seconds. "Thanks for having me." I take several steps back and open my briefcase. "I'm eager to get started." I glance at the door. "When can we expect Janice and Noreen?"

"It'll just be the two of us today."

I get a bad feeling in my stomach. "Oh, I was under the impression this was a business meeting."

"And who says we can't mix business with pleasure?" He goes to the buffet table and picks up a bottle of whiskey.

Whiskey at a business meeting?

"Can I offer you a drink?"

I walk over and get a bottle of water, noticing there's enough food here for a half-dozen people.

He pours a glass, holds it out to me, and leans close. "I'll let you in on a little secret. As I'm the boss around here, it's okay. If you're worried, I won't tell if you won't."

Suddenly I'm wondering if he's just talking about the whiskey.

Now I know why I got the look from Carmen. I wouldn't be surprised if she's been a victim of his misplaced authority. I get it though. I'll bet there are a slew of women in this dealership alone who could file sexual harassment charges against the man. But like most women, me included, we're too afraid of losing a good job. So we put up with it. It's wrong. It's disgusting. It's degrading.

It's for Travis.

All of this is for him.

I can deal with anything if it provides me with the means to get my son back. I mean, I'm not about to piss off the son of the guy who hired me.

I refuse the glass and hold up the bottle of water. "This will do just fine." I walk to the other side of the table and sit, shuffling through my briefcase. "Where would you like to start?"

He brings his whiskey over, sips it, and then leans against the table right next to where I'm sitting. "I'd like to start by getting to know you better."

I swallow hard. I need this job. I need it more than anything. But there are some things I'm just not willing to do.

Please, God, if you're listening, don't make me risk my job. Send someone through the door with an emergency. Cause an earthquake. A freak tornado.

Anything.

Chapter Thirteen

With a sandwich from the break room in one hand and another cup of coffee in the other, I head back to my office. I take off my lab coat, drape it over my chair and sit down to eat. When I go in for the first bite, I realize I'm not the least bit hungry. I'm not hungry because all I can think of is Dakota eating lunch with the 'creepy son of the owner.'

My dad. My own goddamn father is that creepy man.

And she's with him right now.

I know how my father treats women. Like property. Possessions. Toys with which to do what he wants.

Hatred, the color of blood, crawls up my spine, slithering through my every muscle and bone until I'm about to explode.

Tossing my lunch in the trash and grabbing my keys, I punch a button on my phone. "Kara, something's come up. Push all my appointments back an hour."

"Yes, Dr. McQuaid."

In minutes, I'm out the back door, in my car, and burning rubber out of the parking lot.

Fifteen minutes later, I park in the no parking zone at the dealership. But I don't give a fuck. I rip open the front door and rush to the front desk.

The girl looks up. "Hello, Hud—"

"Where's my father?"

She tosses a look over her shoulder. "Private conference room."

"Who else is in there?"

The look on her face tells me what I need to know before she even says it. "Just Ms. Daniels."

"Shit," I say under my breath, already heading down the back hallway.

I stop in front of the door and listen. Because although I know my father, there is a slight possibility that I'm overreacting. After all, Gator Girl has been the product of my every fantasy over the past week. And I'm smart enough to realize that maybe *I'm* the possessive one here.

If I go bursting in there, it could make her look bad. Maybe I need a reason. A reason for skipping out on patients in the middle of the day to save what could be a damsel in distress? Yeah—that's *so* not me. Yet here I am.

And just to prove the point that creepy doesn't fall too far from the tree, I press my ear to the door.

I don't hear anything for a minute. But then… then I hear two words. Two words that make my blood boil.

"Please don't!"

My hand is on the door handle when I hear more words that have me seeing red.

"I said no!"

I rip open the door and slam it shut behind me. Dakota looks like a lost little girl, making herself as small as possible as she sinks into her chair. My father's hand is on her shoulder and his face hovers near her ear.

He looks up at me in surprise. Yet he doesn't move his hand. "Hudson. To what do we owe the pleasure?"

My eyes don't meet his. They are trained on his hand. I walk over and forcibly remove it. "This lunch meeting is over."

Dakota looks embarrassed. Or maybe mortified. "Hudson, what are you doing here?"

Right. She still doesn't know who I am. So to her, I'm way overstepping my neighborly bounds.

"Answer the lady, son."

Dakota's head snaps from me to Dad and back to me. "Son?" Her jaw drops. "You're a McQuaid?"

I give her my keys. "Go wait in my car."

"I, uh…"

She's clearly torn between whether to follow my orders or his.

"Dakota, it's okay," I say with a soft voice that surprises me. "I'll deal with this. It'll all be fine. Please, go wait in the car."

Silently, she gathers her briefcase and walks out the door.

Dad shakes his head. "I'm not sure what had you barging in here." He looks at the door. "Ahhh, now I get it. She's *your* shiny new toy and you don't like to share."

"You entitled mother fucker. She's not anyone's toy."

Devious laughter comes out of his mouth. "Says the pot calling the kettle black."

I pull out my phone and call my grandfather, putting him on speaker.

"Hudson, my boy," he answers.

"Dakota won't be coming back to McQuaid Land Rover. Any dealership but this one. And there will be no repercussions."

Pappy sighs into the phone. "What happened?"

"Tell him," I say to Dad. "Tell him how you can't keep your dick in your pants."

Dad scoffs. "What happened was my overeager, obviously jealous son burst in on a business lunch between me and the Daniels girl." He looks up at me, sneering. "Looks like *you're* the one having a problem with your cock, son."

"I'll deal with this," Pappy says.

"What exactly does that mean?" I ask. I take the phone off speaker and put it to my ear. "Pappy, you can't fire her, she did nothing wrong. She's—"

"I've no intention of firing anyone, Hudson."

"But you'll take care of it?"

"I said I would, and I will."

"And she doesn't have to come back to this location?"

"Unescorted, no. But there may be times it'll be unavoidable, such as tax season."

"I want to know about it. Any time she comes here, I want to be in the loop."

"Hudson," his grim voice scolds. "Remember what I told you."

How could I fucking forget?

"I remember. So we have an understanding?"

"We do. Benny is driving me at the moment, so would you mind taking Ms. Daniels over to Ford-Lincoln where she'll meet with Percy and some others for the afternoon?"

I'm amused at how he reminds me to stay away from her yet in his next breath he asks me to drive her.

"Sure. No problem."

He ends the call. I tuck my phone away and glare at my derelict father. "One day you're going to end up in jail if you keep groping the employees."

He laughs. "Don't you know by now we're untouchable? All those dollar signs behind our names, it makes us kings."

"That's disgusting." I reach for the door. "*You*—you're disgusting. Don't ever touch her again. Don't even look at her."

"As if you can tell me whom I can interact with."

I stomp over to him. "Don't fucking do it. Or I swear to God I'll—"

"You'll what?" He mocks a scared look. "You'll put me in the corner for a time out?"

"Don't you understand what's going on here? Pappy lets you work here because he figures you're better off here than out in the world with nothing to do. You're nothing more than a talking head. A piece of shit. And I'm embarrassed to be your son."

He presses me into the wall with his forearm. "How dare you speak to your father that way."

I bat his arm away. "You haven't been a father to me in a dozen years. The truth is, you never were. No wonder Mom left you for a Calloway. Anyone would be better than the likes of you. Aren't you tired of being a pathetic aging predator with a beer gut who only gets dates because of his bank account?"

"Careful, son, the pot is rearing its head again."

I ignore his statement and go to the buffet table knowing Dakota must be hungry. I put some finger food on a plate and cover it with another. Then I grab a bottle of water and leave. I don't bother saying goodbye. If I had my way, this would be the last time I'd see my old man. But I know in this small town, there's no such luck.

Out front, Dakota is sitting in the passenger seat of my car. And I might like the way she looks in it a little too much. I've never wanted a woman in my car longer than it took to get her to my bed. My head slumps. Because *ding ding ding…* my father is one hundred percent correct. I am the fucking pot.

I push the notion aside and get in the car, handing her the plate. "Didn't want you to miss out on lunch."

As if on cue, her stomach rumbles. "Thanks." She takes the plate and sets it on her lap. "Am I fired?"

"No. But you won't be coming back here anytime soon. I cleared it with Tucker."

"You talked to him?"

"He is my grandfather."

"Why didn't you tell me?"

Why didn't I? Usually, I have no problem going around and flaunting my heritage *and* my money.

I start the car. "You have another meeting to go to. I'll take you."

"Which dealership is your office in?"

"I don't work for my grandfather." I nod to the food. "Eat. You won't be sharp for your meeting on an empty stomach."

She eats and I drive. There are no more words between us. But there are glances. And she blushes when I look over and a bit of shrimp sauce is on her chin. She swipes it with her finger and licks it off.

And my dick turns to stone. Thank God I don't have to get out of the car.

She finishes lunch just as I pull up. "If he ever gives you trouble again, let me know and I'll take care of it."

She doesn't say anything, which gives me the idea she wouldn't let me know. And the idea of her having another confrontation with my father makes me ill.

"Thank you for the ride," she finally says. Then she walks away.

And I watch. I watch her walk away just like I watch her through the hole in the fence. I watch her have a nightly glass of wine on her back porch. I watch her leave her house and go for a walk or a bike ride. I watch her at the window as I back out of my driveway every morning.

Jesus. Maybe my dad isn't the one with the problem here. Maybe it's me.

But when she turns and gives me a look over her shoulder, somehow I get the idea that she doesn't mind me watching.

And I do something I rarely do anymore. I smile.

Chapter Fourteen

As I wait for the cupcakes to finish baking, I whip up Trav's favorite frosting and think of all the things I'm grateful for. And who'd have thought Jellybean Jerkwad next door would top the list. Or should I say the McQuaid next door. I shake my head, still not believing I live next to Tucker's grandson and the son of the asshole who was groping me.

I like to think I'd have stood up to the bastard myself. That I would have kicked him in the balls and told him he has no right to treat women like they exist simply for his pleasure. That I would have chosen my dignity over the job.

But the truth is, I'm not sure I'd have done any of it. Because it's that very job that has allowed me to hire the man Tucker assures me is the best family lawyer on the East Coast. Karl and I had a zoom call earlier and he's confident he can get things moving quickly considering the circumstances. He'll file the appeal right away. He's even having someone interview all my former neighbors about the false allegations made by the Daniels.

Still, though, the Daniels have their own high-priced attorneys. They themselves are high-priced attorneys. I feel it might be a fight to the death. I can only hope I'm not the one who'll be buried.

While I'm frosting the cupcakes, I catch a glimpse of red out the front window. It has to be Hudson's car. As far as I know, he drives the only red Maserati in town. It reeks of wealth. And if memory serves, it even *smells* rich—if rich had a smell.

When I catch myself straining my neck to see if he's walking down the driveway for his mail, I roll my eyes.

He saved me today.

He saved my job.

I look down at the two dozen cupcakes knowing I can't take them all to Travis, and plate some of them on a decorative platter from the cupboard. Heading for the front door, I catch my reflection in the foyer mirror. I set down the platter and change my shirt. Then I convince myself I only did it because I'd dripped batter on the sleeve. When I give my hair a fluff, I know I'm kidding myself.

"You have one job, Dakota." I leave the cupcakes sitting on the front table and park myself on the couch. "To get Travis back." I put my feet up on the coffee table. "Anything else is just a distraction." I sink back into the cushion. "He's not someone you should want, need, or otherwise get entangled with." I look at the ceiling. "Plus, he's… well, he's a McQuaid. He probably sits in his sleek red car counting his millions. And you're a…" I close my eyes. "A poor, unfit mother according to the state of New York."

Wow. I'm pathetic. I can't even win a conversation with myself.

I crane my neck and look at the platter of cupcakes.

"Fuck the state of New York. Who are they to tell me who I am?" I stand and stride over, picking up the cupcakes and walking out of the house and through our connecting yard. My confidence wanes a bit the closer I get to his front door.

But I don't have time to back out. The door opens before I get the chance.

He's surprised to see me.

"Oh, hey," he says. "I was just going for the mail."

Flustered, I hold out the platter and practically shove it into his ribs, getting chocolate frosting on his shirt that no doubt costs more than I make in a day. "Oh my gosh. I'm so sorry. If you take it off I'll wash it." I feel my face heat up. "I mean, not right now. You can take it off later when the time is right." *Not helping.* "Or, you know, whenever." I cover my face with my hands. "This is so not how this was supposed to go. I just wanted to say thanks for today." I motion to the driveway. "I'm just gonna go drink wine and pretend this never happened."

I shake my head at myself as I walk away.

"Thanks, Gator Girl," he calls out after me. "Chocolate is my favorite."

I wave my hand in the air without turning. I've already embarrassed myself enough for one day.

Back in the house, I swap shirts again, taking off the ridiculous one showing a hint of cleavage. What was I thinking? I pour myself a glass of wine, get my phone, and go out onto the back porch.

This is my favorite time of day. The yard faces west, so every evening I watch the sun as it sets and gets swallowed by the trees behind the house. It's beautiful. I can't wait for Travis to watch it with me.

At the same time, this is also the most stressful time of day. Because I never know when I make the call if I'm going to get to talk to him. More often than not, I'm given an excuse for why I can't. I tell myself it won't matter as much tonight because I get to see him tomorrow. But I know I'm lying. It does matter. It matters to me. It matters to him. It matters to our relationship that has become fragile thanks to the conniving people who have been entrusted with his care. I can't bear the thought of my son becoming close with them. Or even the nanny. Is he bonding with her over their soccer games? Is she reading him books at night? Does she hug him?

I stop with the torturous thoughts and pick up the phone. As always, Janet answers.

"Hi, Janet. It's Dakota. Can I speak with Travis please?"

"I'll see ma'am."

And as always, I'm made to wait painfully long minutes—I'm sure as an added form of torture—until someone comes back on the line.

This time, however, my heart soars when I hear my sweet boy's voice. "Hi, Mommy!"

"Hey, baby. I can't wait to see you tomorrow. Only one more sleep and then we'll be together. And I have a surprise for you."

"You do? What is it?"

I laugh. "It wouldn't be a surprise if I tell you."

"Can we play soccer when you come?"

"We can do whatever you like."

"Goody!"

There's a voice in the distance.

"Grammy says it's time for my bath."

Of course it is. "Okay. I'll dream of you tonight. I love you, Travis."

"Love you too, Mommy. Bye."

The line goes dead. Thirty seconds. That's all the time they gave me. And if you add up all the time I've talked with him over the last nine days it's probably less than ten minutes. Ten minutes. I used to get him twenty-four-seven. A tear slips out of the corner of my eye. It's both a happy and a sad one. Because I get to see him tomorrow. I get to see him for six glorious hours.

I finish my wine, go inside, and have one more glass to make me sleepy. Because even though it's only seven-thirty, I want to go to bed and make tomorrow come as quickly as possible.

Sleep eludes me, however, when my mind shifts from my son to the chocolate-stained millionaire next door. Questions I hadn't thought of bombard me. He said he doesn't work for MMC. But then why was he there? And why would he bother coming to my rescue? How did he even know—

My eyes fly open. *Because I told him.*

Earlier this week, I told him about Tucker's creepy son and my lunch plans on Friday.

Did he show up there solely to protect me from his scumbag father?

I drift off to sleep with a strong urge niggling in the back of my mind. The urge to figure out the mercurial man next door. Is he the gallant millionaire who saves damsels in distress? Or is he the jerkwad painted on his garage door?

Chapter Fifteen

I toss and turn all night thinking of Gator Girl. Thinking that no woman has ever made me lose sleep. Thinking that I'm totally fucked that she's the one all up in my head.

For days I went to the mailbox at the same time, dragging my feet, hoping to see her. But she never showed.

She was avoiding me.

I was thinking maybe Lynda Graves got to her after all.

Or Pappy.

But now I know why. Pieces of her back-porch conversation race through my head.

"Hey, baby. I can't wait to see you tomorrow."

"We can do whatever you like."

"I'll dream of you tonight. I love you, Travis."

Travis. So he's the reason she didn't meet me at the mailbox.

But she baked me cupcakes. Then again, maybe she'd have baked them for anyone who got her out of the situation with my father.

I heard the excitement in her voice when she was on that call. She sounded happy. In the few times I've spoken with her, she never sounded that way. It was as if a light switch had been flipped. She's in love. Just fucking great. The only fresh meat in this Podunk town has a boyfriend.

After a few pathetic hours of off-and-on sleep, I decide to get up when a sliver of dawn peeks through the slit of my curtains. I don't look through them as I have every other morning. I refuse to let her take up any more real estate in my head. I take a piss, get dressed, grab a bottle of water, and head out on my bike, peddling the beautiful, off-limits, and decidedly taken girl next door out of my mind.

I punish myself with twenty extra miles today. By the time I'm finished, I have no energy to think. Good, then. Mission accomplished. I make myself a sandwich and take a much-needed nap.

When I wake, the thoughts are back. I curse them. I curse her. But most of all I curse Pappy for his goddamn warning. Because if I'm being honest, ever since he issued it, she's all I fucking think about. And she's everywhere. She's in her yard. She's in her driveway waiting for a ride. She's walking into town or riding through the trails. But she's not everywhere today. Today she's with *him*. I haven't seen a trace of her all day.

Still—she even seems to be in my own goddamn house.

I stare at the cupcakes on the counter. I take one of them and a beer, go out front, and sit on my top step.

Not five minutes later, it's as if fate is playing a cruel trick. Dakota is walking down the sidewalk. As she gets closer, I see her face. Her expression is indescribable. It's like she's happy and sad at the same time. Maybe she's happy because she just got boned, but sad that it might not happen again for a while.

Where is this Travis? In the city most likely.

She doesn't see me as she passes. She doesn't even spare a glance toward my house.

"Hot date?" I ask from my perch on the step.

Finally, she turns my way. "I, uh… didn't see you there. And, no. No hot date."

Liar.

"Where were you then?"

"The city."

"Why did you go to the city?"

She cocks her head. "I'm not allowed to go to the city?"

"I'm just saying, you haven't left your house much except for work and exercise, so I was wondering what's in the city."

Even as the words leave my mouth I realize I'm coming off as a creepy stalker.

Her hands land defensively on her hips. "I did just move from there, you know."

"Why?"

"Why did I move from the city?"

"Yeah. Why not just commute? Especially since you'll work remotely after next week."

Jesus, Hud. Stop with the questions.

"Why the third degree, Hudson?"

"Why the secretiveness, Dakota?"

"Listen, it's been a long day. I'm tired."

I stand. "Hold on. Wait here." I go inside with my uneaten cupcake, dump it along with the rest into the trash, and take the plate out front. "Here."

She takes it and raises a brow. "You ate them already?"

I shrug. "Turns out I don't like chocolate that much after all." I turn and go back inside.

~ ~ ~

It's been weeks since I've talked to her. And, yeah, I get that maybe I acted like a stupid fucking prick. But she's a liar. Why didn't she just tell me about this Travis guy? Every other Saturday she scampers off to the city. Why every other Saturday? Maybe because he's married and that's when they've arranged to have their affair.

I stopped going out back. I stopped listening when she calls him. I don't need to sit here and listen to her fawn over another guy when my dick still gets hard every time I think of her. And every time I think of how Dad treated her, my blood boils.

I've found myself in a position I've never been in before. I think it's called infatuation.

"Dr. McQuaid, exam room five is ready for you."

I'm pulling double duty today as Lyle was called in for an emergency c-section and I'm covering some of his patients. I choke down my protein bar—the only food I've had time for today—and head out of my office. On autopilot, I grab the chart on the outside of the door and absentmindedly flip through it. Nothing special. Annual pap smear.

I knock once and step inside. My heart lodges in my throat when I see Dakota Daniels in a patient gown sitting on the table. I glance down at the chart, finally bothering to read the name. *Holy shit.* "Um… hi."

Her obligatory smile is immediately replaced by shock. Her legs humorously snap together at her thighs, and she pulls the gown tightly around her. Her jaw drops. "You're a *doctor?*"

Chapter Sixteen

Dakota

I can't pick my jaw up off the patient table. My millionaire maybe-jerkwad neighbor is a doctor. And not just any doctor, a gynecologist. Apparently *my* gynecologist.

"Well, you never bothered to ask what I do," he says, setting my chart on the counter.

"I did ask."

"You asked if I worked for McQuaid Motor Corporation."

"Same difference. You could have said something."

"Why would it have mattered?"

"Because," I say, pulling the paper cover over my legs. "It would have. Besides, my appointment was with Dr. Richards."

"He was called into surgery." He pulls the stool over and sits. "I'm covering his patients today. But, hey, you're free to reschedule. I don't want you to be uncomfortable."

I laugh sarcastically. "Hudson, everything about what I'm here for is uncomfortable."

"If it makes you feel any better, men have to be checked for hernias and enlarged prostates."

It's hard not to smile at his attempt to lighten my mood. "Ha ha."

"So are we doing this or not?"

"We're neighbors. Is that allowed?"

"If I wasn't allowed to examine any of my friends, neighbors, or acquaintances, I wouldn't have any patients. This is a small town, Dakota. As long as we're not in a romantic relationship, it's perfectly acceptable."

Romantic relationship. I'm not sure why I feel sad at his words. I mean the guy has avoided me like the plague ever since he gave me back the cupcake platter like a jealous lover. I've thought a lot about it over the past several weeks. He *was* acting jealous. That means he must like me. Or did. And he thinks I have a boyfriend in the city. I could make this right by telling the truth. Maybe then it wouldn't be okay for me to be on this table because he would ask me out.

But I can't tell anyone about Travis. Not yet.

I should reschedule. But then he might think I like him. Or am scared. Or embarrassed. Which—newsflash—I am *all* of those things.

Why do I think me walking out of here would be like letting him win? And if I know anything about myself, it's that I hate losing. I suck up my feelings. "It's fine. I'm already a few months late for my annual, no need putting it off any longer. Especially considering that, yes, we're *just* neighbors."

He doesn't miss my overdramatic emphasis on the word *just.*

"Good. Great. As long as you're sure."

"I'm totally fine with it," I lie. "Unless this would make *you* uncomfortable."

In my head, I'm saying *'Game on.'*

He gets up to wash his hands. "I deal with vaginas for a living, Dakota."

He puts on a good show, but I see his expression. It's almost as if *he's* the one who's scared and embarrassed. And totally uncomfortable.

Oh, my God. Am I really going to let the guy I'm crushing on do this? "Okay, fine. I guess we're good then."

"I guess we are." He presses a button on the phone. "Tech to exam room five."

Right. There needs to be a woman present. Oh God, this is getting more excruciating by the minute.

A woman walks in, smiles, and then stands in the corner working on something. She never makes eye contact.

"Lie back," Hudson says. "I'm going to open your gown for a breast exam."

Oh my God. I was so concerned about the *down there* part, I totally forgot about *this* part.

"Do you perform these yourself?" he asks as I lie back.

I shrug.

"You should. Younger women can have breast issues as well. Do them in the shower when you're soaped up."

My heart thunders as he moves the gown aside and his fingers start rooting around on my left breast. I'm sure he can feel my racing heartbeat. I've never been so embarrassed. Why the hell did I agree to this?

Thankfully, he's not looking at me. He looks thoughtfully at the wall as his fingers work their way in a circular motion from the nipple out. Then he does the same thing with the right one. When he's finished and closing my gown, his eyes finally capture mine, and if I'm not mistaken, we both turn the same shade of crimson.

He clears his throat nervously. "Put your feet in the stirrups and scoot to the edge of the table."

This isn't my first rodeo. I've had men's heads between my legs before. Both sexually and medically. So why does this one particular man both intimidate and infatuate me at the same time?

He pulls his rolling stool over and dons a pair of gloves. "More," he says. "Your butt should almost be falling off the edge."

He's down there. Inches from my most intimate area. With a brighter-than-the-sun light shining directly on my coochie. Can this get any more mortifying?

"Good. I'm going to touch you now."

If I thought my heart was racing a moment ago, that's nothing compared to what it's doing right now. His low, rough, sexy voice telling me he's going to touch me is exactly how he sounds in my dreams. And strike me dead if I haven't had a fantasy or two in my life about a hot gynecologist. I mean, who hasn't? But my fantasy is nothing like this. This is more like being stuck in the dream where you're naked in a crowd of people.

I look at the woman in the corner who is still busy doing whatever she's doing in an attempt to make me less uncomfortable over the fact that I'm about to have a metal speculum shoved up my vagina.

"Relax," Hudson says. "You're too tense. Let your legs fall open."

"Relax?" The laugh that bellows out of me is teetering on maniacal. "You're kidding right?"

He momentarily looks at me. Our eyes lock for a moment. And if I were a betting woman, I'd say his heart is beating almost as fast as mine is. "Just try."

Finally, the assistant steps over, squirts gel on the speculum and then gets the pap smear thingy off the counter.

I blow out a breath, trying to unclench as cold metal enters me, wondering how it's possible that time has completely slowed to a crawl just to draw out this torture.

Then relief strikes as the speculum is removed. It's short lived, however, when Hudson holds up two fingers, lubricated with jelly. "I'm going to manually check your uterus and ovaries."

My head smushes the flat paper pillow underneath it as I pull an arm up to cover my face. The manual exam. Apparently I'd blocked that out as well. "Oh my God, just get it over with."

I swallow as fingers push inside me. I keep my arm in place and my eyes shut, not wanting to know if he's looking at me. His other hand presses down on my lower left belly, and then the lower right.

"Everything looks good," he says as he withdraws. "We're done. You can scoot back."

"You sure?" I say boldly, forgetting about the woman in the corner. "I mean you haven't poked and prodded *all* of my orifices."

He chuckles. "We save the digital rectal exam for when you're older."

Heat crosses my face. Or better yet—my entire upper body. "Well, that's something to look forward to."

I don't miss Hudson's smile as he tosses his gloves in the trash. "Get dressed. I'll meet you in my office right after."

He takes my chart and is followed out the door by the unnamed woman who shall henceforth always be known as the lady with whom is the closest I ever came to a threesome.

I sit up, and my head slumps over into my cupped hands. Did all that really just happen with my gorgeous neighbor?

I'm reading way too much into this. I'm just another patient to him. He's probably seen so many vaginas and felt so many boobs that mine are just one of many he'll forget as soon as he leaves the office. As I pull on my clothes, another thought makes me pause. He's seen thousands of vaginas. Does that mean he loves them outside of work, or hates them? I mean, in my opinion, most people don't like to take their work home with them. At the end of the day, the last thing I want to do in my spare time is crunch numbers. What if he feels the same? What if he's bored with the female body after touching countless numbers of them. Maybe he's even disgusted after seeing what comes out of them.

Or maybe…

Maybe it makes him the ultimate expert on female pleasure.

Stop it, Dakota. You do not need anything else feeding your inappropriate fantasies.

And now. Now I have to go sit across from him in his office. We'll be eye to eye instead of eye to vagina. Can he ever look at me the same way?

I think on it. Was there *a way?*

Yes, there was. Or at least there was before the cupcake debacle.

I finish tying my shoes, take a cleansing breath, and go out the door.

Chapter Seventeen

Hudson

I sit and stare at her chart, not really reading it at all but thinking how that was the strangest ten minutes of my life.

This is my job. My trained profession. Yet I was shaking like an intern. She probably thinks I'm a terrible doctor. Ironically, I've never worked so goddamn hard to do everything right and by the book.

Dakota is different. As a patient. As a neighbor. As a woman. I knew it the first time I saw her. I swear to God something has shifted inside me. Then again, it could just be me fighting back against my grandfather's warning.

This is good. She's a patient now. There's an ethical line I won't cross. Maybe that will get my head back to normal and out of Gator Girl's tractor-beam-like pull.

A throat clears. I look up and she's in my doorway. My pulse races. *Jesus, get it together.*

I motion to the chair on the other side of my desk. "Come in."

She looks at the door. "Do I…?"

"It's fine. Leave it open."

She sits but doesn't make eye contact.

I do my best to pretend that what just happened wasn't the strangest experience of my life. This girl—this *woman*—is fucking perfect inside and out. And now this perfect woman is even more off-limits than before. And fuck me, that only makes her sexier.

I flip open her chart. "As I said, everything looks good. Have you ever had an abnormal pap smear?"

"No."

I go through the patient form she filled out. And even though she answered all the questions, I ask anyway, because something isn't adding up.

"And just some standard questions. Have you had any children?"

She looks at the model of a uterus on my bookshelf. "Um… no."

"Pregnancies?"

She shakes her head.

She's lying. She has a multiparous cervix. Women who haven't had a child have a tight, pinpoint cervix. Hers is a slit—the telltale sign of it having been fully dilated. It never ceases to amaze me how women think trained physicians won't notice such things.

I don't press her on the issue, however, because she most likely has her reasons for lying. Maybe she was pregnant as a teen and gave the baby up for adoption. Perhaps she had a stillborn child. Or even worse, a healthy child who later died. And admitting it out loud would be painful.

"What form of birth control do you use?"

"I don't."

I look her in the eye even though she's still averting hers. "That's not very responsible, Dakota."

Finally she locks eyes with me. "I don't use any birth control because I don't have the occasion to."

"Oh. So you're saying you aren't sexually active."

A blush crosses her face as she shakes her head. "Not lately. No."

I'm not sure which pleases me more, her blush, or the fact that she's not boning anyone.

But something isn't adding up. The *I love you, Travis.* And the every-other-Saturday trips to the city for what I thought was a clandestine affair.

"So you don't need any prescriptions?"

"I was thinking, as long as I'm here, maybe I should get on the pill. You know, just in case."

The way she says it, coupled with the way she's looking at me, has my dick coming to life. *Down, boy.*

I get out my prescription pad and write her a script. "Let me know if you have any issues. Breakthrough bleeding, nausea. You don't smoke, do you?"

"No. Never."

She says it with such authority it's like she's trying to prove a point.

"Good. Unless you have any other concerns then, you're free to go." I hand her the chart. "Take this to the counter and they'll check you out."

"Okay." She takes it and heads for the door. Before crossing the threshold, she turns, hesitating momentarily. "Hudson, was that as God-awful strange for you as it was for me?"

Finally, I let my guard down. I sigh deeply then laugh. "Like you wouldn't believe."

She cocks her head. "So it wasn't just me?"

"It wasn't just you."

She cracks a hint of a smile. "See you around the neighborhood?"

I nod. "That you will."

Once she's gone, I get up and close the door. Then I crouch over, putting my hands on my knees. Because… *fuck*. I am totally screwed.

~ ~ ~

Pulling up to the house, there seems to be a lot of activity next door. A plumbing truck. A pickup. And my grandfather and his girlfriend, Rose, are standing out front with Dakota.

I park in my garage and cross the yard. "What's up?"

"Busted pipe," Pappy says. "Flooded most of the damn house. All the flooring has to be replaced along with most of the baseboards."

"Dang." I look at Dakota who naturally seems upset.

Two men walk out of the house. One is wearing overalls with *Gray's Plumbing Inc* stitched over the left breast. The other man's shirt has a faded name of a construction company I can't quite make out. But the guy seems familiar.

"Hey," the familiar one says as he walks over. "Hudson, how's it hangin'?"

When I look at him with drawn brows he adds, "Billy Nickle from Cal Creek High. We played baseball together."

"Right," I say, not really remembering him at all. "How are you?"

He thumbs to his pickup. "Got my own company now. I realize that don't put me anywhere with the likes of you all, but hey, it's somethin'."

"It's very impressive," Rose says. "You should be proud of owning your own company."

"So, Ms. Daniels," he says to Dakota.

"It's just Dakota."

"Well, Dakota. I can do the whole job in a week after the materials come in, which will take at least five business days. I'm sorry to say you won't want to live here during that time."

Dakota looks at the ground.

Billy puts a hand on her shoulder. "But don't you worry, I'll have it done as fast as I can."

There is conversation going on around me, but all I can see is his hand lingering on her. And I don't fucking like it.

"It's the perfect solution," Rose says. "Hudson?"

"Oh… what?"

"You're right next door. You'll be out of the house most days. She'll be here where her things are. And she can keep an eye on the repairs."

"Um… *what?*"

"Your guest room. It'll be ideal for Dakota, don't you think?"

I stare at Rose, not quite believing what she's suggesting. "You want her to stay with me. In my house?"

Dakota shifts nervously. "I'm not sure that's a—"

"Nonsense," Rose says. "Hudson will be happy to help. And he will be quite the gentleman, I assure you." She turns to me. "Isn't that right, Hudson?"

I look at my grandfather. Surely he's going to strike down Rose's idiotic idea. "Will you ladies give us a moment?" He walks to the side of the yard, and I follow. "You know how I hate to disappoint Rose. If this is what she thinks is best, I won't argue. But, grandson, you will do as she said. And you'll do good to remember our agreement. *Gentleman.* Got it?"

"Agreement?" I scoff. "You mean your threat."

"Do we understand each other?"

"I don't like houseguests." *Translation: I don't want the beautiful woman of my goddamn wet dreams whose business I was all up in mere hours ago to sleep in the bedroom next to mine with only four inches of drywall between us.*

"You'll deal with it." He nods to his girlfriend. "For Rose."

I huff out a long breath. "Fine."

He escorts me back to the ladies. "It's settled then. Hudson will help you bring whatever things you need over to his house where you'll stay throughout the renovations."

Dakota looks hesitant. "I don't want to be a burden."

"It's fine."

The contractors leave, the leak having been repaired, and Tucker and Rose start down the sidewalk. Something occurs to me, and I step up behind them. "Pappy?"

He turns.

"Why were you here? I mean this is Uncle Paul's property. Shouldn't *he* be dealing with it?"

"We were walking by on our evening stroll when Dakota came home and discovered the flooding."

"I guess it's good luck you were around to take charge then."

Rose looks at him strangely. "I'd say that *was* a bit of good luck."

"Come now, darling. We want to finish our walk before dark."

I go back over to Dakota, then motion to my house. "Let me change and I'll come help you get your things."

"You really don't have to. I feel terrible about putting you out."

"It's not a big deal. My house is big enough for the two of us. It's even got a nice back deck where you can take your nightly wine."

Her head cocks to the side. *Shit.* My stalker side is coming out.

I backpedal. "I mean, if you like that sort of thing."

She thumbs to her house. "I'll just go get started."

"See you in a few."

I walk casually back to my house, then race inside, change clothes, tidy up the guest bedroom and the kitchen, and then take a breath. And then another. Because suddenly I feel like an adolescent whose wish has just been granted by a big blue fucking genie.

Chapter Eighteen

I remove my shoes and slosh barefoot across my soaked bedroom carpet, packing only one suitcase with the necessities. After all, I'll only be right next door if I need anything else. I take my favorite framed picture of Travis off the nightstand, place it on top of the clothes, and zip up the bag.

How am I moving into the guest room of the doctor who examined me mere hours ago? The very man I'm drawn to for inexplicable reasons. The man I know nothing about except that he's from an uber-rich family and has a pissed-off ex-girlfriend who leaves nasty epithets on his garage door. It's just all too surreal.

The doorbell rings. I drag my suitcase through the drenched carpet, then across the wet hardwood floors that, despite the many fans set up to dry them, are already warping.

When I open the door, Hudson and I stand in silence. It's as if we're both replaying the events of earlier in our minds and neither of us know quite what to say.

Finally he steps inside. "How can I help?"

I motion to the suitcase. "I'm just bringing this one. I can always pop over for more clothes. Let me just grab my purse and my work stuff." Work. I almost forgot about that little complication. "Hudson, you know I work from home, don't you? I hope that won't be a problem."

"It won't be."

The shortness of his words sends guilt climbing my spine. "I'm sorry you got roped into this. If it becomes too much of an inconvenience, I'll find a hotel."

"I said it won't be a problem." He pulls up the handle of the suitcase. "Now are you coming or what, Gator Girl?"

Somehow, him calling me that breaks the tension and I follow him out the door. "I'm right behind you, Jellybean."

He stops and I almost trip over the suitcase. He turns. "Just… no."

"Well it's hardly fair that you have a nickname for me and I can't have one for you."

His face twitches into a half-grin. "If you insist on having one, call me Hud."

"Hud?" I scrunch my nose.

"It's short for Hudson."

I purse my lips. "I wasn't born yesterday. It's just so… boring." I study him, my head moving from side to side, and I think. "How about *Doctor* Jellybean?"

He silently laughs. "Better, but still no."

Hudson rolls my bag across the driveway then picks it up when we walk through the grass connecting our yards. I don't miss how his muscles ripple and bulge as he carries the heavy suitcase with one hand. Wow—how is someone who basically sits for a living in such good shape? Then I think of his bike. Or should I say, bikes. I've seen him on several different ones. He doesn't know I watch him sometimes when he's in his driveway tinkering with one or the other.

He escorts me through his front door and parks my suitcase in the foyer, both of us standing here like we don't know what to do next.

"Is it always going to be this weird between us?" I ask.

"You think it's weird? You mean because of earlier? It's no big deal."

"No big deal?" I raise a brow. "Are you telling me you weren't the least bit uncomfortable?"

"It's my job, Dakota."

"That's not what I asked."

He leans against the wall. "Fine, yeah, it was a little strange. Didn't we already cover this topic in my office?"

"Hudson, honestly, it was strange even before I walked into your exam room."

"You think I'm strange?"

"That's not what I said. This, us, we have some strange kind of energy between us."

Oh my God, did I just say that?

He blows out a long breath. "So I'm not the only one who felt it. Come on, I'll give you a tour and then you can unpack."

We walk into the large open living room, and it is definitely not what I expected. The walls are painted a crisp cream color with glossy double crown molding. Decorative abstract art hangs along one long wall. A large wrought-iron clock hangs on another. "Huh."

He follows the direction of my gaze as I peruse our surroundings. "What?"

"Not exactly the bachelor pad I was anticipating."

"You thought there would be empty beer cans and pizza boxes lying around?"

I shrug. "Or something." I step over and run a finger along the edge of an interesting sculpture on his bookshelf. "Did you decorate it yourself?"

"My mom has a knack for these things."

I narrow my eyes. "Your mom? As in the woman married to your dad?"

He scoffs. "Hardly. She divorced him when I was a kid. I guess you have firsthand knowledge of why that might have happened."

"Well, then. Good for her."

As we pass the large windows overlooking his back yard, I admire his huge deck. It's quite possibly three times the size of mine and has two levels. And, oh—he has a hot tub.

"You're free to use it," he says, seeing me stare at the large spa. "The controls are right over here." He points to a panel on the wall by the French doors leading outside. "It's great for relaxing after a long day."

"Thanks. I'll keep that in mind."

He leads me through his kitchen. Like the deck, it's larger than mine, with a big island in the center with a prep sink, a double oven on the back wall, and a six-burner cooktop. I could do some real cooking in this place.

Leading me down the hallway, he stops at the first doorway. "This is my home office." I step inside and take in the large desk, bookshelves lined with dozens of medical journals and books, and a credenza. His medical degree hangs prominently on the wall behind the desk and more tasteful artwork lines another wall. A picture of Hudson and two similar-looking men—one of whom I recognize—catches my eye.

"Your brothers? I met Hunter. Who's the other one?"

"That's Hawk."

"So it's just the three of you?"

He points to another picture of a woman and a girl. "Five actually. That's my sister Holland and my half-sister, Dani."

"So your mom remarried."

"Yup.

"Do you like your stepdad?"

He chuckles. "I didn't. None of us did. He's a Calloway."

Curiosity wrinkles my brow. "As in Calloway Creek Calloway? Like the owners of the town?"

"Yes, but no. Not exactly. Long story. But we don't hate him so much anymore." He nods to the picture of his brothers. "Hawk is marrying a Calloway so we kind of had to bury the hatchet."

"It's good that you're giving him a chance."

"You say that like you have experience."

"My mom was married three times," I say. "None of them were my father."

He makes a face. "Ouch. Sorry. You said *was*. Did she get divorced again?"

"She gave up after the three failed marriages. I was thirteen when the last one ended. But she's gone now. She died when I was in college."

"Dang. That's tough."

I walk back into the hallway, escaping the conversation. "Show me the rest."

The next room has more bookshelves filled mostly with sports memorabilia. I recognize some of the teams. In a large, framed glass case hanging on the wall there's a #8 jersey from the New York Nighthawks signed by Caden Kessler. I walk to the next one. "Who is Lawrence?"

"Mason Lawrence. He used to play for the Giants back in the day. Took them to the super bowl. One of the best quarterbacks the franchise had ever seen."

"So you're a collector?"

"I didn't set out to be. It just sort of happened over the years. My brothers and I are into sports." He thumbs to the hallway. "Come on, I'll show you your room."

Across from the 'sports' room is a tastefully decorated guest room with a queen bed, a dresser with a large mirror hanging over it, and a small desk. I place my purse on the desk thinking it's not as big as the one I have next door, but it'll do for a few weeks.

"You can use my office," he says as if reading my mind.

"I'll be fine here."

"Dakota, you're the CPA for a multi-million-dollar corporation. You need to be able to spread out and do your work. Use my office. I insist."

Even though I'm still finding it hard to look him in the eye after the events of earlier, I raise my brow at his demand. "You *insist?*"

He turns and leaves the room. "I'll get your bag," he calls from the hallway.

Ten minutes later, I'm unpacked. I get the picture of Travis out and look at the empty nightstand. I can't put it there; Hudson might see it. I kiss my fingers and touch them to Trav's photo before hiding it away in a drawer like a dirty little secret.

Guilt sinks in as I settle onto the bed. Travis is not a dirty secret. And I've done nothing wrong. But a judge—a highly respected government-elected individual—called me an unfit mother. If I didn't know me, I wouldn't believe my story either. The records show only what the Daniels want them to. Drugs that weren't mine and that I didn't know were in the apartment.

It's almost seven. I'm craving a glass of wine, but I forgot to bring some over. It's become a habit, sitting out back, having a glass, and calling—mostly unsuccessfully—my son.

Walking out into the unfamiliar hallway, I look into the strange living room, and go for the front door.

"Going somewhere?"

I turn to see Hudson peeking around the corner of the kitchen holding the phone to his ear.

"I forgot something. Be right back."

"Hold on," he says into the phone. He holds it away from his ear. "Pizza toppings."

I give him a sideways look.

"I'm ordering pizza, what do you want on it?"

"Uh… spinach and onion."

"One large spinach and onion," he says into the phone. "Put pepperoni on half."

"And pepperoni," I say.

He laughs and relays my wishes to whomever is on the other end.

I trot across the yard, into my house and through my wet, mildewy kitchen where I retrieve two bottles of wine then return to Hudson's.

He's nowhere to be found. I stand in the middle of his kitchen, not really wanting to go through his stuff, but needing to find a wine glass. I spy a glass cabinet to the left of the refrigerator. Ah—there we go. I pour myself a glass and take it out back, settling on a comfortable lounger on the upper part of the deck.

Across the yard, the sun is setting. Somehow the view is better from here. But I'm not sure why. "So beautiful."

Movement from below scares me and I almost spill my wine. It's Hudson's head. His upper body comes into view when he stands.

"Oh," I say. "I didn't know you were out here. I can go inside."

"You don't have to stay in your room, Gator Girl. You have the run of the house."

He climbs the five deck stairs and sits on the lounger next to me, taking a sip of what I assume is whiskey.

I lean back and put my phone away. The call will have to wait. "Can I ask you a question, *Doctor?*"

He snorts. "I suppose that's an improvement over the others. Okay, shoot."

"Why did you fix my bike?"

"You had a flat. And the brakes were shit. You would have flown right over the handlebars."

"And you knew that how?"

"I heard the moving guy tell you it was flat."

"You mean when you were spying on me out the window?"

He sets his glass on the small table between us and scolds me with his stare. "Like you don't ever look at me out of yours?"

I shrug. "Like I said… strange energy."

"Oh, is that what you call it?" He motions around. "So what do you think?"

"I think your deck is massive. I love it."

He laughs out loud.

"What's so funny?"

"For a second there, I thought you said something else."

I replay my words in my head and then I'm certain my face turns bright red. "See—this is the strange I was talking about."

"Sorry," he says, still laughing.

"Can I ask you something else?"

He raises a palm, inviting the question.

"Why do you live here? I mean, you're a doctor. And a McQuaid. You can obviously afford so much more."

"You don't think my house is good enough?"

"God, no. That's not what I meant. Your house is nicer than anything I ever used to dream about. It's just that, knowing what I know about Tucker and the business, you're pretty much set for life. And you do drive a flashy car. So I guess it seemed like something just didn't add up."

"The truth is I work a lot. I don't see the need to waste money on a mansion that would be empty most of the time."

"Hmm."

"What does that mean?"

"Nothing. It wasn't the answer I expected."

"What would have been?"

I shrug. "Maybe that you had a house in the hills. Upstate or in Cape Cod. And you just keep this as your love nest or whatever."

"Love nest?" He laughs again. It's a deep grumbly laugh from the pit of his stomach. And it does things to the pit of mine.

"Well, with the affectionate love notes left on your garage by who I can only assume is a jilted lover or girlfriend…"

"I don't have a girlfriend."

"I assumed as much based on the wording of those love notes."

"No, I mean it wasn't a girlfriend who left them. It was a woman I dated a few times. She wanted more."

"Maybe she was misled."

"She wasn't."

The way he says it with such confidence and authority has me wanting to believe him. But there are always two sides to every story.

I stand and take my wine.

"Running you off, am I?" he asks.

I hold up my phone. "I need to make a call."

He looks at my phone as if it's his enemy. Then he turns away and takes a drink. "Dinner will be here in fifteen."

"Thanks for that, by the way. I'll pay for my half."

"Your half of twenty-five dollars?" He chuckles haughtily. "Don't bother, Dakota."

"*Now* you're sounding like a spoiled rich kid. I'll leave the money on the counter."

"Suit yourself."

Back in my bedroom, I close the door and go to call Travis when an email pops up. It's from Karl Wheeler. He assures me he's making good progress on the appeal. He says there's been success interviewing Brian's friends and our old neighbors. None of them attested to ever seeing me use drugs. He states that while it will take time to prove Travis's paternity with all the red tape, he's sure the pressure he's putting on the Daniels will soon result in better visitation.

I look to the ceiling and smile, tears clogging my throat. Short of the days I get to see my son, this is the happiest I've felt since he was taken from me five weeks ago.

I close the email, dial the Daniels' number, and say my nightly prayer.

Chapter Nineteen

Strange energy. That's what she called it. I call it super-charged sexual attraction. Attraction she doesn't seem to want to admit and that I can't act on even if she did.

Today is Saturday. She left this morning with a huge smile on her face. Didn't say where she was going. Barely even said goodbye.

Part of me wanted to follow her. But that would cross the line into seriously chargeable offense territory. Instead, I went on yet another grueling bike ride that has my legs still shaking even hours later.

I'm not sure what has me so much in a fucking tizzy. Based on her testimony in my office, she's not sleeping with anyone. Then again, she did ask me for a prescription 'just in case.'

Just in case what? Just in case this Travis guy on the other end of the phone finally agrees to become a bonafide adulterer and sleep with her? Just in case she finds someone here in Cal Creek? Just in case… *me?*

It's the last thought that has me opening a new bottle of whiskey.

The front door opens and I lean against the kitchen counter and wait for her to come around the corner. Then I hear voices, and my brothers appear. And they aren't alone. Right, I forgot we're watching the Hawks game here. But… why would they bring Addy and Willow?

Hunter laughs. "Based on the look on your face, brother, we weren't who you were expecting."

Before I can come back at him with a snarky comment, Dakota comes around the corner and glances at everyone in the room. "You have company." She motions to the hallway. "I'll just go get some work done."

Addy steps over to her and holds out her hand. "Dakota, I'm Addison Calloway-soon-to-be-McQuaid, and I hope you'll change your mind and hang out with us. It's why we came."

Dakota looks surprised. "It is?"

Willow holds up a bottle of wine. "When we found out what happened with the broken pipe, we decided to save you from having to listen to guys night all alone. I hope we didn't overstep."

"No, of course not. That's very nice of you. And it's great to meet you, Addison."

"Addy, please. And this is my fiancé, Hudson's oldest brother, Hawk."

Hawk and Dakota shake hands. Then he chuckles under his breath as he looks at me.

Hunter slaps my shoulder. "Come on, let's turn on the game."

"I thought you weren't betting anymore."

"That doesn't mean I don't still have a boner for sports."

The three of us go into the living room and I turn on my large-screen TV. Hawk, Hunter, and I alternate places where we watch games. Their houses are set up far better for it, with their large outside viewing areas with outdoor bars and kitchens. Still, they never complain about coming to my humble abode.

I hear laughter coming from the kitchen and strain to hear what they're saying, all but ignoring my brothers' banter and the game.

"Dude," Hunter hits my arm. "You've got it fucking bad."

I snap my eyes to his. "What are you talking about?"

"The girl in the kitchen. Your neighbor and temporary roommate."

"What am I missing?" Hawk says. "Wait, are you and Dakota—"

"Dakota and I aren't anything," I scoff. "Except neighbors, and yes, temporary roommates."

Hunter raises his brows and studies me. "Oh. My. God. You *do* have it bad. But based on the way you're acting, I'd say the feeling is not mutual."

I swat him. "Shut the fuck up, Hunt. I do not *'have it bad'*. She's my goddamn patient."

Both of them double over laughing.

The women join us in the living room, and I shoot a warning glance at my brothers.

Willow sits next to Hunter on the small couch while Addy plops right down on Hawk's lap in the oversize chair. Dakota looks like she has no idea what to do. The only seat left is on the sofa next to me. She puts her glass of wine on the table and sits, leaving a cushion between us.

I lean over. "Have a good day?" I ask, petulantly.

"As a matter of fact, I had a great day. Thanks for asking." She takes a drink and looks away.

Fuck.

I stare at her for a few more seconds and then glance at Hawk and Addy who are both watching me like I'm one of their kids. And speaking of kids… "Where are all the rugrats?"

"We got a sitter," Addy says. She pulls out her phone and hands it to Dakota. "This is our little angel, Rivi. Funny story." She nods to the television. "She was actually named after a Nighthawks player."

Dakota takes the phone, looks at the photo, hands it back, then toes her shoes off and pulls her legs up beneath her. While she seemed happy a few minutes ago, she's anything but right now. "She's gorgeous."

Willow gets her phone out, too, and proudly shows everyone the newest pictures of Myles and Izzy. Her face breaks out into a smile. "Myles laughed for the first time this week. Here let me show you the video we got."

The girls pass the phone between them. When Dakota watches the video and the kid starts laughing, I could swear it looks like she wants to cry.

"He's adorable." She hands the phone back and picks up her wine. "Excuse me, I'm going to refill."

Am I the only one who noticed her glass wasn't even half empty?

I go into the kitchen after her. She's turned away from me, leaning against the counter, head slumped. Oh, shit, I almost forgot. Dakota has most definitely been pregnant. And looking at the pictures seemed to gut her. I have the urge to go to her. Ask her about it. Comfort her, even. Which is strange. I never comfort women. Not unless they're patients of mine.

I close my eyes—which she *is*.

I stand here, watching her in pain, having absolutely no idea what to do.

She turns, sees me in the doorway, and pastes a smile on her face. "Everyone seems very nice. You're lucky to have siblings." She gets the bottle of wine from the counter, tops off her glass, and goes back to the couch.

Dakota perks up after another glass of wine and no more talk of children. It looks like she's making friends. In fact, it almost seems like these are her first friends. Which would be unusual considering she's been in town for over a month. It has me wondering why she hasn't been more social.

When she laughs along with Addy and Willow, I'm entranced. Her laughter is captivating. It's sexy. It's goddamn beautiful. And the sound of it has me silently vowing to make it happen again.

Hunter comes out from the kitchen and leans down on his way by. "You planning on watching *any* of the game? Or do you only plan on watching *her*?"

I ignore him, and then do my very best to keep my eyes focused on the television. But her voice makes it hard not to look. Her smell. Her mere presence. It's like trying not to look at the most amazing sunset. Or maybe a train wreck. I'm trying to decide which.

Chapter Twenty

Dakota

Saturday night was nice. I've been living in Calloway Creek for six weeks. And despite invitations like the one I got from Regan Lucas, I've not spent any time seeking out friendships. Every ounce of energy I have goes into two things: work and getting Travis back.

Then my eyes flit to a photo of Hudson on his office wall and I admit that's not exactly true.

I was relieved to have other women around. Especially since it's been so awkward being in Hudson's house the past several days. The glances. The forced politeness. The... strange energy.

When my laptop pings with a Zoom call from Percy, I'm happy for the distraction. Happy I don't have to sit here entrenched in Hudson McQuaid. His photos. His leather chair. His scent.

An hour later, after fixing myself lunch and settling back at the desk in Hudson's office, I catch movement in the driveway out of the window.

I roll the chair over and peek out. Oh, my gosh, a woman is spray-painting words on Hudson's garage door. B A S, and it looks like she's working on a T.

I have two choices here. I can let it happen, or I can use this as an opportunity to find out more about my mercurial roommate.

Curiosity getting the better of me, I make my way outside.

The woman is surprised when she hears the front door shut. She stops mid-spray and puts a hand on her hip. Her eyes travel the length of my body from head to toe and back. "So you're his flavor of the month? And you're *living* with him? Good luck with that."

I walk out onto the driveway. "Actually, no. I'm Dakota. I live next door, but my house flooded when a pipe burst. I'm only crashing here for a few weeks. I'm not with him." I nod to the half-painted graffiti on the garage. "But it looks like you were."

"Are you going to call the police?"

"Not my house, not my place."

She looks relieved. "Thanks for that, I guess."

"So he used to be your boyfriend?"

She shrugs. "I mean, not technically, but after going out five times, it was implied."

Going out? Or having sex. I know the answer. And it's not lost on me that I'm jealous of the woman defacing Hudson's property.

"He's a seducer. A user. You're new around here, so maybe you haven't had the chance to find out. But I'm surprised you haven't. Seems he would have already used you and tossed you aside."

"If what you say is true, then why haven't I seen him have women over? And, he barely goes out."

The woman laughs. "Then my plan is working."

"Plan?"

"To get every woman in this town to boycott him."

Oh, so that's what Regan was talking about. It was Hudson she was referring to. I'm slightly amused. Because since I met him, I've gotten zero creepy playboy vibes. In fact, the guy seems nothing like his sleazebag father. She's mixing up the two.

"Just to confirm, we're talking about *Hudson* McQuaid?"

"Of course, Hudson, why?"

"I just… haven't seen him behave in the way one might anticipate the player you described."

For the second time, her eyes scan me, this time with more obvious spite. "Who exactly are you?"

"I told you. My name is Dakota."

"That's not really answering my question, now is it?"

"Considering you haven't even offered me your name, I feel no obligation to do so." I thumb to the house. "Now I have work to do. Just finish here and leave before one of the other neighbors actually *does* call the police."

Back inside, from the office window, I see her look over at me, clearly knowing I'm watching, and then back at the garage. She completes the word, glances back at me, then adds the word 'RAT' in front of the other epithet. She changed the color and used red for that one.

I wave at her when she tosses me one last glance over her shoulder. I half expect her to wave her middle finger back at me. Because I'm standing in his house. And apparently it's where she wants to be. And dozens of women before her.

And I wonder just why I haven't seen the same side of Hudson McQuaid as everyone else in this town.

~ ~ ~

Done with work by six, I look back outside at the words that have been glaring at me all day and decide to do something about it.

I change into workout clothes and go to his garage. I know he's got paint in here. I've seen him using it no less than twice before. The woman is persistent and dedicated to the task if nothing else.

Taking the paint outside, I shut the garage and get to work.

Why am I even doing this? To stay busy? For exercise? To protect him somehow?

I hone in on the last thought. Why would I want to protect him? If Hudson and I did end up together, it's quite possible I'd just be another… whatever her name is. Maybe he's all about the chase. Catch and release. Wanting what he can't have.

Can't he have me?

I sigh, refusing to let myself fall into another schoolgirl fantasy. One that has him picking up a paintbrush, painting side-by-side, then, oops—I'd accidentally spatter paint on him. He'd look down at his shirt then coyly dip his brush into the paint and dab it on the end of my nose. I'd pretend to be mad and wipe my brush down his bicep. His jaw—lush and dark with five-day stubble—would fall open and he'd dip his brush again and touch it to my ankle, teasing my sensitive skin as he brushes his way up my shin, along the inside of my knee and along my inner thigh. I'd throw down my brush. He'd toss his, then he'd push me—

A car door slams shut. "Well, shit."

I turn. Hudson is standing in the driveway behind me, looking pissed as he scans his garage door.

"I was hoping to have this done before you got home."

He shakes his head at the half-covered word. "You don't have to do this. Give me a second to get changed and I'll finish the job."

As he trots up the driveway and through the front door, I'm all too aware of the thoughts going through my head as my eyes follow him. And I'm also conscious of the dampness between my legs. So much for *not* fantasizing.

What I didn't anticipate is the disappointment I feel when he comes back out, takes my brush, and finishes the job without so much as a word, glance, spatter, or stroke.

As I step back and watch, I accept what I've tried so hard to suppress. I think I'm completely head-over-heels for the rat bastard.

Chapter Twenty-one

Hudson

After seeing my last patient of the day, I'm sitting at my desk when Angie, one of the nurses, parks herself in my doorway. I can feel her staring. I don't really feel like getting another lecture, so I ignore her. But she doesn't go away. I close the patient chart and look up. "Did you need something?"

"I was wondering if you were sick. Actually, several of us are wondering."

"Sick? No. I haven't even as much as sneezed, why would you ask?"

A bewildered look crosses her face. "You haven't made any suggestive sexual comments, not even a dirty look. So you *must* be feeling under the weather."

I shake my head. "Never felt better."

Her eyes narrow. She stares. Then her jaw slackens. "Why, Hudson McQuaid, there's only one possible explanation. You must be in love."

I cough, and grunt, "That's ridiculous. What the hell, Angie?"

"Hudson, for four years you teetered on the line of sexual harassment with every female in this practice. You ask us out, stare at our breasts, talk inappropriately about us to others. Yet lately, it's almost like…"

I lean back in my chair. "Almost like what?"

"Like you're one of them. Richards, Peterman and the other attendings." She rolls her eyes. "I can't believe I'm even going to say it because it feels like I should see pigs flying outside your window, but you're acting like a true respected physician."

I recognize the predicament she's putting me in here. On the one hand, being a respected physician is something I crave. But if I agree with her on any of those fronts, would I be admitting to what I've been accused of?

And I'm not in fucking love. Not even close. Just because my cock stands at attention when I see Gator Girl taking a late-night dip in my hot tub does not mean I'm whipped like my brothers. And those feelings I get inside whenever she's around—it just means I've gone so long without sex that I'm wound as tight as a cocked gun ready to fire. I'm sure I'd have the same feelings toward *any* woman living under my roof.

I tuck some files into my satchel. "I'll do these dictations at home. See you tomorrow, Angie."

She doesn't move. "Whatever you say, Dr. McQuaid."

I close up my office and head to the back door, but not before I see no less than three other staffers whispering to Angie—all of them staring in my direction.

"Gossipy women with nothing better to do," I grumble on the way to my car.

It's only six fifteen. I normally don't leave this early. Deciding to get takeout on the way home, I call ahead to Lloyd's and order a steak. When the hostess asks if that's all, I spontaneously tell her to add an order of the seafood pasta. Dakota likes seafood. She also likes pasta. I know this because for the past week, she's cooked every night. She's always busy cooking something or other when I get home. Cooking for *me*. I think she feels like she has to. Like she's an imposition.

The truth is, she's a welcome and unexpected breath of fresh air. I've always scoffed at the idea of living with a woman. I need my space. I have my own routines. I don't like change.

Then I look at the empty passenger seat and realization hits me like a hundred-mile-an-hour curveball. I like the way she's changed things. I *want* her in my space. I want her *everywhere*.

At a stop sign, I scrub a hand across my jaw at the epiphany. Because, mother fucker, Angie was fucking right.

~ ~ ~

I set down the bag of takeout, thankful the kitchen isn't already smelling of another meal she's slaved over. "Dinner!" I call out.

Dakota comes around the corner, and I'm stunned into silence. I haven't seen her this put together since those first few days she would stand in her driveway waiting on Benny. Her hair is down in long flowing waves. Her eyes pop with heavier-than-normal makeup. Her lips look juicy and pink.

Down, boy.

But my cock only dances for a brief second. Because when I realize what this means, an emotion I seldom feel—except when it comes to Gator Girl apparently—rears its ugly green head. "Going somewhere?"

"Yes."

I swear she's being obtuse just to get to me. And I know this because I see the hint of a smirk.

"With...?"

She rolls her eyes. "Don't worry, Dad. I'll be home by midnight."

I stride over and lean in next to her ear. "Let's get one thing straight, I'm most definitely not your father."

Jesus, her scent. It's all fruity and light. Peaches or something. It makes me want to feast on *her* instead of the prime ribeye on the counter.

She draws in a breath then side-steps me, heading straight for the food. "What smells so good?"

"I got Lloyd's takeout. Brought you some, too. But I guess I'll be eating both since your skirt is so short it appears you'll be trolling for a meal somewhere else."

Yes, I realize I sound like a child, but damn it, I'm fucking pissed.

She cocks an amused brow. "Do you have a problem with me going out, Doctor?"

Doctor? I swear she only calls me that when she's being flirty. Why would she be flirty with me when she's on her way out with another man?

"Do what you want, Dakota."

"What I want is to eat whatever is in that bag. I'm meeting Regan Lucas and her friends, Ava and Maddie, for coffee behind the ice-cream place. I was going to skip dinner—but now that I smell this..."

She roots through the bag, pulls everything out, opens the two containers, and hands me the one with the steak. She gets out plates, utensils and napkins, knowing her way around my kitchen as much as her own—something I like just a little too much.

"You're making friends," I say when she sits. "That's nice. So you plan on hanging around Calloway Creek?"

"Why would I not?"

I shrug. "It just seems like you're so guarded. I thought maybe all of this was temporary."

"This?" she asks, taking a bite.

"The job, your house, this town."

"I guess it's hard to say what the future will bring. But I do like it here. I like it a lot."

I don't miss how she's looking at me when those words leave her luscious pink lips. Then, *fuuuuck me*, my balls tingle when a smidgeon of pasta sauce settles to the left of her mouth. Before thinking twice about it, I reach across the table and wipe it off with my thumb.

Other than when doing her exam, this is the first time I've touched her. And it's just her chin, not even her amazing fucking breasts, or her…*Shit*, don't even go there. It's her chin for Christ sake. But my cock thinks it's sexier than a stripper on a pole.

Our eyes lock. Her face and neck turn crimson. I lick my thumb and then go back to my meal. She draws in another deep, deep breath and goes back to hers.

Fifteen minutes later, she's out the door. And I've never been more relieved watching her walk away knowing she's meeting Regan and her friends. She's not going to the train station. Not going to *him*. Then again, it's only Tuesday, not Saturday.

My patient or not, the next time she tries to go to the city, I'm going to make it my mission to give her a reason to stay.

I clean up, put the leftovers away, and rub one out in the shower thinking of her lips and what they could do to me if I hadn't been covering for Lyle fucking Richards.

Chapter Twenty-two

Who knew girls' night could be so fun when alcohol isn't involved? I'm having a great time, but it makes me miss Heidi. I've wanted to stop at her place before coming home every time I've gone to the city, but I couldn't get myself to do it. After spending the day with Trav, I'm too worn out and sad to do anything else. Sad that I have to wait two whole weeks to see him again. Him— my son. *My* flesh and blood, not theirs.

Every day, I check my email obsessively for word from the lawyer. He said he was working on more visitation. I'll take anything. I'll make the train ride to the city three times a week if I have to. I'll lose sleep. I'll miss work and make it up at midnight. Anything to fill the missing void in my life.

My eyes close, dredging up another thought from my lonely subconscious. Is Travis the only thing missing?

My mind flashes back to dinner. The way he looked at me. The *'I'm anything but your father'* comment. The seductive way his finger swiped my chin.

"Dakota?"

I look up to see three pairs of eyes on me.

"Sorry, what?"

"Ava asked if you had met any nice men yet." Maddie chuckles. "But from the way you were just biting your lip, I'd say you already have."

I can feel my face heat up. "I'm really only focused on work right now."

Ava stares me down. "Word around town is you're crashing in Hudson McQuaid's spare room."

My eyes snap between all of theirs as they look at me expectantly.

Regan chuckles. "You can't fart in this town without everyone smelling it, Dakota. So spill. Did you break your pipes on purpose? Did you orchestrate the flooding so your dreamy neighbor would have to step up?"

"Dreamy?" Maddie scoffs. "Hudson McQuaid? He's probably got ten STDs."

"Nah," Regan says. "He's a doctor. He's smarter than that."

"Doesn't mean he's not a toad," Ava adds then turns to Maddie. "And you… seriously? Tag was even worse than Hudson before you came along. All it takes is one good woman to turn a man around."

Regan nods in agreement. "She's got a point."

"You guys, stop," I say. "I'm only staying there for another week. I had nothing to do with the pipes bursting. It wasn't even my idea to crash with Hudson. It was Tucker McQuaid's girlfriend who insisted."

Maddie about snorts coffee through her nose. "Rose? She's my grandmother." She shares a look with the others who all laugh.

"What is it?" I ask, clearly missing something.

"If anyone knows Rose Gianogi," Ava scoffs playfully, "they know she's a master matchmaker."

"Matchmaker?" I scoff. "So you think Rose, a nice seventy-something-year-old woman snuck into my house, broke my pipes and then suggested I move in next door?"

"Wouldn't put it past her," Maddie says. "She's got herself a reformed bad-boy herself, just like me."

"Really?"

"Oh, yeah. Tucker was just like the lot of them. Maybe even worse than his son, Robert. He had mistresses—many of them. He didn't give a thought to anything but his own pleasure and his own money. Until his wife died. I think that was a wake-up call for him. He did a complete one-eighty. And now… knock us all over with a feather… now he's the most doting boyfriend I could have asked for for my grandmother."

"Do you think they'll ever get married?" Regan asks. "It's not like they're getting any younger."

Maddie shrugs. "I doubt it. He's eighty-six now and perfectly fine with how things are."

"And your grandmother is okay with that?" I ask.

"She says she is. But sometimes I get the feeling she'd like to make it official."

The air changes around us. Several people walk past us crying. A few are running. More are on their phones, jaws open, shocked looks on their faces. Something bad has happened.

A woman comes over from the direction of Donovan's Pub. She looks to be on the verge of hysterics.

"Serenity," Regan calls, waving her hand around. "What's going on?" Regan motions to me. "This is Dakota. Dakota, this is Ren—she runs the pub with her father and her husband Cooper Calloway."

"Hi," I say, getting the feeling this isn't the time for a normal meet-and-greet.

She nods hello and sits heavily on the bench next to Maddie. Maddie puts an arm around her. "Ren, why is everyone freaking out?"

"It's Phoebe and"—her eyes close tightly and a tear slips out—"little DJ. They... they're dead."

Gasps come from the three other women at the table and chills run up my spine.

"What?" Ava asks. "How?"

"Details are still coming in, but apparently it was carbon monoxide. They think she accidentally left the gas stove on all day long without a flame. And when Dallas"—Maddie squeezes her tightly—"When he came home, he found them. I just got off the phone with his sister Allie. News is spreading all over town."

Everyone's eyes are flooded with tears. Including mine. I have no idea who Phoebe and DJ are. Zero clue who Dallas is. All I know is that this Dallas and I... we now have way too much in common.

Ava wipes her tears and turns to me. "Dallas Montana is the middle brother of three. His family owns a winery just outside of town. Phoebe is... *was*... his wife. And, oh my God." She chokes up. "DJ was only six months old."

Serenity stands. "We should go find Allie."

I get up as well. "I should go. You all know them. I'd only be in the way."

As they follow Serenity back to the pub, Regan turns. "We'll do this again soon," she says with a sad smile.

I swallow hard. "I know they don't know me, but please give them my condolences."

She nods and continues on with the rest of them.

I fight tears the entire walk home. It's as if demons have invaded my head and come to torture me. Thankfully, when I get there, Hudson is on the back deck. He doesn't see me come in. I head straight for the bedroom, shut the door, and cry myself to sleep.

~ ~ ~

"What should we do this weekend?" Brian asks. "My folks are in Europe. Want to go invade their palace and pretend we're the King and Queen?"

I laugh as I change the diaper of our little prince.

Brian picks Travis up when I'm done and flies him around the room in his arms. Trav squeals, "Fly, Daddy!"

God, I love watching the two of them together. And I especially love watching how at ease Brian is when his parents are out of town and not hovering. If you looked up helicopter parents in the dictionary, you'd see a picture of Wayne and Patricia Daniels. They mapped out every detail of every facet of all three of their kids' lives. Right down to what kind of law they would practice and who they would marry.

Brian threw a huge wrench into their plans when he met me.

As I watch the two of them together—my boys—I know Travis is as much Brian's as he would have been if they shared blood.

"I have a better idea," I say with a sultry grin. "Why don't I call Sarina down the hall and see if she can babysit. It's been a minute since we've had a real night out." I run a finger down his chest and then walk around behind him and whisper in his ear, "Trav can sleep over at her place, and we can, well... not sleep."

"Dakota, I'm not exactly comfortable getting a boner while holding our son."

I laugh and take Travis. "We have an afternoon playdate with Lara and Freddie." I point to his books on the kitchen table. "You study while we're gone. You have finals coming up and you definitely won't be studying later tonight."

"Yes, ma'am." He pulls me close. "I love you, Mrs. Daniels."

I kiss him. "You better."

I grab Travis's bag and stroller and we stop by Sarina's on the way to the park. Three hours later, with Travis exhausted and ready for a nap, we're back at the apartment.

"Guess what?" I say as we enter. "Sarina's all good—" I stop talking when I see the back of Brian's head slumped over onto his books. He's asleep. Asleep on his open law books. Going to law school is slowly sucking all the life from him. "Shh," I say to Trav, putting my finger to his lips when he fusses. "Daddy's sleeping."

I whisk Travis off to his room and get him settled for a nap, the whole time smiling because I'm so excited about this evening. I wasn't overexaggerating when I said it had been a minute. It's probably been months since we've gone out. Brian is in his last year of law school. He's not only studying for finals, but the Bar Exam. It's only offered twice a year. He'll graduate in May and take the exam in July. As a Daniels, it is expected he'll pass on the very first try as both his parents, his older sister, and his uncle had, despite the passing rate only being in the thirty-percent range.

That's a lot of pressure on anyone, let alone someone who doesn't even want to be a lawyer.

But Brian conceded. He said we need to pick our battles. And he reminds me constantly that the only battle he really needed to win was the one over me. He has me. He has Travis. He considers himself the ultimate victor because of that. But it's because of that that he puts up with the demands of his parents. The expectation to follow in their footsteps and become a corporate lawyer. To rank near the top of his class. To pass the Bar with flying colors.

It's all so much. And I haven't failed to notice the increase in Brian's extracurricular activities. Namely his use of Adderall and cocaine. It worries me so much, but he's never let his drug use interfere with our relationship, or his with Travis. And my hope is after he passes the bar, it will become a thing of the past.

Part of me knows his parents will keep moving the bar higher. Pleasing them is like a rabbit chasing a carrot tied to a stick over its head. It's impossible to ever actually obtain. I should know, I gave up eons ago.

I kiss Travis's soft tuft of dark hair and quietly go out into the other room. I walk up behind Brian and run a hand across his hair hoping to wake him nicely. Hoping he got enough studying done that he'll be able to relax on our date.

I lean down and whisper, "Brian."

He doesn't respond. I sigh, knowing I should probably just let him sleep. But he can't be comfortable.

I shake him gently. "Babe."

He still doesn't move.

Then I see his phone on the floor. The screen is cracked. I pick it up and touch it to wake it. There's one unread text. It's from his father.

Dad: Don't ever hang up on me again. Never forget who runs things around here. Who controls the very future of this family. Of YOUR family.

I blow out a long breath. His father called. Leave it to Wayne to ruin our 'vacation' from them. I'm sure Wayne was reminding him how it will reflect upon him if Brian doesn't rank in the top ten percent. It's ludicrous that they're even putting so much pressure on him when it doesn't matter. As long as he graduates and passes the Bar, it doesn't matter. He's going to work for his family's law firm. He's got a guaranteed job. I swear they just taunt him for sport.

"Babe, wake up."

I look at the pill container next to his books. Adderall. And the other container that's not exactly a prescription. I look back at the phone and the cracked screen. Did he throw it, or did it fall?

"Brian!" I shake him harder, knowing that if he did either of the drugs on the table he should most definitely not be sleeping. "Brian!"

My heart is pumping out of my body. He's overdosed. It happened once before, but that was years ago when he was given bad drugs.

"Baby!"

Tears roll down my face as I take my phone from my pocket and call an ambulance. That's when it happens. That's when my whole world changes. That's when the woman on the other end of the phone asks me to find a pulse.

There is none.

Or if he's breathing.

He's not.

My entire existence implodes.

And the only reason I don't use the entire contents of the two little bottles on the table is the tiny person down the hall.

Paramedics burst through the door. I'm crying. I'm screaming. I feel like I'm dying.

One of them wraps me in his arms. "Dakota, it's okay. Wake up, Dakota!"

My husband is dead. My son has no father. But all I'm wondering is how the paramedic knows my name.

Chapter Twenty-three

Hudson

She's thrashing around, sobs bellowing out of her. I climb in bed next to her and try to get her to hold still. "Dakota!"

I say her name over and over until she calms. Finally her eyes open and she looks at me like she has no idea who I am. She's completely disoriented.

"It's Hudson. Are you okay?"

She stares at me, breathing heavily, still trying to overcome whatever nightmare had a grip on her.

I have no idea when she got home last night. She never said a word and I didn't hear her. Then again, I was on the phone, talking to my brothers and everyone else in the family about the news of Phoebe and DJ.

Maybe I'm scaring her. I pull away and sit on the side of the bed. Light coming from the hallway illuminates the room.

Suddenly, she snaps out of it as if remembering who she is, who I am, and why she is where she is. She sits up, scoots against the headboard, and pulls the sheets around her.

"What happened?" I ask.

She wipes sweat from her cleavage as I vow not to gawk at her creamy breasts spilling out from her UF spaghetti-strap pajama top with a blue and orange alligator. But she still doesn't speak.

"Stay here. I'll be right back." I hurry to the kitchen for a bottle of water. I hand it to her when I return. "Drink this."

She takes a sip. Then she looks at me. *All* of me. And it dawns on me that all I'm wearing are my skivvies.

Her gaze falls to the bed. "I heard about the woman and baby who died."

"Yeah. Fucking horrible."

"Did you know them?"

"Everyone knows everyone in this town, but we weren't close if that's what you mean. The McQuaids and the Montanas haven't exactly been friends."

"I thought it was the Calloways you had a beef with."

"The Montanas come in a close second. I went to school with Dallas—the woman's husband. We weren't in the same grade. He's younger than me. They run a winery."

She nods. "The girls told me. What a tragedy."

I narrow my eyes. "Is that why you had a bad dream? You didn't know them, did you?"

"It just… brought up bad memories."

Memories of what? The desire to ask her is strong. Phoebe died. And DJ. And that brought bad memories. Maybe my intuition is right, and she lost a child rather than gave one up. If that's the case, I shouldn't pry. I can't. During residency I saw firsthand how devastating it is for someone to lose a baby.

"Is there anything I can do?"

She holds up the bottle. "You did it. Thanks. But, uh, maybe you could sit for a while. It's just…" She looks anywhere but at me. "Maybe you could cover up?"

I chuckle and get the throw blanket at the foot of the bed and wrap it around me. "Better?"

She nods.

"You're a bit distracting yourself." I motion to her chest.

She pulls the sheets up higher. It's not light enough in here to see, but I can imagine her face pinking up. "Talk to me about something other than what happened. Tell me about the woman who paints disparaging words on your garage."

"Of all the things we could talk about, *that's* what you choose?"

She pulls a pillow onto her lap and hugs it. "I met her, you know. Caught her in the act."

"You met Lynda?"

"I didn't know that was her name, but yes. She acted quite jealous that a woman was living in your house. I got the idea she felt she should be here instead. She says you went on five dates, and thought it was implied that she was your girlfriend."

I sniff hard and shake my head. "It wasn't. I know this makes me sound like all the stuff she painted on my garage door, but I never led her on. I never led anyone on. I was never interested enough. It was all"—I scrub and hand across my jaw knowing what a jerk this makes me sound like—"sexual."

"Hudson, I'm not going to judge you. You're a twenty-something guy with a lot of life ahead of you. If you don't want to settle down, you shouldn't have to. And if these women can't understand that, it's their problem, not yours. As long as you were up front with them."

I stare at her, surprised that a woman would even take my side. "I was always clear about it. I swear I was."

Her eyebrows go up. "Was?"

"Yeah, well, there seems to be a club of which Lynda is the founder and CEO."

She laughs.

I'm smart enough to recognize why I haven't been fucking around. It's not any club, or lack thereof. It's not Lynda Graves. It's the Gator Girl sitting two feet away from me.

"Have there been a lot of them?" she asks. "Jealous women?"

I shrug. "You have to understand my position. A lot of women in this town see me not as a respected physician, they see me as an heir. They only see dollar signs. A meal ticket. A sugar daddy who will give them everything."

Her punishing stare scolds me. "Surely not everyone you've dated feels that way. Maybe you just think they do. Or…"

She stops talking.

"Or what?"

She picks at a spot on the bed. "Or maybe you just haven't found the right person."

Well, holy shit. The amount of sexual tension that just erupted inside this bedroom is thicker than maple syrup.

"I suppose I haven't."

"Do you think you'll ever settle down?"

"I never really think about it."

Or I didn't until recently.

"Word around here is that your brothers were the same way."

"That is the word. So, I have a question for you, Gator Girl."

She pretends to hate it when I call her that. But I know she secretly likes it.

"What is it, *Doctor?*"

"If you caught Lynda in the act of trespassing and vandalization, why didn't you call the police?"

"Because I thought she might have had a good reason for doing it."

"What if she comes back and you catch her doing it again?"

"I'm only here for a few more days, Hudson. I doubt very much that will happen."

Her words are like a punch to the gut. Because I like having her here. I like it a whole fucking lot. I scoot closer. "But what if it does happen?"

My eyes go to her throat, and I watch her swallow.

"I'd go out and paint over it like before."

"Why?"

"You didn't see the way she looked at me. The girl obviously had or has serious feelings for you. And I feel sorry for her. So I'd rather just let her get her frustrations out and paint over it than see the poor woman end up arrested. Plus, that would only make things worse."

"Mmm."

She tilts her head. "What does that mean?"

"Nothing. Just that you impress me more than most."

She cocks a brow. "Meaning?"

"You're young, yet the CPA of a Fortune 500 company. You're independent. Strong. And you don't give any indication that you need a man to justify you or complete you or whatever the hell women are looking for. And you don't seem the type to take shit from anyone. Yet you're very empathetic."

"And when you say I don't take shit from anyone, you mean from you."

I chuckle. "Yeah, that too."

She yawns. Her arms stretch out to the side, the sheet falls down and I get a view of major side-boob. It's fucking sexy.

Our gazes lock. I'm still close. I can smell her. Hell, we aren't touching but I can *feel* her. Every damn inch of my body is screaming at me to lean in a few more inches and kiss her already. But I'd be breaking so many rules. Pappy's. The Board of Medicine's. *Mine.*

Those magnificent dark eyes. She wants me to kiss her. Maybe even as badly as *I* want it.

I skitter off the bed. "Goodnight, Gator Girl." I make it as far as the door then throw the blanket at her.

She doesn't catch it.

She's too busy staring at my tented skivvies.

I turn, flick off the hall light, and go take a cold shower.

Chapter Twenty-four

Dakota

"We're hoping to finish up today," Billy Nickle says as I stand in the foyer and look at the new hardwood floors. "If we don't, I'll come by and complete the job in the morning. You'll be in by tomorrow afternoon for sure."

"You shouldn't have to work on a Saturday. Besides, I won't be here all day anyway."

"It's really no problem. I'm sure the sooner you can get out of his house, the better, eh?"

My eyes scrunch together. Why does everyone in this town think so negatively of Hudson?

"Listen." He stands, takes a step toward me, and leans against the wall. "I know I asked before, but you can't blame a guy for trying. Dinner on Sunday?"

"I'm flattered, Billy. But I must respectfully decline."

He looks in the direction of Hudson's house. "It's him, isn't it? Be careful, Dakota. He'll use you like an old rag and toss you aside just as easily."

"Nobody is using anyone, Billy. Well, I'd better get back to work."

Exiting the house, I look back at him over my shoulder. Billy is attractive. Muscular. Nice. Handy for sure. But looking at him… being around him… does nothing to me.

My skin doesn't prickle when he walks into the room. My heart doesn't pound when he looks at me with bedroom eyes. My breath doesn't catch when I get a whiff of him as he passes. And my panties don't dampen when he sits inches away from me on my bed. No—those only seem to happen with one man.

What is so darn confusing is that I've been in town for about two months now. I've been asked out by several men—four in fact. But not *him*. Not the one guy everyone in Calloway Creek tells me is the king of broken hearts and scorned women. Not the guy who sleeps twenty feet away. Not the guy who walked out of my room with an erection that had my mind swimming and my fingers wandering.

"Ugh!" I scream on my way through our yards, frustrated with Hudson. Mad at myself because I even care.

I immerse myself in work for the rest of the afternoon. Tucker seems pleased with my progress. Percy fully retired two weeks ago at Tucker's insistence that I was capable of taking over. He was right. I underestimated myself. I could do this. I *am* doing this.

If only Travis were here, everything would be perfect. I glance up at the wall, at the picture of Hudson and his brothers. *Well, almost everything.* I scoff at the thought, shake my head, and am getting ready to finish up early when I hear the front door open.

I go on high alert because one, I didn't see Hudson's car come up the drive, and two, I'm questioning if I forgot to lock the front door. I scan the room looking for a weapon. There is none. I hurry to the adjacent room and grab one of Hudson's signed baseball bats off of a display on the wall. Then I stand in the hallway, prepared to defend myself.

When Hudson stumbles past the hallway and into the living room, I scold myself. This isn't the city. People don't just go breaking into random places. Happy that I wasn't seen looking like a paranoid crazy lady, I put the bat back in its place and go to investigate.

Hudson is at his bar cart, pouring himself a shot of tequila.

"You okay?" I can smell from here he's already had a good bit of alcohol. I look at the time. It's four o'clock in the afternoon. Hudson never comes home this early.

He doesn't turn. He doesn't speak. He just pours another and tosses it back.

"Hudson?"

He gets out a glass, grabs a bottle of whiskey and heads out to the back porch.

I stand inside and watch him collapse onto a lounger, almost losing hold of the bottle in the process. He fills his glass and sets the whiskey aside. He sips, sets the glass on the table, and then his head slumps into his hands and his shoulders shake. Is he… crying?

I realize the predicament I'm in. He didn't speak to me, not even when I spoke to him. He went right outside. He wants to be alone. But he looks broken. And nobody should have to be alone when they're feeling broken. I should know.

Then I realize what might be going on. The funeral was today. But I believe it was this morning. Has he been drinking since then? It doesn't make sense. He said he wasn't even close with them. Yes, it's sad. Horrible. Devastating. But something doesn't add up.

Despite the early hour, I make a decision. I get a bottle of wine and a glass and go out back. Without saying a word, I take the lounger next to him, pour myself a glass, and sip.

After several minutes, he looks up, lost and despondent. His bloodshot eyes question my presence.

I smile sadly. "In my experience, misery loves company."

He stretches out on his lounger, sipping his drink, looking everywhere and nowhere.

"Funerals can be difficult," I say. "Even when you didn't know the deceased well, they still make you aware of how little time we have and how precious that time is."

His head shakes. "I didn't go."

This surprises me. "Oh. I thought everyone went."

"They did. The whole town practically shut down. I intended to go but a patient went into labor."

Some of his words come out slurred. As I suspected, he's been drinking for a while. "Are you okay, Hudson?"

He holds up his drink. "No. But I will be after a few more of these."

"Do you want to talk about it?"

"You know, normally, after a bad day—like the one I had today—I grab a bottle, come out here, and drink myself to sleep." He turns to me. "*Without* being hounded by anyone to share my fucking feelings."

I gather my bottle and glass and stand. I'm walking around him to go inside when he reaches for me and grabs my arm. "Hey, listen. I'm sorry. I'm not used to having anyone here when… when…" He drops my arm. "Stay. Sit down."

Ordinarily after being spoken to like he did, I'd keep walking. But he's clearly in pain. And if I know anything, I know pain. So I sit.

We lie in silence, two feet apart, only a small table and bottles of whiskey and wine separating us. But somehow I feel connected to him. He looks as devastated as I felt when Travis was taken from me.

He sips slowly. I do the same. Time passes. Ten minutes? Twenty? The only sounds come from a distant lawnmower and the occasional shutting of car doors. There's some indistinct chatter coming from the men working over at my house.

Hudson flinches when he hears the faint sound of a baby crying. He refills his drink. "I lost one today."

I turn and face him, using my arm as a pillow as I silently give him the opportunity to elaborate.

"A baby," he stutters. "I lost a baby."

My eyes close. I imagine that must be the very worst part of his job. "I'm so sorry."

He stands, pacing the deck, shaking his head. He stumbles once then catches himself on the railing. "Odds are it would happen eventually. I deliver over eighty babies a year and this happens to one out of one-sixty." He swallows heavily. "I've seen it before, during residency. But I never…" He looks down at his hands, studying them. Then he strides over, picks up the whiskey bottle and throws it against the side of the house. It shatters into several large pieces. "Fuck!" he yells at the world. "Fuck, fuck, fuck!"

I race over to him, instinctively wrapping him in a hug. And he doesn't push me away. In fact, he holds onto me for dear life. Then he sinks to the ground, pulling me with him, and we sit, embraced in a ball of human agony. Him thinking about his lost patient. Me thinking about my son.

"Thirty-nine weeks," he says. "Thirty-nine fucking weeks without so much as elevated BP. It was the perfect textbook pregnancy." He leans against the house, still holding onto me. "She was so excited when I showed up. They tried for years to conceive. But when we got her hooked up to the monitor, there wasn't a heartbeat." His whole body shakes. "There wasn't a fucking heartbeat, and she was forced to deliver a dead baby."

I squeeze him tightly, not knowing what to say, only knowing I can be here.

"I failed. I have one goddamn job and I failed."

"You think this was *your* fault?" I try to pull back, but his embrace tightens. "You said there was no heartbeat when you got there. It wasn't your fault, Hudson."

Finally, he lets me go. I settle next to him against the house.

"Stillborn babies don't even look dead," he says. "Did you know that? Right after birth, when they're still attached to the placenta, they look like every other baby. They just aren't moving." Suddenly, he looks up at me as if he's horrified. "Oh, shit, Dakota. I didn't mean to bring this up with you."

"It's okay. And I get it. I know exactly how you feel. I've seen a dead body too. And he didn't look dead. He just looked… asleep."

"Ah, fuck. I'm sorry. How far along were you?"

I shake my head. "I didn't lose a baby. I lost a—" I look away. I haven't told anyone in this town anything about me. So I hesitate. But only for a second. He's hurting. We have something in common. So I tell him. I tell him despite how much it hurts. "I was married once. He died. I found him right after it happened."

Hudson is more than a little surprised. "You lost a *husband?*"

The way he says it is as if he didn't understand me.

I nod. "He died of a heart attack because he used too many drugs. He wasn't a bad person. His parents put a lot of pressure on him. He was about to graduate from law school when it happened."

"Shit, Dakota. I had no idea. I'm sorry."

I look at a piece of the shattered whiskey bottle to my right. "Sometimes I think it was my fault."

"Why do you think that?"

"I knew he was doing drugs. I looked the other way because he was always so good to me. I figured maybe he would stop once he passed the Bar Exam. He was just months away. Months."

"It wasn't your fault," he says.

"And today wasn't yours."

He sighs. "I know that. Logically, I do. It's just there's so much expectation to hand every mother a perfect pink baby. And ninety-nine percent of the time, it happens. Nobody goes into labor thinking two hours later they'll deliver a dead baby. It has to be the worst thing I've ever witnessed."

I wipe my eyes—sure they're now horribly streaked with mascara. "Look at us," I say. "We must be a sight."

He touches the ring finger of my left hand. There's no longer a tell-tale white circle that had been protected from the sun. "How long ago?"

"Two years."

He looks at me. Our eyes lock. They connect. They bond us because of our shared experiences. Our gazes are intense. My eyes are still wet with tears. His are red and unwavering. If I didn't know any better, I'd say he was about to kiss me. Which is strange because this is not the time to be kissing when he recently lost a patient and I just told him about my dead husband. But for some strange reason, that almost makes it feel right.

Then, he breaks our stare. And I realize how sad it makes me. I want him and his brokenness. I want him and his cockiness. I just want him.

In a bold move, I climb onto his lap, lower my lips to his, and kiss him. His lips are salty. Or maybe it's the salt from my own tears that I taste. He doesn't kiss me back. He doesn't even move. I've made a mistake. I've been misreading him. I go to pull away when his arms come around my back and hold me prisoner against him. His mouth opens and he deepens the kiss. He welcomes my tongue. He inhales my breath.

I can feel his desperation. His despair. It's palpable. He's holding onto me as if I'm his lifeboat. Unfortunately, I'm all too familiar with the storm he's in. So I let him squeeze me as tightly as he needs. Because right now, I know he needs to feel life. And alive is exactly what I feel with him.

His lips are as soft as they are strong. They're everything I've been missing. They feel like home.

It's the most intense kiss I've ever experienced.

He hardens beneath me and I push myself into him, never needing a man as much as I do right now. I want to make him feel like he's not the failure he believes himself to be. I need him to make me feel like the woman I long to be.

We're breathless as we break apart. I put my lips against his neck. "Hudson…"

Unexpectedly, he puts his hands on my waist and guides me off his lap. "Dakota, I can't."

"Hello?" someone shouts from the gate at the fence. "Dakota, you back there?"

Hudson and I look at each other knowing so much has been left unsaid.

I close my eyes and answer. "Yes. Give me a sec."

Apparently he didn't hear me correctly, or he doesn't care, because Billy opens the gate and comes to the deck. I stand quickly as Hudson crawls over and starts cleaning up the broken bottle.

"Everything okay here?" Billy asks.

"Fine. Happy hour got a little crazy. You know how it goes."

He eyes me suspiciously then turns his gaze on Hudson, who refuses to make eye contact, probably because he doesn't want Billy to know he was crying. "Your place is done. You can move back in."

"Oh." I glance back at Hudson, who has stopped cleaning and is just sitting still. "Well, thanks, Billy."

"You need help moving your things?"

I shake my head. "I don't have much, but thanks. Thanks for everything."

Billy leaves. Hudson stays seated. He doesn't even look at me when he says, "I guess you should get going then."

I grab the bottle of wine. "I guess so."

Fifteen minutes later, I'm next door. To my knowledge, Hudson never went back inside.

I'm as confused as an atheist in a room full of Catholics.

Chapter Twenty-five

Hudson

I've never been one to believe in fate or fairy tales. But call me a blind fool if Gator Girl isn't destined to be mine.

Her lips. Her perfect goddamn lips. They kept me awake all night. I've never been kissed by a woman that way. There was a desperation in her kiss that came from the circumstances, but there was so much truth to it. I could feel it. Taste it.

Slowly, I watch the time pass on my phone, tapping it every so often until it reaches 9:20. I pull on sweatpants and a shirt, fetch a cup of coffee, and sit on my front porch knowing she'll walk by in a few minutes. Because that's what she does every other Saturday. She walks to the train station and goes to the city for the day.

Today, I plan to stop her.

Right on time, I hear her front door shut. When she comes into view as she nears the end of her driveway, all I can think of is how she was on my lap. How I wanted nothing more than to take her right there. How I've never wanted any woman as badly as in that moment.

She's on the sidewalk. She doesn't see me. She doesn't even look in my direction.

"Going somewhere?" I shout from my porch.

She startles and stops walking. "To the city. But you already knew that."

I nod to the small shopping bag in her right hand. "What's in the bag?"

"Nothing."

"A gift?"

"Hudson, I really have to go."

I stand and lean against the porch pillar. "Don't go to the city."

Her chest visibly rises and falls. "I have to."

"Why? Why do you have to, Dakota?"

"I have a commitment."

"Break it."

"I can't. I'm sorry. I really need to go."

I contemplate going after her. I want to. But Hudson McQuaid isn't a beggar. I watch her walk down the sidewalk and disappear around the corner, then I go inside, slam the door like a tantruming teenager and realize that's exactly what I was for the last thirty seconds—a pathetic beggar.

How have I sunk so goddamn low?

~ ~ ~

"You expecting a call?" Hunter asks.

"What's that?" I look up from my phone.

"You've been checking your phone every two minutes for the last hour. What's so important?"

Hawk gets a beer from his outdoor fridge and replaces my empty. "It's the neighbor, isn't it? Fuck." He gets out his wallet.

I twist the cap off my beer. "Neighbor?"

"Dakota. She's got to be the reason you're in such a foul mood this afternoon."

Hunter grabs the remote and turns down the sound of the baseball game on the outdoor TV. "I knew it." He holds out his palm to Hawk. "Pay up."

"Knew what? And why does he have to pay up?"

"When Hawk and I left your house last week I bet him a hundred bucks you'd end up chasing her like a dog after a squirrel."

I slap away his hand. "I'm not chasing anyone."

"Then do you mind telling us why you're in such a shitty mood?"

Hawk cocks his head. "She moved back home, didn't she? That's it. She moved home and now you're sad." He laughs. "Oh, this is precious."

"Says the guy who has his nose so far up his fiancée's ass he can't even see daylight."

"It's us," Hunter says. "There's nobody else around, Hud. You can talk about it."

I shake my head. I take a drink. I look off in the distance. "I have no fucking clue how it happened."

"It?" Hawk says.

"Yeah... *it*," I snarl. "You want me to say it? Fine. I like the girl. Happy? But it can't happen."

"Well, why the hell not?"

"For one, she's a patient and there's this little fine print that says I'm not allowed to screw patients."

"That can be remedied," Hunter says.

"And secondly, the old man forbade it."

Hawk and Hunter look at each other and break out laughing.

"What's so goddamn funny?"

"It makes so much sense now," Hawk says, tucking his money back into his wallet. "Pappy told you to stay away from the company CPA. He probably doesn't want to lose an employee over your philandering. Hell, he already has to deal with that enough with Dad. But now she's forbidden in so many more ways and you can't stand it when someone tells you something is off limits. It's one thing to be bound by the confines of your job, quite another to want to go against our meddling grandfather."

"Damn," Hunter scoffs. "I was sure this was one bet I'd win."

I stand, needing to take a piss. But I turn before I go inside. "Give him the goddamn money," I say to Hawk.

His eyebrows shoot up. "Why, Hud?"

I scold my idiotic behavior for the tenth time today. "Because I practically begged her not to go to the city today to see whoever the fuck she goes to see every other week. Because we kissed last night. And because I decided she's the only damn woman I want to be kissing." I step through the back door, shake my head, and admit to them what I haven't even been able to admit to myself. "Because I think I'm in fucking love with her."

I never go back outside. I take a leak and walk home. Then I sit and wait. Wait for her to get back. Wait for this foreign feeling to abate. Wait for this storm called Dakota Daniels to pass.

Three hours and as many whiskeys later, I know she must be home. She never stops anywhere after. But why? If she were going to meet a friend, she wouldn't be so secretive about it. Yet she flat out told me she wasn't having sex.

I stare down into my empty glass as it dawns on me. Her husband died. I'll bet she goes to visit his grave. She's the one who found him. That can really mess with a person's head. Maybe she sees a shrink while she's there. Maybe—and this is the one that really stings—maybe she's visiting *two* graves. Because Dakota has most definitely had a baby.

But she kissed me. Does that mean she's over him? Could last night have been her first kiss since it happened? And I turned her away. I was going to explain. Damn Billy Nickle interrupted. And I was drunk. I didn't want to go throwing around words I wasn't sure I meant while under the influence.

Visiting graves. It can't be that. It wouldn't explain the phone calls I've heard. The *"I love you, Travis."*

I have to get to the bottom of this. I count up the number of drinks I've had over the course of the afternoon. I assess my current state of consciousness. I'm good. Inebriated enough to say what I need, not drunk enough to say stupid shit that shouldn't be said.

My forearms come to rest on my knees as I slump forward, realizing I'm in a position I've never been in before. All this time. All these years. I've always laughed at women who were infatuated with me. Women who seemed like they'd stop at nothing to get me. I never understood it. Never got it. Never fucking felt it all the way to my soul. Until now.

I walk through the house, determined. I go out the front door, confident. I stroll through the yard, very aware of my beating heart. I approach her door, pulse now racing. I ring the bell, praying.

She answers. A million things I was going to say race through my head, and I can barely put two words together. Because when I look at her, I know what I told my brothers is one-hundred-percent true. I'm in love with her.

"You didn't let me finish last night," I manage to string together.

"You pretty much said it all when you pushed me off your lap and told me you couldn't."

"Will you shut up and let me finish?"

She backs against the wall and motions for me to come inside. Surprising, considering I just told her to shut up. "Do you think I didn't want to keep kissing you? That I didn't want to take you inside and do a lot more? That I haven't wanted to since the first day I saw you out the window? But there are lines. Ethical lines. You're my patient."

"And if I wasn't?"

"If you weren't my patient, Gator Girl, I'd push you up against that wall and show you what a real kiss from Hudson McQuaid feels like—Tucker be damned."

"Tucker?"

"He forbade me to take up with you."

"Oh, he did, did he?" Her lips turn up with a half-smile. "Wait here." She walks into the kitchen and comes back with her phone. She makes a call. "Hello, this is Dakota Daniels. Effective immediately, I'd like to be assigned to another doctor. Thank you." She puts the phone on a nearby table and looks up. "There. I left a message. You're officially fired, *Doctor*. Now what are you going to do about it? Are you going to listen to your grandfather, or your own heart?" Her tongue comes out to swipe her lower lip as she waits.

My pants tighten. No one has ever fired me before. I was always the one who severed the doctor-patient relationship. For my benefit. But this girl—this woman—she's doing it for *hers*.

Damn, I feel like a kid on Christmas as I stride over to her with a huge fucking grin.

Chapter Twenty-six

He pins me against the wall with authority. This time it's *his* lips doing the claiming. And I'm an all-too-willing participant. Having a man's body against me again is empowering. Especially when I feel I may be holding all the cards.

I'm not exactly sure why I feel that way except that I've heard things about him over the past few months. Things that simply don't jive with his behavior toward me. Things that let me know Hudson has never been the pursuer in any relationship—only the pursued. Yet he seems completely enamored with me. One might even say obsessed. Something isn't adding up.

As our lips come apart and he works his mouth down my neck, I ask the million-dollar question. "Hudson, are you only doing this because you want what you can't have?"

He stops kissing my neck and looks into my eyes. "Nobody tells me what I can't have."

"Exactly." I slink out from under him and walk into my living room. "Your grandfather told you to stay away. That makes me forbidden. Until a few minutes ago, I was your patient. Double forbidden. Is this all about the chase?"

He walks up next to me and pushes a chunk of hair behind my ear. He leans in and holds my head closely against his lips. "Are you refusing to be caught, Gator Girl?"

When I don't answer, he pulls away.

I walk to the other side of the couch, contemplating my options. I like this guy. I like him a lot. The attraction between us is electric. There's something there. But I'm not going to be made a fool of.

"I won't be another Lynda."

"What's that supposed to mean?"

"Listen, Hudson. I'm not asking for anything but honesty. What is this exactly? Are you looking for some kind of neighbors-with-benefits thing? Because if you—"

"Dak—"

"Now *you* shut up, okay? Let me finish. If you want that, I might be okay with it. I just need to know up front so there aren't any misconceptions. I don't want to have to buy a can of black paint after joining the *I fucked Hudson McQuaid* club."

He strides over with purpose and traps me against another wall. Oh, how I love the way he does that. It's so caveman. "What if I told you I wasn't looking for neighbors-with-benefits?"

His scent overpowers me. I'm drowning in it. And I have a feeling that no matter what he tells me, I'm about to be putty in his hands. "What are you looking for then?"

"Something different." He kisses my neck and tingles shoot up and down my spine.

"Different how?"

"From all the others." His lips settle over my collar bone.

"You're going to have to elaborate."

He stops kissing me and buries his forehead in the crook of my neck. "Jesus, are you really going to make me say it?"

I have to bite my lip. I'm tempted to smile because I'm pretty sure I know what he's going to say. "Yes."

He sighs into my neck and pulls back. "Fine. I like you, Dakota. And I'm not looking for just another romp in the hay. I'd like to explore the opportunity for… more."

"More?" I raise a brow, rather liking this game.

He rolls his eyes. "Yeah, you know, dinner, movies, holding hands and shit like that."

Though the delivery could use some work, the meaning behind his words is everything I've wanted to hear. It's what I've dreamed of. What I crave. But now that he's said it, all I can think of is how wrong it would be. He's putting himself out there but doesn't know anything about me.

"Hudson, while I appreciate that, I'm not sure I'm in the right place for a relationship."

"You're…" He steps away and paces behind the couch. "Wow. This is new."

I approach him and put a hand on his arm. "I like you. Obviously I do. I mean, I just fired you so we could, you know, do stuff. But I may need a little time to go from neighbors-with-benefits to anything else."

He laughs.

"What's so funny?" I ask.

"*I'm* normally the one setting the rules."

"There are no rules, Hudson."

"Oh, there are rules," he says with a mischievous grin.

"Such as?"

He sits on the couch and draws me onto his lap. "Rules like I'm going to be the only neighbor you're *benefiting* with."

I smile. "I suppose I can live with that."

He pulls my head toward his. "Not just the only neighbor. The only *anyone*."

"I'm not one to sleep around, Doctor."

"So we're on the same page?" he whispers into my mouth.

"If I'm not *benefiting* on the side, neither can you."

"Gator Girl, my left hand has been the only thing I've been benefiting lately." His tongue juts out and swipes across my lips. "That's all about to change."

He reclaims my lips. This time I have no thoughts about what his intentions are. I just let go and enjoy this feeling. This feeling I've craved ever since Brian died. The feeling of being wanted. Needed. Dare I say, loved? Because right now, that's what this feels like. It feels like I'm being kissed by a man who loves me.

And it's everything.

The more his lips and his hands work over me, the more I know I'm kidding myself. I don't want a friends-with-benefits relationship. I want more. I want all of him. And I'm pretty sure I love him. But love is complicated. *I'm* complicated. And complications are not what a man like Hudson wants.

So I decide to live in the moment. Let this go wherever it takes us. And let the rest work itself out.

I sit up and remove my shirt, then my bra. Hudson stares at my chest as if he's never seen it before. As if he's never seen *any* breasts before—which is ludicrous because he's surely seen thousands. But the way he's looking at me, how he's revering me, it's how every woman longs to be looked at.

"Fuck, you're beautiful."

I close my eyes as he captures one of my nipples in his mouth. Bolts of electricity sizzle through my body from head to toe as he toys with it, flicks it, sucks it. He caresses my other breast with a hand, pinching the nipple between his fingers with just enough pressure to make me moan unabashedly.

I'm trying to understand myself right now. I've always enjoyed sex, but I've never been this forward. This driven. This freaking needy.

He stops to take off his shirt. Now *I'm* the one gawking. I've seen his bare chest plenty of times. The night he rescued me from the bug. When he was in his driveway after a bike ride and took his shirt off to cool down. When he came into my bedroom after my nightmare. But I've never been able to touch it. When I reach out and put a hand over his pec, he shivers. It makes me feel powerful.

I take the power one step further and pull off my shorts.

He ups the ante and takes off his.

We sit on the couch, both in our underwear, staring at each other.

My panties are wet. His boxers are tented.

"Oh, the things I want to do to you," he says.

I let out a long, slow breath. "So do them."

He slips onto the floor, gently pushes me back into the couch cushion, and hooks his thumbs around the waistband of my panties. He locks eyes with me as he takes them off. I raise my rear end and let him. He tosses them aside and his eyes shift down. It's a place he's been before. But before it was clinical. Professional. Now it's personal.

He puts a hand on my thigh. "I'm going to touch you now."

They're the same words he said to me before my exam. But they're delivered with vastly different intentions. My entire body shivers knowing what comes next. His mouth is inches from me. He's going to kiss me there. Lick me there. He's going to do things to me he's only done in my fantasies.

"Jesus, Dakota." He looks up. "You're fucking perfect in every way." He slips a finger inside me. "I'm going to make you come with my fingers. With my tongue. I'm going to make you come hard."

He pulls my butt to the very edge of the couch, and I practically explode before his mouth even touches me. I'm coiled up so tightly I know it won't take long. I can feel myself building. It's the kind of warmth spreading inside that lets you know it's going to happen. The cliff you know you're about to fall over. It's hovering right there. And he's about to give me the final push.

I watch as his tongue finds my clit, circling it with increasing pressure. Then he lightens up, then more pressure again, then he pulls back, then starts again. All the while his fingers work around inside me. And, suddenly, *oh*—I groan loudly when he massages a spot inside me.

"That's it isn't it?" he says, briefly taking his lips off me.

I can't even speak. I'm experiencing sensations I've never experienced. My God, I was right. The man knows his way around a woman's body. I've always thought the g-spot was a mythical thing. He's proving it's not only real, it's the most amazing thing I've ever felt. A warm, cozy, flushing feeling rolls through my body in waves. It's a freight train I can't stop, and his tongue swirling around my clit just edges me closer.

My body explodes with shudders. I yell at the ceiling. He doesn't stop stroking me inside, giving me the longest, most intense orgasm I've ever had.

When I stop moving, completely spent, he sits back on his haunches looking mighty satisfied with himself.

"Oh, my God," I say, embarrassed. "That was so good I think I just peed a little."

"You didn't pee. You had an FE. A female ejaculation." He shakes his head as if amazed. "I've read about it in medical journals, but I've never actually seen it. Christ, that was sexy."

I sit up straight. "Female ejaculation? Is that really a thing?"

"It is."

"It's not just pee?"

"FE is the secretion of a very small amount of fluid from the paraurethral glands."

I laugh at his clinical explanation. "Careful, you might turn me on again with that kind of talk."

"Oh, believe me. I plan to turn you on again." He rises to his knees and looks me right in the eyes. "You have to be completely relaxed for it to happen." He smirks. "Neighbors-with-benefits my ass. You want more, Gator Girl. Just like I do. And we're going to have it."

I want to tell him yes, I want more. Because I do. I want so much more.

"Let's just enjoy each other, Hudson. Leave the rest to chance."

His head shakes slowly back and forth. "Dakota—after what I just witnessed, I promise you there's no fucking chance I want to ever do that with anyone else."

My heart turns over in my chest. Because if I wasn't sure I was in love with him before, I know I am now. But he has no idea I come as a package deal.

He stands up, gathers me in his arms, and walks in the direction of my bedroom.

I stiffen. There's a picture of Travis on my nightstand. I wiggle free. "Give me a minute. Wait here." I rush in, put away the picture, and then go into the bathroom. I look at the selfish woman in the mirror knowing Hudson wouldn't be with her if he knew everything. I promise myself I'll tell him. But not yet. Tonight I'm going to be selfish. Because if I've learned anything in life, it's that there are no guarantees.

When I open the door, Hudson is standing in the bedroom doorway, naked. His penis is erect. It twitches when he looks at me.

"Do you have any condoms?" I ask. "Because I don't."

"We don't need any."

I scold him with a punishing stare. "Uh, yes, Doctor, we do."

He strides over, grabs my hand, pulls me to the bed, guides me down on it, and climbs over my body. "Actually we don't." He leans close. His hot breath flows over my neck. "Because until you admit it, we're not doing the deed."

"Until I admit what?" I press my hips up into his erection.

"That you want more."

I turn and look at the bare nightstand. "Hudson."

"Okay, fine. You don't want to admit it? Then I'm going to torture you in every way possible. By the time I'm done with you, you won't be able to stand. You won't be able to talk." He bites my earlobe. "You won't even know your own name."

The thought of him making me come yet again is thrilling. But if what he said is true, and the only action he's had is his left hand, I think it's only fair that I repay the favor. I reach between us and take him in my hand. "Maybe you're the one who won't even know yours."

He grunts, laughs, and sighs at the same time. "Game on, Gator Girl. Game on."

Chapter Twenty-seven

Hudson

Something smells different. I turn over in bed and open my eyes. When I see Dakota, everything from last night comes rushing back. The way she kissed me. How she held my dick in her hands. Her perfect lips around my cock.

Jesus, I'm hard again even after the three extraordinary orgasms I had last night. *Three.* And not one of them from penetration. I'm going to stay true to my word. She won't be another Lynda. I won't let her.

Her eyes flutter open. She stares quietly. As if she's surprised I'm still here.

Hell, *I'm* surprised I'm still here. I never sleep over.

I brush a stray hair off her cheek. "Good morning."

"Morning." She stretches her arms above her in a waking yawn.

"You seem well rested."

"Three orgasms will do that to a girl."

"You know, I'm not really sure what I'm supposed to do now. Do I make you coffee? Stay for breakfast? Get the hell out?"

She blinks. "I'm confused."

"I've never done this before. Not sure of the protocol."

"You've never done what before?"

"Slept with a woman. In her bed. All night."

Her eyes widen. "Never?"

"You're the first."

Her lips curve up into a smile. "You're the first man to give me three orgasms in one night."

I scoot closer and pull her against me. "It doesn't have to end there."

"Actually, it does. I'm going on a bike ride with Regan this morning." She cranes her neck to see the clock. "I have one hour." She snuggles into the crook of my neck. "Last night was nice."

I run a hand across her bare shoulder and down her soft arm. "So… no more going to the city?"

She tenses. Then she sighs. "I have to keep going to the city." She looks up at me. "I'm not seeing anyone else, Hudson."

"Then why do you go?"

"I had a life there."

"Is it about your late husband?"

She shrugs. "I don't know, in a way I guess." She pulls away, sits on the side of the bed and gets her robe off the bed post. "I really should get ready. I don't want to be late."

She's giving me my walking papers and I don't like it one fucking bit. I stare at her back. She's really not going to tell me. After last night. After I slept here. She's not going to open up to me. It dawns on me how little I know about her. She never talks about her past. Other than telling me about Brian on Friday, I don't know thing one about her. Women are usually eager to tell me all about themselves. But Dakota is a closed book.

"I'd invite you along, but I'm trying to establish friendships here."

I wave it off. "Chicks are too slow anyway."

She turns and offers me a puckish grin. "Is that a challenge, Doctor?"

"Anytime, anywhere."

"Help yourself to coffee and bagels if you want. I'm going to take a shower. See you later?"

She's not even going to eat breakfast with me. I sit and pull on my skivvies. "Yeah, see you later."

My eyes follow her as she walks to the bathroom. I get dressed, feeling, I don't even know… stupid? Rejected? *Jesus, Hud, quit being such a pussy.*

But then, as I make the proverbial walk of shame back to my house, I realize what the feeling really is. And suddenly it makes me empathize with all the women in my past.

My door is unlocked. I wasn't aware I'd left it that way. When I get as far as my kitchen, I see why. My grandfather is at the table with a cup of coffee. I scoff. "Help yourself, Pappy."

I don't bother telling him that it's *my* name on the deed to this house, not his. Because then he'll remind me that it's his money paying for all of it. Or it *was* his money paying for everything until I made attending. I'm making good money now. So if he's here to try and bribe me again, he's shit out of luck.

"Pour yourself a cup and sit," he commands.

I do it. Because arguing with him is not the way I'd planned on starting this day.

He looks at the clock. "Expected to find you here. I've been waiting an hour."

"You could have called."

"Where were you?"

"Out."

"I didn't hear your car pull up."

If I know Pappy, he already knows it's still in the garage. "I wasn't in my car."

"And you're not dressed for exercise. Were you with a woman?"

I sigh in irritation as I run a hand down my face. "Pappy, why are you here?"

"I was walking by and thought I'd pay my grandson a visit. Rose has me on this program." He raises his arm and taps on his Apple Watch. "She wants me getting in my steps." He pounds on his chest. "Keeps the ol' ticker working."

"You never pay a visit for no reason. What is it you want?"

He pulls a slip of paper from his pocket. "I've jotted down the names of a few women I thought you'd be a good match for."

I pinch the bridge of my nose. "Pappy, why do you feel the need to meddle in everyone's life?"

"Told you before. I want you to be happy, Hudson. I want all my grandchildren to be happy."

"I'm happy."

"Hudson, you've painted your garage no less than three times in the past few months. Your only friends are your brothers. You work and you bike and you sleep. How is that a meaningful existence? Now, I've spoken to each of these women. They are all amenable to entering into a relationship with you."

"Amenable? Jeez, Pappy, why not just say it's a business transaction?"

"You do realize that many countries still participate in the practice of arranged marriages. You can look at it like that if you prefer."

I choke on my coffee. "Marriage?" I get up from the table and dump my cup angrily in the sink. "If you're here to strong arm me into settling down with some woman on your list who has agreed to marry the grandson of a billionaire, you can—"

"I can what? Choose your words carefully, Hudson."

His punishing stare burns into me.

I make a good living. I don't need his money. But I'm not out to burn any bridges.

"Pappy, I'm twenty-eight. I just became an attending. My job is demanding. I'm not ready for any commitments yet." I hear myself talking, but when I say the word commitment, Dakota's face is the only thing I see. "Someday, I might be. So can you cool it with this pressure? Give me a few years. Revisit this when I hit thirty."

"Thirty," he grumbles. "Mmm."

As I sit back at the table, he works his scruffy jaw with his thumb and forefinger. I can practically see his head spinning with ideas. Or conspiracies.

"Where were you this morning?" he asks again.

Part of me is relieved he keeps asking. Because if he knew where I was, he'd bring the hammer down. "I thought you knew everything, Pappy." If this is the game he wants to play, I'll play along for now.

He stands and presses his palms onto the table, hovering over me. "I *do* know everything, boy. So watch yourself. And do not test me. Are we clear?"

I try to read his eyes. Does he know where I was? Is this just another threat for me to stay away? Or is he bluffing?

"Crystal."

"Good. Now walk me out."

He hands me his cup. I put it on the counter and follow him to the door. We're standing on the front porch when Dakota pedals by. She glances over, a smile on her face, but it fades when she sees Tucker next to me. She waves. At me? At him? And then she's gone.

Pappy is staring again. At me. He leans in. "Stay in your lane, Hudson." Then he walks away.

Stay in my lane? What the hell does that mean? What even happened here?

I go back inside, slamming my front door, confused about my grandfather. About Dakota. About every goddamn feeling inside me. Because what I really wanted to do when he pulled out that list was get a pen and add a name to it. Dakota Daniels. I wanted to strike a line through the others and tell him hers was the only name I'd consider. That she's the only person I've ever wanted a relationship with.

Ironically, however, she is the only female in the tri-state area who doesn't want the same thing. How fucking poetic. I finally find the girl of my dreams and all she wants is to be my fuck buddy.

Chapter Twenty-eight

Dakota

Strange energy. The past week has been filled with it. There has been a battle of wills going on between me and Doctor Jerkwad. I'm waiting for him to come back over and proposition me; bed me thoroughly and properly; give me another one of those FEs that had my head spinning. He's holding sex hostage, waiting for me to give in and admit my deep feelings for him.

Oh, if Lynda could see him now. The irony of the town playboy not 'playing' on principle.

Drinking my morning coffee, I sigh and stare at the swing in the back yard, knowing exactly why I won't give in to Hudson. He would see me differently if he knew I was a package deal. A package deal with five tons of baggage that comes in the form of ex-in-laws who have painted me as an inept mom.

Hudson isn't the kind of man who is eager to take on a family. And call me selfish if I just want to enjoy the company of a man without thinking about the future. A future that may not even include my son if the Daniels have their way.

I close my eyes, guilt seeping in through every pore. How could I let myself enjoy that night with Hudson knowing Travis is stuck with those horrible people? How could I have forgotten about court dates, supervised visitation, and retainer payments to lawyers?

Maybe they're right. Maybe I am a bad mom.

Travis needs to be my sole focus. Playing doctor with the man next door should be the last thing on my mind.

I see a sliver of red as I pass the dining room window. I go over and lean on the sill, watching him pull out of his driveway as I've done so many times before. And as he's done all those times, he looks over. We lock eyes from afar. But this time it's different. We have a connection now. We bonded on some other-worldly level. I'm not even sure how that's possible when we didn't even have sex.

What is it about him? And what does he see in me? I'm no different from Lynda and every other woman in this town. Except that his grandfather made me off-limits.

He lifts his chin. I wave a hand. He drives off.

My phone rings and I rush over to answer it. My heart stops when I see Karl Wheeler's name. Why is my lawyer calling me at seven in the morning? Has something happened? To Travis?

"Hello?"

"Dakota," he says happily. "I've got good news."

"Thank goodness. I could use a bit of that."

"Do you have any plans for the weekend?"

"Tomorrow is not my Saturday to see Travis, so no."

"How would you like to see him this weekend? *All* weekend? For an unsupervised overnight visit at your house?"

I let his words replay in my head. "What? Really? They agreed to that?"

"They know we're getting closer to the truth, Dakota. We've interviewed dozens of neighbors and witnesses. We're investigating paternity. They surely didn't anticipate you hiring a firm like mine, one that has the resources and expertise to put up a fight. They had no choice but to capitulate to this demand."

"Will this be a one-time thing?"

I hold my breath, hoping it's not.

"Dakota, while I don't know the answer to that, I'm hoping this will be the first step into getting you full custody. As you know, getting in front of a judge takes time. And it's not something we plan to do until we have all the evidence we need."

A tear slips down my cheek. I get him for the whole entire weekend. I feel like I've won the lottery. Maybe not the grand prize lottery, but more than just the Powerball number. And it's progress. Movement in the right direction. Most of all, it gives me hope.

"Thank you, Karl."

He gives me details of how it will happen, and I write down every last word with a huge smile on my face.

Then, before starting work for the day, I go into the second bedroom and open some boxes. I didn't dare touch Trav's things before. I didn't want to tempt fate. Now, however, I empty every single one, getting out all his clothes, books, and toys, setting up the room so it feels like home to him. Because that's exactly what I want this house to feel like: home. And with him in it, I know it will.

With Travis's room set up, I lean against the wall, admiring my hard work. While envisioning him sleeping in the bed, an overlooked part of that reality creeps into my happy thoughts—Hudson will be next door. He may see us. Hear us. He might even catch me walking with Travis to or from town or the train station.

I'm about to be outed to the whole town as a single mom without custody.

I pick up one of Travis's stuffed animals and convince myself I don't care. My son is the only thing that matters. And if people can't see that, screw them.

I fly through work today, getting a full eight hour's worth done in less than seven. I go to the grocery store and pick up all of Trav's favorites. Fruit Loops. Nerd ropes. And all the fixings for smiley-faced waffles. I'm going to spoil the bejezus out of that boy. I'm going to savor every single moment.

Oddly, the thing I'm looking forward to the most is watching him sleep. I used to do that often. He goes to sleep early, long before I do. Sometimes I'd stand in his doorway and admire the innocence of a sweet slumbering boy without a care in the world. Does he sleep peacefully at Wayne and Patty's? It's been months. Has he gotten used to them by now?

As I carry my grocery bags home, I swallow the huge lump in my throat. All my visits have been supervised. There hasn't been an occasion to ask Travis about any of it. Every time I come close, Laura interrupts and diverts his attention. She's clearly been instructed not to allow personal conversations. Which is why I'm terrified they're trying to indoctrinate him somehow while painting me as someone of the past who isn't worthy of them or him.

But tomorrow there will be no Wayne. No Patty. Not even Laura. I'm going to have thirty-two hours of uninterrupted, uncensored time with my son. It's a gift I intend to treasure no matter who in this town happens to notice.

"That's quite a load," Hudson says, coming out of his garage as I approach my house. "You expecting company?"

"You're home early."

"I'm on call this weekend. I only do it every six weeks as we rotate the schedule, but it means leaving early on Friday to catch up on sleep. For some reason, women tend to go into spontaneous labor more often at night."

"Oh, well… then I guess you should go get some sleep."

"Or"—he raises a seductive brow—"we could stop playing this game and you could put on a swimsuit and join me in my hot tub. Better yet, *don't* put on a swimsuit and join me in my hot tub."

"Game?" I ask, shifting my bags around to distribute the weight while trying to ignore the pang in my gut verifying I want nothing more than to do what he asks.

"You ignoring the feelings you have for me. Me pretending it doesn't bother me. That game."

"Maybe we could talk about this some other time, Hudson. After your busy weekend."

He nods to my bags. "Or after yours. Who are you expecting?"

I contemplate coming clean. More than likely, he'll find out anyway. Then again, he is on call. He'll either be asleep or at the hospital. And this is definitely not a conversation I want to have on our shared sidewalk where it's possible nosey neighbors could be listening.

Tell him, the angel on my right shoulder says, knowing it's the right thing to do.

Don't, the devil on my left one retorts, not wanting to ruin what I have—elation over being wanted by a man, and excitement over seeing my son. If I tell him, both of those could disappear. Today, I've been happier than I've been since arriving nine weeks ago.

I let the devil win this one. "We can talk Sunday. Come for dinner?"

"I'm on call until 8:00 p.m."

"Then dinner will be at 8:30."

He closes the gap between us, puts an arm around me, and pulls me against him. "Dinner might be at 8:30, but I assure you, it's not the food I'm looking forward to feasting on." He kisses my neck in a place he must remember drives me wild.

My breath hitches. My body hums. My head spins. Yes, I'm most definitely in deep.

I just hope I don't end up drowning.

Chapter Twenty-nine

Hudson

I know I should sleep. On-call weekends are the worst. It seems like every time you finish with one patient and pull up in the driveway, another page comes.

I get out of bed and open the curtains. The sun is just beginning to set. There's no activity at her house. No lights on in the back yard. No cars in the driveway. Nothing.

She's being secretive again. Why wouldn't she tell me about the groceries?

Don't read too much into it, Hud. She's probably having girls over for margarita night.

Just when I'm about to close the curtains and crawl back into bed, I see movement behind her house. My window gives me a clear view into her unfenced yard. It makes me feel less stalkerish than the times I've watched her through the hole in my fence. But only a little.

She pours herself a glass of wine, watches the sun dip below the trees, and then... *holy God...* then she dances.

I'm in a trance, glued to the window as I watch her float around the wooden deck in a long T-shirt and bare feet. She glides in graceful, fluid motions as if she's a practiced ballerina. One over-energetic twirl sends wine sloshing out of her glass and onto her shirt. She looks down at the red stain and laughs. Jesus, her laugh. I've heard it before, but not like this. Her laugh, her smile, her dance—I've never seen her so relaxed and carefree.

Dakota Daniels has a secret. That I'm sure of. And whatever that secret is, it keeps her from achieving true happiness. This—what I'm witnessing right here—is about as close as I've seen her get. She's been nice, generous, and sometimes funny. But there's always something under the surface. Something that holds her back. Keeps her guard up. Something that's keeping her a prisoner of sorts.

Whatever it is, it's not something she wants to tell me. Not even after the connection we had last weekend. Not after the three orgasms. Not after I slept in her bed. Not even after I told her I wanted more.

Jesus, what is it about this girl that has me going so far out of my lane? My head is full of her, and my gut is twisted in knots. I want her. I want her so fucking bad. And the pathetic part of all this is that she knows it. And that means she holds all the cards.

I shake my head and close the curtains knowing this is not a position I ever intended to be in. I crawl back into bed, punch my pillow, and fall asleep dreaming of the dancing girl next door. Only in my dreams, she dances with me. And in my dreams, she wears white.

~ ~ ~

I've never been so happy to have been paged three times in a twelve-hour period. Two vaginal births and a c-section. Must be the full moon. I swear it's a thing.

At two in the afternoon, I pull into my garage. In the house, I eat a protein bar and wash it down with two glasses of water before heading to bed to hopefully grab a few hours of sleep before the next page. It doesn't take me long to relax. I'm exhausted. My eyelids are heavy, and I feel myself drifting off when laughter awakens me. And not just any laughter. *Kid laughter.* Coming from Gator Girl's back yard.

I throw the sheet off and dart to the window, but I don't see anything for a moment. Then I see a glimpse of someone's feet swing briefly into view. And then again. More laughter.

She's pushing a kid on a swing. She has visitors.

Suddenly, I'm not tired anymore. I can't see the other side of her yard from here, so I go to the kitchen, pour a cup of coffee, and head out back. Standing on the deck, I hear voices but can't make out words. I should give her and her guests privacy. I should go back to bed. I know I'm intruding on so many levels. And I don't care. All social decency tossed aside, I wander over to the hole in the fence.

And what I see amazes me.

If I thought Dakota was happy last night, that was nothing compared to the elation on her face right now. Even from fifty feet away her eyes sparkle. Her skin is radiant. Her smile is luminous. She's fucking beaming. Damn she's beautiful.

Sadness washes over me. I want to be the one to make her look like that. To make her smile and laugh and—

A small boy runs into view. "Mommy, I want to swing again. Push me higher this time!"

My brain isn't firing on all cylinders. I'm overworked and sleep deprived, because I could swear I just heard him call her Mommy.

"Higher, Mommy. Higher!"

Laugher from both of them dances across the yard as my jaw hits the dirt. *Mommy?* She has a fucking kid?

My head doesn't know what to do with this information. I'm as confused as a goat on astroturf. She never said anything about a kid. I mean, I knew she had to have been pregnant at some point. But how is this the first time he's at her house? The boy must be four or five years old. How could she live next door for nearly two months—live *with me* for two weeks—and not reveal this monumental truth?

Dakota stops pushing. "My arms are tired, Trav. Want to play soccer instead?"

He yelps in delight and hops off the swing.

Trav. This is Travis. The Travis she calls. The Travis she says 'I love you' to. Her kid. Her son.

I don't know why I keep expecting someone else to walk into the yard. A man. Travis's father perhaps. Is Travis her only secret? Or is there more?

Then again, her husband died. He must be Travis's father. But then why is the boy not living with her?

I need answers. Answers I'm not going to get spying through the fence.

Then, as if fate heard my plea, a ball flies overhead. Dakota looks over and I hide.

"We'll fetch it later," she says. "Come on, let's see what else we have."

I pick up the ball, turning it over in my hands, and head for the gate. She doesn't even see me coming, she's rooting through a toy bin on the deck. The boy sees me though, and he tugs on her shirt. "Mommy."

He moves behind her, wary of the stranger I am.

Dakota looks up and immediately her smile falls. She knows I know her secret. She knows she's been deceiving me. She knows she'll have to explain.

I throw the ball into the air and catch it. "Lose something?" I look at the boy. "This must be yours. It bounced into my yard." Dakota is clearly at a loss for words. She looks like a deer in headlights. I approach. "Aren't you going to introduce us?"

She swallows. "Of course. Travis, this is my neighbor, Mr. McQuaid."

I step closer and hold out my hand. "Hudson. It's nice to meet you, Travis."

He looks at his mom. She nods. "You can shake his hand, baby."

Baby. I look at her lips, wishing she was using the endearment on *me.*

No—stop. She has a child.

It should matter. It should matter that she didn't tell me. It should matter that she didn't trust me. It should matter that she lied, even if by omission.

But somehow, it doesn't. Knock me over with a ten-ton feather, but it doesn't. I still want her. I want the single mother next door. Her and her secrets. Her and her baggage. *Her.*

Travis puts his small hand in mine, and we shake. "That must be quite the leg you have if you kicked the ball all the way over the fence. You're strong."

Travis smiles proudly. "I'm gonna be a soccer player."

"I guess you are." I turn to Dakota. "Any other surprises I need to know about?" I motion to her house. "Older brother? Younger sister? Baby daddies?"

The piercing sound of my pager goes off. Of course it fucking does.

"What's that?" Travis asks as I press the button to silence it.

"Hudson is a doctor," Dakota says. "That sound means he's needed."

Travis seems quite interested. "You're a doctor?"

"I am."

"Can you help my mom?"

I cock my head. "Help her with what, champ?"

"Grammy said she's sick."

Dakota's eyes flood with tears. She drops to her knees. "Oh, baby. She's wrong. I'm not sick. I promise I'm not."

Five minutes ago Dakota looked like the happiest woman alive. Now, she just looks broken. I want to stay. I want to stay and find out the answers to a million looming questions. But I can't. "I... have to go."

She nods and takes her son's hand. I get the feeling playtime is over.

"Hudson!" she calls after me when I'm at the gate.

I turn.

"No more surprises. It's just us."

"Okay then." I walk through the gate, wanting to throw my pager against the house. Because, fuck, my life just got a hell of a lot more complicated.

Chapter Thirty

Dakota

It's the moment I've looked forward to the most. Bedtime. I get Trav's favorite book and crawl into the queen-sized bed next to him.

"This bed isn't as big as my bed at Grammy's."

"Not many things are." I snuggle closer. How do I explain to a four-year-old that his grandparents are lying to him? Furthermore, how do I explain to the man I love that I'm not the woman he must see me as—the single mom who isn't capable of raising her own child.

"Travis, I want to talk to you about what you said earlier. Your grandmother is confused, baby. I'm not sick. In fact I've been to a doctor, and he says I'm totally healthy."

"Is that man your doctor?"

"Hudson? No." *Not anymore.*

"Do you think I could be a doctor?"

I chuckle. "What happened to you being a soccer player?"

"I could be a doctor who plays soccer. Couldn't I?"

I kiss the top of his head. "Yes, baby. You can be whatever you want. Now, should I read?"

He nods and leans his head on my shoulder. I open the book and almost can't read it through my tears. Being able to do this again is everything. But knowing this can only happen occasionally and not every night rips me apart. But I muddle through. I even do all the voices just as he likes.

"Mommy?" he says sleepily when I close the book.

"Mmm?"

"If you aren't sick, how come I can't live with you?"

My heart breaks in two. This isn't the first time he's asked. He asked during my very first supervised visit, but Patty wouldn't let me answer. After that, I suppose she told him more lies.

"Oh, Travis. I wish I could explain it in a way you'd understand. Just believe me when I say I'm doing everything in my power to make it so you can live with me again. Would you like that? Would you like to live here with me in this house?"

I hold my breath knowing I shouldn't have asked. The place he lives now is a castle compared to this—even though this is the nicest house I've ever lived in. He has acres of land on which to play. Servants making his meals. Drivers taking him places.

"Who will play with Archie?"

"There are a lot of people at Grammy's who could play with their dog."

"But he likes *me*."

How can I compete with everything he's become accustomed to over the past few months? Of course he wants to stay.

"I like the swing." He stretches his neck around and looks up at me. "If I live here, can we get a dog?"

Tears prickle the backs of my eyes. "Yes, baby. We can get a dog. We'll pick one out together."

"Can I name it?"

"You bet."

"Will you take care of him when I go away to school?"

"What's this now?"

"Grammy and Grandpa say I'm going away to school. It's school where you sleep there. Daddy went there, and so did Aunt Bethy and Uncle Benji."

Boarding school. I sigh. They're planning on sending Travis away to boarding school in the fall. When he's only five? How could they claim to want him so badly and then turn around and ship him off for someone else to raise?

"Calloway Creek has a great school, Travis. If you like the swings here, you should see what they have. And it's just around the block. I could walk you there every day."

He beams with excitement. "With the dog?"

"Yes. With the dog."

One of his hands slips behind me and he squeezes me hard. "I love you, Mommy."

"I love you too, Travis. I love you so much it hurts."

"How come it hurts?"

I put my hand over his heart. "Your heart is where you keep all your love. And sometimes you can love someone so much that your heart isn't big enough and it tries to expand to hold all of it." A tear falls. "But I'm not sure my heart could ever be big enough to contain all my love for you."

"Don't cry, Mommy."

"It's okay. It's a good cry."

"My heart hurts too."

I nod and swipe a lock of hair off his forehead.

He looks down at the bed. "Is it bad that my heart doesn't hurt for Grammy and Grandpa?"

"No. It's not bad."

He taps the cover of the book. "Can we read it again?"

I smile big and read it to him two more times. Then I turn off the light and watch my son sleep by the moonlight coming through the window. I watch him sleep and wonder if there has ever been any mother who loves her son as much as I love him.

I watch him until I can't keep my eyes open anymore. Then I fall asleep next to him on the bed, needing to hold onto every moment I can.

Because tomorrow, I'll sleep alone.

~ ~ ~

It's the worst form of torture walking into the house without Travis. Taking him back to the city today was one of the hardest things I've ever done. I contemplated not doing it. Taking what little money I have and running off with him.

But I know they'd find us. They have means. They have connections. And then they'd take him from me for good.

I have to trust Karl. And I have to believe they agreed to overnight visits because they feel they're getting backed into a corner. The best thing I can do is wait it out and hope they aren't successful in brainwashing Travis any further.

How is this the same house I left just a few hours ago? I've lived here for over two months, but now everything has changed. Travis is everywhere. I can't walk past the kitchen without seeing him eating waffles. Or the living room without seeing him building a Lego set. Or the back yard—that's where I see him the most. On the swing. Kicking a ball. Smiling up at me.

Suddenly, being without him just became ten times harder. And my resolve to get him back is even stronger. I don't have room in my life or my heart for anyone else. *Do I?*

I take a bottle of wine outside, pour myself a glass, and settle into the lounge chair as I stare at the swing, willing Travis to appear. My eyelids become heavy, and I give in to the emotional exhaustion of the weekend.

~ ~ ~

Fingers tickle my forehead and I smile. *Travis.*

But when I open my eyes, it's Hudson who towers over me. I blink and look around. It's almost dark. I must have fallen asleep.

I sit up so quickly I get a head rush. "I, uh… forgot. I'm sorry. I haven't cooked anything. Raincheck?"

He holds out a bag of food from Lloyd's. "It's a good thing I brought dinner then."

I swing my legs over the side of the lounger. "Honestly, I'm not sure I'd be very good company right now."

"I'll put this in the refrigerator." He disappears and comes back a minute later with a wine glass, pours himself a drink, tops off mine, and sits on the chair next to me. "Usually after a weekend like this, I'd have something stronger, but this will have to do."

We drink in silence as we watch the sunset. Neither of us speaks for what seems like forever. I know he has questions. He might even be mad at me. But he's here. That has to mean something.

Once the sun has dipped beneath the trees, he turns to me. "I knew you had a child."

"You did?"

Of course he did. Tucker is his grandfather. I'm sure Hudson knows everything. Then again, he seemed more than a little surprised yesterday when he brought the soccer ball over.

"It's amazing what women think their gynecologists don't know. Your cervix gave you up."

"Why didn't you say anything?"

"Wasn't my place. You could have had a stillborn baby. Or given a child up for adoption. You could have had a kid who died."

"I'm sorry I didn't tell you."

"Why didn't you?"

"It wasn't just you. I didn't tell anyone. I didn't want to be seen as a failure."

"Why would anyone think that?"

I scoff. "Why *wouldn't* they? I'm a single mother who barely gets to see her son."

"My mother used to tell us never to judge anyone until you've walked a mile in their shoes." He laughs. "I didn't listen to her. I judged *everyone.* I judged them for being poor. For being bad at sports. Hell, I judged them for being ugly."

"Yet here you are." I finally make eye contact. "Why is that, Hudson? I figured you for a guy who would run the other way rather than get caught up with a girl like me."

He nods. "A few months ago I'd say you were dead on."

"So what changed?"

"If you don't know the answer to that, Gator Girl, you're not as smart as I thought you were."

His eyes burn into me. I swallow, wanting to get devoured by his heated stare, but at the same time knowing it's not a good idea.

"You've been here for twenty minutes, and you haven't asked why I don't have custody."

He shrugs. "Figured you'd tell me if you wanted me to know."

"If I tell you, you'll decide I'm too much trouble. Because I have a lot of baggage, Hudson. And I'm not talking about Travis."

"Maybe I should be the judge of that."

"Says the guy who just admitted to judging everyone."

"Touché." He lifts his glass.

I gulp a few large swallows of wine. "Travis doesn't remember his father. He was two when it happened."

"He's four now?"

"Five in September." I get a bad taste in my mouth thinking about what that could mean for him. "He'll be ready for kindergarten in the fall."

"You say it like it's a bad thing."

"Brian's parents want him to go to boarding school."

"Why should Brian's parents get to decide?"

I look off in the distance. "Because they are his legal guardians."

"Well… shit. By the look on your face, I'm guessing that's the baggage you mentioned."

"You have no idea."

"Enlighten me."

"How much time do you have?"

He leans back onto the lounger pillow. "As much as it takes."

I top off my glass and take a sip, knowing the time has come to fess up. "I didn't come from the proper pedigree. His parents hated me from the start, from the very moment they met me on a weekend visit to Gainesville where we both went to the University of Florida. They put so many expectations on him. They expected him to graduate with honors. Get into a top law school. Join the family law practice. And he was expected to marry well. I threw a wrench into those plans. We knew they'd never let us marry without severe repercussions, so we forced their hand and got pregnant."

"Wow. Bold move."

"It was Brian's idea. But one I've never regretted."

"Yeah, I could see that."

"When Brian died, they cut me off. Brian had always gotten a living allowance. We rented a nice apartment in the city, close to NYU where he went to law school."

"I went to NYU for med school."

I cock my head. "Is it weird to think we might have been on campus at the same time? I went there a lot to have lunch with him. He loved eating at this little Italian place—"

"Giovanni's?"

"Yes. That's the one."

"Red-and-white striped tablecloths. Lasagna to die for. And Giovanni, he always said—"

"Buon appetito!"

He laughs. "Small world."

"I haven't thought about those days in a long time."

"Sorry. Didn't mean to go off track. You were saying about your apartment?"

"Oh, right. On my salary, I couldn't afford the rent. I had to find another place. Smaller. Dirtier. Less desirable neighborhood."

"They were okay letting their grandchild grow up that way?"

I shake my head. "It was all part of their plan. But first, before we moved, they called protective services on me claiming I was doing drugs. CPS brought a search warrant and found Brian's stash. I was arrested but never charged thanks to the lawyer I hired. And Travis wasn't taken away. Not then anyway. No, they waited and built their case against me.

"I'd spent every last dime I had on my lawyer and was forced to move a second time, into an even smaller place. I maxed out my credit cards. Missed one too many utility payments. And that's when they came in for the kill. They're all lawyers—his whole family—and they have unscrupulous people working for them. They made up stories about me. Painted me as an unfit parent. And the judge who granted them guardianship went to law school with Brian's father."

Hudson sits up, forearms on his knees, clearly pissed. "First thing tomorrow, I'm finding you a new lawyer."

I shake my head. "No need. I fired the old one after I got this job. And the new lawyer is the reason I was able to have Travis for the whole weekend. He's making good progress."

"Dakota, I have connections too, you know. Or my family does anyway. I can help."

"Thank you, but everything that can be done is being done. They have someone looking into their false allegations. But these things take time. It's just so hard. All the waiting. Knowing they're badmouthing me in front of him. They're telling him I'm sick, Hudson. They are brainwashing him." Tears I've been able to hold in until now start to fall. "Every day he's with them, I feel more of him slipping away."

He pushes off his chair and sits on the edge of mine. "Hey, it's okay. You said yourself they're making progress."

"It's not fast enough. It'll never be fast enough." I lean into him, needing comfort. His body is lean and strong. His arm comes around me making me feel safe. Protected. I look up. "Make me forget, Hudson. Make me forget about them and what they're doing to my son. Make me forget—just for tonight."

He looks into my eyes, and I can see the war going on behind his.

He scoops me into his arms and carries me inside. He walks through the living room, down the hall, and into my bedroom. He puts me on the bed, turns off the light, and crawls in next to me—fully clothed.

"Sometimes it's best not to forget," he says, spooning me from behind. "That way you know what you're fighting for. Now sleep, Gator Girl. I'm not going anywhere."

His words. His strong arms. His refusal to take advantage of me when I'm at my most vulnerable. They all make my heart hurt. And I can feel it expanding so much, I fear it might explode.

Chapter Thirty-one

For the second time in as many weeks, I wake up in a strange bed. But it doesn't feel strange. It feels right. It's early and still dark out, but I can make out her face. It's peaceful now, unlike the turmoil displayed on it last night. I can't imagine what she must be going through. And she's doing it all alone.

I'm not sure how long I lie here looking at her. And as I lie here, I can feel my heart opening and her walking right on in as if she owns the place. And that scares the devil out of me. I barely know her. And what I'm learning is some seriously jacked up shit. A dead husband who overdosed. Crazy in-laws who lie about her. An innocent four-year-old being used as a pawn. What else don't I know? Somehow, I feel there's more to the story than what I've been told. Which is why I'm so goddamn confused about how I feel every time I look at her.

I want to help her. I want to help her kid. I want to wake up every day looking at her.

"Mmm." Her hand moves along my chest. "You're still here."

"I told you I wasn't going anywhere."

Her eyes open. "You're a much better man than your reputation would have one thinking."

I chuckle. "Tell that to the woman who has made a sport out of defacing my garage door."

Dakota pulls away, wiggling her lower half. She throws her shorts on the floor and puts her panties on my chest. "I want you to be bad, Hudson. For the next thirty minutes—be bad."

I loop her pink lacy underwear around a finger as she strips off her top half. She's lying naked in bed next to me and I'm fully clothed. My cock likes her idea. It really wants to come out and play. It's been a long time since he's seen the inside of a woman.

"Dako—"

She puts a finger to my lips. "Huh-uh." She climbs on top of me, her smooth skin luminescent in the breaking dawn. "I'm Gator Girl." She tugs up my shirt and I lift my shoulders so she can pull it off. "Do you have a problem with that, Doctor?" She sweeps two fingers beneath my waistband, grazing my hard-as-stone cock.

"Not as long as you're sure about this."

She leans down, her face inches from mine as she hovers. "All week I've dreamed of you inside me. If I'm being honest, I dreamed of it long before that. I may have even fantasized about it. Your fingers. Your tongue. What they did to me last week." Her lips graze my ear. "I touched myself remembering how you made me come."

I'm about to jizz in my pants. I want to flip her around, press her into the mattress. Dominate her until she's screaming my name. But the part of me that wants to wake up to her every day holds me back.

I pull her hand out from under my pants. "That's not what I meant, Dakota. I need to know you're serious about *this. Us.*"

I hear myself say it and I can't believe the words. I've somehow transformed into an insecure fool who needs reassurance that there'll be a tomorrow. Jesus—when the fuck did this happen?

She sits up, pensive now, but doesn't move from on top of me. "I'm serious about getting my son back. About doing my job and keeping a stable environment for him. About staying in Calloway Creek."

"You're going to have to do better than that." I run my hands up her rib cage, over her breasts, and then I pinch her nipples. "You have to say it."

Her eyes burn into mine. "Tell me what you want me to say."

My hands fall to her hips where I grip her and flip her onto her back. I straddle her and pin her hands up by her head. I lean in and kiss her jawline. I trace my tongue along the cords of her neck as she mewls to the ceiling. I work my way to her ear and whisper, "Tell me you want more. Tell me we're not just neighbors. Tell me I'm the only man you want to touch. Tell me you feel alive when we're together. Tell me your head spins and your vision blurs when you see me." I pull back and stare at her in the breaking dawn. "Tell me you fucking want me as badly as I want you, Gator Girl."

She swallows as she looks up at me. "If I tell you all those things, will you make love to me already?"

Make love. Not fuck. It's all the same thing—but it's not. With her it's different. *Everything* is different.

I take her hand and place it over my heart. "Only if you mean it."

"You want me to tell you I think about you all the time? That I wonder if you're thinking about me? That I can't breathe when I see you because the feelings inside me take up all the space in my lungs? That I feel guilty because I've only known you for months and have emotions I didn't even have with my own husband? Is that what you want to hear?"

My lips come crashing down on hers. She may not have said exactly what I wanted to hear, but she said enough. She said her truth, and right now that's everything. And as I kiss her, words swim in my head. Three of them. Words I've never wanted to say to another woman.

Her fingers tear at the button on my pants. In seconds, I'm shedding the rest of my clothes. I can't do it fast enough. I need us together, skin-on-skin, nothing between us. I need it like I need air. I need her like I need my next breath. I need us like I've never needed anything before.

My dick throbs against her as I explore every inch of her skin with my fingers. My mouth. My tongue. She squirms beneath me, doing some exploration of her own. Her soft hands trace every muscle of my back, the curve of my ass, my thighs. When she takes my cock in her hand I have to bite my lower lip to keep from coming too soon. Because when I come, I'm doing it inside of her. Just as I've imagined for weeks.

I groan out loud when I run a finger through her slick folds. I spread the wetness around her clit, knowing just what motion drives her insane.

"Hudson."

The soft word is spoken like a prayer. Hudson. Not Doctor. It's me she wants. Not some forbidden relationship with her gynecologist. Not some romp with her elusive neighbor. *Me.* I feel powerful yet so un-fucking-deserving.

She fingers my balls and teases my perineum until I can't take another second. I pin her to the bed, my eyes locking with hers as I guide myself inside her. Her hips lift and take me in all the way, both of us moaning when I hit the end of her.

I stop moving. I stop breathing. I'm climbing a mountain. Diving beneath the sea. Flying through the air. I'm having a deeply religious experience. One that is forever changing me.

"More," she says, gripping the sides of my head. "I want more."

The way she's looking at me. She doesn't mean more cock. More movement. More sex. She means more *me*. It may not be the three words I was hoping for, but it may as well have been with the tears pooling in her eyes.

I do what she asks. I give her more. More of my heart. My goddamn soul. I want to give her more than more. I want to give her everything.

And I do something I've never done in all of my twenty-eight years. I make love.

Slowly, I begin to move within her. She holds onto me, urging me to move faster. I pull out so the head of my cock is only a few inches inside her. I twist a bit, hoping to find the spot that drives her wild. I know in an instant when I've found it. Her eyes close and she exhales. Her fingers tighten on my ass. Her breath hisses between clenched teeth as I hit the spot over and over.

I'm not sure why I've never looked at a woman during sex. Because it's amazing. It's why songs are sung. Why sculptures are created. Why wars are fought.

The moment before she comes, her eyes fly open. She stares at me. Into me. Right fucking through me. And I know right now there will never be anyone else for me. I should claim her here and now. Tell her I love her. Put a ring on her finger. Drag her to Vegas and make her marry me. Because damn it—I want it all, every goddamn piece of her. Even the pieces that will never be mine—her virginity, her past. Her kid.

She shouts out my name. I call out hers. And as we come together, it's a meeting of hearts, souls, minds.

I collapse down onto her, drained physically and emotionally. But I have enough energy for one more word.

"Mine."

Chapter Thirty-two

Dakota

Mine.

The word echoes through my head as he rolls off me and lies by my side. There are words I want to say back, but I can't. My head tells me it's too soon to feel what my heart is feeling. I'm emotional. I just had Travis for the weekend. And the sex. Oh. My. God. I know it's been a long time since I've been with a man, but wow—there are just no words.

Except maybe that one. *Mine.*

It's the way I feel. It's exactly what I want. But there are so many other things I need to work out in my life before I can consider what *I* want.

I lay my head on his chest, loving the sound of his beating heart. Wanting to hear it every day.

"Why did you become a doctor?"

His chest bounces up and down with a chuckle. "That's not exactly the pillow talk I was expecting after what we just did."

I peek up. "What we just did was amazing. But it's something I've wondered for a while. You're an heir to a massive corporation, not to mention Tucker's own personal portfolio. Not to seem blasé about it, but why did you bother?"

"You mean why would a spoiled rich kid like me want to go through the rigors of med school when I could have just sat back and done nothing?"

"Well… yes."

"You really want to know?"

"I do."

"It was my dad."

I stiffen thinking of my horrible encounter with Robert McQuaid.

"Sorry to bring him into this, especially when we're naked in bed, but you did ask."

"Tell me more."

He shifts uncomfortably. "My father was a shitty role model. Once I became old enough to realize it, I swore I wasn't going to end up like him. And the opposite of my Barcalounger-beer-drinking-car-selling father was going to med school. It started out as a joke, me being interested in medicine. And it pissed him off, probably because he wanted me to amount to nothing. Just like he had. But the more I looked into it, the more serious I became about making it a reality.

"So you did it to prove to yourself that you weren't like him?"

"You could say that. The irony is, I turned out exactly like him. The only difference is I have a medical degree."

I perch my head on my hand and look him straight in the eyes. "You are nothing like your father."

He shakes his head. "You didn't know me then."

"When?"

"Before."

"Before what?"

"Before you."

I'm stunned. Finally, the answer to the question in my head about why I haven't seen the side of him everyone else sees. It's *me*. *Us*. We're the reason he's not that man anymore.

This moment is monumental. I want to bask in it. I want to bask in *him*. But he's opening himself to me—maybe because he now knows my secret—and I plan to take advantage of it and learn all I can.

The *basking* will have to wait.

He brushes a hair off my forehead. "What else do you want to know?"

"Why obstetrics and gynecology?" I roll my eyes. "I mean except for the obvious reason."

He laughs. "Everyone gets the wrong idea. I didn't go into it for the naked women. It's a job. I might as well be typing on a keyboard. It's clinical."

"Is that what it was like when you were examining me?"

"The truth? I was terrified. I felt like I was an intern again and you were my first patient. I was sure you could feel me shaking."

"I was sure you could feel *me* shaking."

"I could. But that's nothing new. Most women are nervous to some degree."

"Did you know back then that you wanted this to happen?"

"I didn't think it was a possibility. Not with Tucker forbidding it. And not with you making secret phone calls to someone I thought was a lover."

"Secret phone calls?" I raise my brow.

"I may have heard you once or twice on your back porch."

I chuckle. "And you thought I went off to the city to have some torrid affair."

"I was insanely jealous."

I can't help my smile. "Good. Now you know how I feel when I hear the women in this town speak of their interludes with you."

He scoots out from under me, pulls my back to his front and spoons me. He whispers in my ear, "There will be no more interluding with anyone who is not you."

My smile gets wider. "Well, okay then. But you still haven't answered my question. Why obstetrics?"

"Early on, it was clear being a doctor is mostly about dealing with the sick and elderly. It can get depressing, and the outcomes are not all that great. But with obstetrics, there's excitement. Patients are happy to be seeing me. And in the end, they get a perfect little person. There isn't much death. Not much cancer. Few bad outcomes. And there's a lot of variety between pregnancies, surgeries, new patients. And gynecologic surgery is very sophisticated and technical and uses cutting-edge robotics."

I laugh. "You like playing with the cool new toys."

"Hell yeah, I do."

"And it fulfills you."

"I thought it did. But now I know something was missing."

"What?"

He leans in. His hot breath flows over my ear. "You."

I turn around in his arms. "You don't think this is all going a little fast?"

"Dakota, I've spent the last decade bedding women for sport. It's a harsh reality, but it's true. When you're someone like me, a guy with a fat trust fund and a billionaire grandfather, women come out of the woodwork. They all want one thing, though. Money."

He squeezes my arm. "With you it's different. We had something before you knew I was a McQuaid. It might not have been much, but it was a connection I've never experienced. And it's funny, because I was sure you knew who I was when you moved in. I was positive my grandfather would have warned you away as he did me with you. I can't tell you how nice it was when I found out you had no idea who was living next to you. It felt so normal to banter with a woman who wasn't after my bank account. To think what you were feeling for me was because of me and not my name. Not my portfolio."

"I think you misread the intentions of a lot of women, Hudson. I'm sure not all of them were after your money. But I get how you might think so. And, selfishly, I'm glad you didn't give any of them a chance, even if they do keep painting crap on your garage." I sigh. "Poor Lynda."

"So you don't think I should send her a bill for all the paint?"

I laugh. "You should do no such thing. Give her time. I get the feeling you're not an easy man to get over."

"Good thing you'll never have to get over me then."

"And now we're back to things moving fast. Hudson, I don't even know how old you are."

"Twenty-eight. You?"

"Twenty-seven." I narrow my eyes. "How is a twenty-eight-year-old a full-fledged doctor? Don't you go to school for like ten years and then residency? I thought you were at least thirty."

"Don't let the forehead lines fool you. They came from years of pulling all-nighters. I had so many AP credits coming out of high school, college only took three years. And NYU Med School has an accelerated three-year program for students who already know what specialty they want to go into. So what normally takes one person eight years only took me six. My four-year residency ended early this year."

"So you're some kind of prodigy?"

"No. I'm just determined." He lays me flat and hovers over me. "And right now I'm determined to make you late for work."

"Don't *you* have to go to work?"

"Not after an on-call weekend. I'm free all day."

My face curls up into an impish grin "Well, then. It's a good thing I have flexible hours."

He snickers as his lips draw closer to mine. "The doctor is in, Gator Girl."

Chapter Thirty-three

Hudson

Reluctantly, at nine-thirty, I leave her house. As I walk across the yard back to mine, I momentarily wonder something: *do I have a girlfriend?*

"Girlfriend." I try the word out loud. "Dakota Daniels is my girlfriend."

"What's that you say?"

I look up at my porch to see Pappy sipping a cup of coffee. And the cup is from my own personal collection. The man truly has no boundaries. "I'd say make yourself at home, but I see you already have."

"Considering it's my money that purchased it, I figure I have the right."

Not wanting to argue and kill my good mood just yet, I climb the porch stairs, open the front door, and leave it open for him. I go to the kitchen, pour myself a cup of coffee, and sit at the kitchen table. And I wait. Because I know he knows where I was. And he's about to give me a goddamn earful.

He takes his time making his way in. He knows hesitation is the best form of torture.

The whole time I'm wondering what he'll do. I don't care what he does to me, I just don't want Dakota to pay for my disobedience. Her having this job is the only thing affording her the opportunity to get her son back.

Pappy strolls into the room. He doesn't look at me. He goes to top off his coffee. Then he slowly gets creamer from the fridge. He stirs it into his cup at a glacial pace. My God the man is intimidating as hell.

Finally, he takes a seat across the table. He sniffs and clears his throat. "Seems you've taken up with the McQuaid Motor Corp CPA."

"As you already know the answer to that, I don't see the need for this conversation."

"Oh, there's need alright. If I recall, I explicitly told you to stay away from her."

"She's my neighbor, Pappy. We're the same age. Both single. We were bound to cross paths. If you were so adamantly against it, you should have put her up in a different property."

"This was the only one available." He stares at me over the rim of his cup as he takes a long, slow sip. "What are your intentions?"

I glance at the clock. "Well, I intend to have breakfast. Then maybe a bike ride. The yard needs cutting."

"Don't disrespect me, boy. You know very well what I'm asking. And you know why I'm asking it."

"Do not take this out on her," I say, struggling to keep my cool. "She needs the job, Pappy. She has a son. Did you know that? A son who was taken away from her. Working for MMC means she can afford a good lawyer and get him back."

He cocks his head and studies me. "Mmm."

My grandfather may be old as dirt, but his mind is sharp. And it's always working. I don't know what he's thinking right now, but I can bet it's how to end my relationship with Dakota without hurting her.

"You didn't answer my question. What are your intentions?"

I shrug. "I don't know."

"I think you do."

"No, I don't. You want to know why? Because I've never been in this situation before. I've never had to think about intentions or consequences or four-year-olds in the city being brainwashed by corrupt in-laws. I've never had to take anyone else's feelings or circumstances into consideration. So when I say I don't know, I mean it, Pappy. I have no damn idea what I'm doing, and I'm in way over my head."

I could swear I see the hint of a smile. But it fades quickly. "You mean to tell me you are aware of the fact that Dakota has a child, and you still intend to be her suitor?"

I scoff. "Suitor. That's an interesting word for it."

His stare scolds me. "I was trying to be gentlemanly about it. Now answer the question."

"If I say yes. If I say she's my girlfriend. If I say I'm willing to do whatever it takes to be with her and help her get her kid back, what will you do? Because I really don't care if you threaten me, Pappy. You want to take away my trust fund—do it. Hell, it's more of a crutch than anything. But none of this is Dakota's fault. We were in deep long before I told her about you forbidding me to date her. She keeps the house and the job. And she'll know nothing about this."

He raises a fluffy white eyebrow. "You telling me what I can and can't do?"

"Pappy, please."

There's that inkling of a grin again. He clears his throat and stands, puts his cup in the sink, and goes for the front door. I quietly follow him out, waiting for him to drop the hammer. He turns. "I'll do nothing for now. I'll do nothing because I know exactly the kind of man you are, Hudson. You'll get your fill and move on. It's good fortune the tot isn't living next door. Best he doesn't get too attached as you'll no doubt leave his mother for the next pretty face."

"Did you not hear what I said?"

"Every word. But Hudson, a leopard can't change his spots."

"Well, *you* did."

He takes a step toward me. "She's fragile. When you let her down, do it gently. I'd hate to lose a good CPA."

"You're not going to lose anything. And neither am I."

He laughs and walks out the door. "When pigs fly, Hudson." He walks down the porch steps and turns. "Tread very carefully, grandson."

I watch him walk away. He thinks he knows everything. He's so sure I'll fuck this up that he isn't even forbidding the relationship anymore. And he said nothing about my trust fund. Twice now, I thought he'd try and use it to his advantage. And twice I've been wrong. But if I know anything about my grandfather, I know he hates to lose. So what's his angle?

~ ~ ~

I do exactly what I told Pappy I'd do. Breakfast. Bike. Lawn. The whole time I think about Dakota. Is she able to do her work today? Or is she thinking about this morning? Because it's all I'm thinking about. Is she staring at the same thing on her laptop over and over trying to concentrate? Gazing out her window to catch a glimpse of me? Looking at her bed remembering how we made each other come? How we said things. Meaningful things.

Still in sweaty clothes, I sit on my back porch and open a beer. Is this how it happened with Hawk and Hunter? Because two months ago, I'd have bet my entire inheritance I wouldn't end up like them—whipped by a girl who could walk me around by the leash attached to my fucking balls. But the thing is, I'm not sure that's where the leash is. I'm pretty sure it's around another part of my anatomy. It's around my goddamn heart.

No matter how much Pappy warns me away; no matter what Dakota says about moving too fast; no matter what I think about how screwed up it is that I've turned into my lovesick brothers; one thing is true… I'm in love with the woman next door. I'm in love with Gator Girl. Dakota Daniels. Travis's mom.

My world just became a whole new ballgame. One I've every intention of winning.

Chapter Thirty-four

Dakota

I can't stop smiling. Which makes me feel guilty every time I walk through the quiet house. Or look at the empty back yard. Even Travis's clean room.

How can a person be both happy and sad at the same time? It's as if there are two of me. The mother without a son. And the new girlfriend of Hudson McQuaid. I've been asking myself all day how they can co-exist. I never thought it possible for me to feel one iota of joy while my son is living thirty minutes away with people who couldn't ever love him like I do. I never thought it possible for my heart to explode with affection and desire every time I catch a glimpse of the man next door.

I never thought it possible to fall in love again after Brian.

Yet here I sit, a stupid grin on my face as I think of our time in bed this morning.

When the doorbell rings, my heart thunders. It must be him. Has he been thinking about me all day, or simply waiting until after five o-clock to come over, having no idea I've been too distracted to get much done.

I slip off my pants, letting my casual button-down flow freely to my thighs. I unbutton the top three buttons and let the right sleeve fall off my shoulder. I fluff my hair and make my way to the door.

"See something you li—"

I stop cold, stiffen, and cover up my shoulder when Patty Daniels stares back at me. She scoffs, and her judgmental eyes travel up and down my half-naked body as if she's appraising a serial killer. "I suppose I shouldn't be surprised." She waves a hand around my front porch. "A place like this must come with expectations." She sneers at my barely covered thighs. "Expectations you seem all too eager to fulfill."

"Wait here." I shut the door, close my eyes and shake my head in disgust. What is she doing here? And why did I have to answer the door this way? I hurry to where I shed my pants, pull them on, button my top, and go out front. I have no intention of inviting her inside.

She eyes the front door as I lean against it. "No invitation? That's not very neighborly."

"You aren't my neighbor. Why are you here, Patty?"

She walks over to the bench on the porch, dusts it off with a tissue, and sits. "You need to stop lying to Travis or we won't allow him here."

"Please tell me how I'm lying."

"You told him he would be living here. And that you'd get a dog. And he could go to a school with a big playground."

"Oh, *I'm* the one who's lying? Patty, you told him I was sick for Christ sake. And that he'd be going to sleepaway school."

"All my children went to boarding school. It's how it's done in my circle, Dakota."

"Except that Travis is not your child. He's not even your grandchild."

"Lies." She shakes her head slowly, her lips in a sneer. "More lies."

"If you are so sure I'm lying, why haven't you submitted to a blood test?"

"How could you claim to love Brian as much as you did and then spread lies about him being incapable of fathering children? The truth is, you wouldn't. You made up an elaborate story to try and hold onto Travis. Do you really expect us—not to mention a judge—to believe you and my son conspired to force us to allow you into the family by having a child that wasn't his? I'd say it's more likely you got knocked up and tried to pass the child off as his so you wouldn't have to give up the lifestyle that came with him."

"If you believe that, why are you so adamant to have Travis? If he isn't your flesh and blood, what good is he to you?"

"First of all, I believe he most certainly is a Daniels, something I don't need a test to confirm. He has Brian's hair. His eyes. And if by some twist of fate he's not, well… it'll all be worth it to see a lying, manipulating tramp like yourself suffer."

"Oh, my God. You really are a monster. You'd keep him from me out of spite? And of course he looks like Brian, we planned it that way."

"More lies."

"It's all true, Patty. Every word. And you must know it. Why else would you have let Travis come for the weekend?"

"Perhaps I wanted you to have those last moments with him. See what you'll be missing when we go before the judge with evidence of your ill-fated attempt at manipulation and he terminates any and all visitation."

"That's not going to happen."

She laughs and looks at her manicured tips. "You're forgetting who and what we are. You think whoring yourself out to get to live in a nice house and afford an expensive attorney will help you?"

My jaw drops. "Is that what you think I'm doing here?"

"We know everything, Dakota. We know you're living here rent-free. We know you can't afford someone like Karl Wheeler. And who do you think you're fooling, pretending to be a sophisticated CPA for a multi-million-dollar corporation? So who exactly are you fucking to make all this happen?"

"You have people spying on me?"

"It's all part of the business, dear. No offense."

My skin crawls. These people—they're even worse than I thought. She'd keep my own son from me knowing he's not even her flesh and blood just because she hates me. Just because her son defied their orders and married me? I should have run away with Trav yesterday. I should have gone far away and found one of those organizations that will give women and children new identities.

She stands and approaches. Her breath reeks of coffee when she leans in close. "It seems you'll stop at nothing, Dakota. You should know, neither will we. And given who you are and what you're up against, honestly, do you think you even have a chance? So enjoy these last few visits. Because I predict you'll never see him again. And don't think of doing anything crazy like running off with him. We have people watching."

Tears flow down my cheeks. Because I know everything she says is true. They aren't just empty threats. She despises me. She hates that I took her son away.

"You'll never get over it, will you?" I ask, trying to hold my head high.

"Get over what?"

"The fact that your son loved me more than he loved you."

My face burns with the slap she delivers to my cheek. "How poetic then that you'll come to know that exact feeling."

She turns to leave but I yell after her. "That's what this is all about then! You don't care about Travis. All you want is to get back at me for stealing your precious son. Is that it?"

She stops. "It's a shame really, a boy that young first being ripped away from his mother and then being shipped off to a school to be raised by strangers. Who knows what happens behind closed doors. Especially when a child that age misbehaves. I've already seen signs of it, him lashing out. He's going to be a feral one that boy. The discipline will do him good."

"You know!" I yell. "You know he's not Brian's. You've known all along, haven't you? All of this is to punish me. Punish a little boy who is innocent in all of this."

"I told you years ago you weren't meant to be a part of this family, Dakota. You didn't heed my warnings. And now it's time to pay."

I point to her car and yell, "Get off my property!"

She laughs. "As it's not yours, you really have no right to order me to do anything, dear. We hold the cards. *All* of them."

"I believe the lady asked you to leave."

Patty and I both turn. Hudson is approaching. And he looks pissed. He passes Patty and comes to stand next to me. She appraises him the same way she did me. "Who are you?"

"The person who's kicking your ass off this property if you don't get in your car and leave."

She doesn't even seem rattled. She takes two steps toward us. "Your name, you inconsiderate shit. What's your name?"

"McQuaid. Not that it's any of your business."

"McQuaid." She stares at him and scoffs. "So I was right. You've made her your whore. Given her a job. Funded her legal battles." She laughs. "The girl must suck one hell of a cock."

Hudson gets in her face. "I don't know who the fuck you think you are, but if you think you can beat my family, go ahead and try. We'll take you down with one hand tied behind our backs." He pulls out his phone. "Now I suggest you get off her property in the next ten seconds or be thrown in jail for trespassing."

His threat doesn't faze her. "I've said what I came to say. And believe me, even if you had the authority to get me arrested, I'd be out in hours, and the first thing I'd do is have the judge rescind all visitation. So, I don't give a fuck what your last name is, back off or she'll never see her son again."

Neither of them moves for several eternal seconds. It's a battle of wills, both of them trying to prove they're more powerful than the other.

Patty is the first one to break the silence. "I must be off. I promised Travis a trip to the pet store. I'm thinking the next time he's set to come here, he'll go kicking and screaming. And I'll tell him it's your fault, Dakota. It's your fault he has to leave his new puppy. And he'll know he won't ever see the pup again if he lives with you. The boy is four. Who do you think he'll choose?"

With that, she gets into her BMW, backs out of the driveway, and races off.

I run inside the house and just make it into the bathroom before losing my lunch in the toilet.

Chapter Thirty-five

Hudson

It's been a long week. A week of not seeing Dakota. She claims she's been busy with work, but I know it's the woman. She really did a number on her. I didn't hear the entire conversation, and Dakota hasn't talked about it, but I get the idea there's a lot more to the story than grandparents wanting to hold on to a piece of their dead son.

Friday rolls around and I'm done waiting. If she won't come to me, I'm going to her. I shower and change after work, put on a nice shirt and slacks, and ring her doorbell.

She answers wearing sweatpants and a UF T-shirt. I step inside and trap her against the wall. "Do you know how much I want to see you wearing *only* this shirt?" I kiss her neck. "But that can wait until later. Get dressed. We're going out."

"Out?"

"To dinner."

She sighs. "Hudson, I'm not really in the mood."

"That's exactly why you need to go out. You've been sulking in the house all week. You need fresh air. Great food. Good company." I run my tongue down the side of her jaw. "And after, we'll get in my hot tub and I'll make you scream my name."

"It sounds lovely, but I'm not sure I'd be very good company."

"Lovely?" I snicker. "Perhaps I need to better explain the screaming my name part." I reach under her shirt and cup her bare breasts. "First I'm going to kiss these. Tease your stiff nipples with my tongue." I run a hand down her rib cage and along the elastic waistband of her pants. I cup her crotch. "Then I'm going to put my tongue down here. I'm going to lick you. My fingers will be inside you, rubbing that little spot that's going to make you come all over my face. And then—"

"God, Hudson, can we just skip dinner already?"

I laugh, remove my hands, and step back. "No we cannot. You need a night out. Drinks at Donovan's then dinner at Lloyd's."

She touches her head. "My hair."

"You look amazing, Dakota."

"Fine. But I'm putting makeup on at least. Give me five?"

I follow her back to her bedroom and sit on the edge of the bed while she does whatever it is women do in the bathroom. Travis smiles at me from the picture on her nightstand. What will it be like when he's back with her? There will be no spontaneous dates. No fucking on the couch. No late-night hot tub adventures.

The strange thing is, I might be okay with that. For ten years I've done all that other shit. Fucking whenever and wherever. Living by nobody's timetable but my own. Maybe that was the problem.

I get up and walk into the hallway, lean in the doorway of Travis's bedroom, and have the weirdest fantasy. And it has nothing to do with sex. I imagine the three of us outside kicking a soccer ball. Running and laughing and falling into a pile of autumn leaves. Travis jumping into my arms. And I see Dakota smiling. Damn, I love to see her smile.

"I'm not sure I have anything to wear," she calls from her bathroom.

I turn and walk back to her room. "You don't need to dress up." I go to her closet and look through her clothes. There must be something here she can wear.

It's odd, though, how few clothes she has. And she doesn't have anything fancy. No little black dress. A few pants suits. I touch the lavender one she was wearing on her first day at work. I push aside the other one she wore when Dad came onto her. There are a few blouses. Mostly T-shirts and sweaters.

"What are you doing?" she asks, stepping next to me.

"Helping you find something."

"I can do it myself."

I can't tell if she's upset with me or embarrassed by her lack of dressy clothing. "Like I said, anything is fine."

She holds up a long sweater. "How about this? It's long enough to pass as a dress. I can class it up with a belt."

I put my arm around her waist. "Sweetheart, I hate to tell you this, but you're already classy."

She lowers the sweater to her side and cocks her head. "Did you just call me sweetheart?"

I replay my words in my mind and scoff. "Well, fuck, I guess so. That's a first."

"For me, too."

"Really?" My brows dip. "What did Brian call you?"

"Dakota."

I can't help my smile.

"What?" she asks.

"Nothing." I shrug. "Just that we've only known each other a short time and I already have *two* nicknames for you."

Her hands land on her hips. "Are you really making this a competition between you and my late husband?"

"Of course not." I sit on the bed, schooling my features, not wanting her to know that sometimes I do think about it. I think about how none of this would be happening if her husband hadn't died. How we'd never have met. How I wouldn't be falling head over fucking heels with the single mom next door.

I thought I'd gotten past my dickhead phase. Apparently not, however, because the thought of Dakota with another man makes me see red. And *that* man—she was married to him; pledged her life to him; had a kid with him. Jesus—I'm jealous of a dead man.

She undresses as if I'm not a red-blooded man sitting three feet from her. Naked but for her scant panties, she pulls a bra from the dresser and hooks it on.

"We may never make it to dinner," I say, as my cock enjoys the show.

"You're not the only one who can tease, Doctor." She slips the sweater over her head and steps over to me. "Good things come to those who wait."

I reach my hand under the sweater dress and cup her between the legs. "Oh, there will be good things *coming* tonight, alright."

She puts on a belt and twirls around. "Hopefully this will suffice."

I appraise her from head to toe, noting how gorgeous she is no matter what she wears. "Sufficient *and* easy to remove. I approve."

She laughs and I realize it's the first time I've heard the sound since her former monster-in-law showed up at her door.

We lock up and go to my garage. I open the car door for her—another first, but I don't tell her that. I don't need her knowing just how true Lynda's graffiti was.

"This is only the second time I've been in your car," she muses. "Despite the fact that we're…" Her words trail off. She shifts in her seat and looks at me. "Hudson, what are we exactly?"

"I—"

She holds up a hand. "Don't answer that. I didn't mean to sound like a desperate woman who needs validation."

I start the car. "Fine then, I won't tell you what I was going to say."

She's silent on the short car ride to Donovan's. It only takes a few minutes to get there being that it's just blocks away. I park and race around to open her door. She takes my hand and looks up as I help her out. "Okay, fine. What were you going to say?"

I chuckle and squeeze her hand, lacing her fingers with mine. "Come on. There's probably some people inside who might be interested in meeting my girlfriend."

"Your girlfriend?" Her lower lip becomes trapped by her teeth.

I nod. "We're sleeping together. We said stuff. We both want more. So yes, Gator Girl. My girlfriend."

"But what about Travis? And horrible mothers-in-law who harass me? What about all that?"

"All part of your charm and mystery, sweetheart."

She smiles.

I lean in. "You like it when I call you that." I touch my lips to her ear as I speak. "I'll be calling you that tonight in the hot tub when I make you come."

"Well if it isn't the infamous playboy of Calloway Creek with his new flavor of the month."

Both of us turn to see Lynda Graves walking by with friends. All of them are sneering at me. Dakota squeezes then releases my hand.

"Lynda, do you have a sec?" I ask.

Her brows shoot up. "If you're looking for a threesome, I'll pass."

"I wanted to apologize."

Surprise crosses her face. I've rendered the woman speechless.

"I'm sorry for making you feel the way you did. I should have been clearer from the start. And I shouldn't have led you on in any way. I deserved what you did. And I hope we can be friends."

Lynda's eyes dart between Dakota and me. "She's the one who was at your house that day."

"Lynda Graves, this is Dakota Daniels."

Dakota holds out a hand. "Nice to formally meet you, Lynda. And might I say bravo for your creativity."

Lynda eyes her hand as if she might refuse it, then she shakes. "Are you going to the pub?"

"We were," I say. "But it's getting late. I think we'll go straight to dinner instead." I open the car door for Dakota. "Goodbye, Lynda."

Inside the car, Dakota watches Lynda and her friends walk into the pub before she turns to me with questioning eyes.

"I didn't think it would be nice to go in and flaunt our relationship in front of her."

She smiles. "Why do I get the feeling you just graduated from Jellybean Jerkwad High and now you're a full-fledged member of Respectable Adult U?"

We're both laughing. And damn it feels good.

I start the car and head toward Lloyd's. "You won't think I'm so respectable later, Gator Girl."

"A gentleman in public and an animal in bed. What more could a girl ask for?"

Five minutes later, we're being seated in a private booth at my uncle's restaurant. I ignore the stares of the other patrons. I get it. Hudson McQuaid is taking a woman out for a nice dinner. It's something that's never happened until tonight. Sure, I've been out with girls before. Usually to Donovan's or some other low rent place. Never to Lloyd's. And never have I sat on the same side of the table as my date.

"Welcome to Lloyd's. Can I get you some dr—"

The waitress falters when she sees me. When she sees my hand and Dakota's clasped on the table.

"Um… what can I get you?" she scoffs, staring daggers at my date.

We order drinks, and as she stalks away, Dakota snickers. "You slept with her, didn't you? God, Hudson, do you even know her name?"

"It's Jenna."

Her eyes narrow. "Would you have known it if it wasn't on her name tag?"

"Probably not."

She sighs. "Why do I get the feeling everyone in this town is going to hate me?"

"You've landed one of the most eligible bachelors in Cal Creek, sweetheart. Deal with it."

"It's a good thing you're so humble about it."

I shrug. "It's a fact. Why hide from it?"

"You said *one* of the most eligible bachelors. Who are the others?"

I motion across the room. "See the guy over there in the corner having dinner with the older man? That's Blake Montana. And that's his father, Chris."

"Montana? Is he the one who just lost his family?"

"No, that was Blake's brother, Dallas. Blake is the youngest. He just earned his masters degree. Now he's helping run his family's winery like the others."

"A winery. Impressive."

A twinge of jealousy burns in my gut. "Hey now, it's not as impressive as, say, being a doctor, is it?"

She giggles. "Oh, no. Of course not."

"Thanks for stroking my ego."

She leans in. "I plan on stroking a lot more than that."

My left hand lands on her right leg. I start to trail a finger under the hem of her dress when Jenna returns with our drinks and we order.

"Who else?" Dakota asks. "Who are the other sought-after bachelors?"

"Blake's oldest brother, Lucas, is technically single but engaged. We all have bets going on if there will even be a wedding. He's known as the runaway groom of Cal Creek. He's left several women at the altar. Then you have the Cruz brothers. I suppose you could say they're eligible, but they don't come from money."

"You think you have to come from money to be sought after?"

"Probably not. But it helps."

"I thought you said you didn't appreciate the fact that women only like you for your money."

I tune out everything else and ask, "Why do *you* like me, Dakota?"

She stares into my eyes and thinks about it. "I suppose because you're the kind of guy who puts air in bike tires when people aren't looking. And because you think you're all professional but get nervous when the girl next door comes for an appointment. But mostly, because you didn't run for the hills when you found out about Travis."

The way she sees me. It's different. It's unlike how any other woman has ever seen me. I'm a different man around her. I'm a better man *for* her. And I'm rather liking this opportunity for us to get to know more about each other.

"Where did you work before starting at MMC?"

"A boutique firm in the city. I dealt with small business owners primarily. Nothing like what I do for your grandfather."

I'm about to ask her how she went from that to a high-profile job with my grandfather. We've never talked about it, but now I'm curious. How did such a small-time CPA land a job at a Fortune 500 company? I open my mouth to ask, but am interrupted by Blake.

"McQuaid," he says, stopping at our table. "Are you going to introduce me to the new girl in town?"

"Dakota Daniels, this is Blake Montana."

"Nice to meet you," she says politely.

His hand holds onto hers just a little too long for my liking, so I add, "Dakota is my girlfriend."

He chokes on spit. "Sorry," he sputters. "I thought you said girlfriend."

"I did."

He looks between the two of us, surprised. "Oh, wow. I guess… good for you then."

"How's your brother?" Dakota asks. "It's just awful what happened."

Blake's head bobs up and down sorrowfully. "It wrecked him. After the funeral, he up and took off. Got himself some remote cabin up north where he's been hiding out ever since. He hasn't been back, and he won't let anyone visit."

"Losing someone that unexpectedly is hard," she says. "It will take time. A lot of time."

I squeeze her hand, wondering not for the first time if she's over him.

"You say that like you have firsthand experience," Blake says.

"She does."

"Ah, damn. Sorry."

Dakota smiles sadly. "It was a long time ago."

"Mr. Montana," a passing waitress says, "your steak is ready."

"Nice to meet you, Dakota. See you around, McQuaid."

"That poor family," Dakota says. "They're already dealing with a lot and now they probably feel like they've lost their son as well."

"Sweetheart?"

Her lips curl into a half smile. "Yes?"

Wanting to take her focus off things that make her sad, I ask, "Do you mind if we move onto more enticing subjects?"

She bites her lip. "Such as?"

"Such as how long I can sit here and tease you before you beg me to take you home and give you more FEs."

A hand covers her blushing face. "That is so embarrassing."

"Are you crazy?" I remove her hand. "It was the sexiest thing I've ever seen. And I'm on a mission to make it happen again."

My finger rubs slow circles on her thigh. It's dark in the restaurant, the table's only light coming from a muted sconce on the wall. Nobody knows what I'm doing to her. Our eyes lock as I run my hand higher, under her sweater and up to her panties.

They're already wet. I push them aside and slide a finger inside. I leave my finger there even as our salads get placed on the table. I love the fact that she doesn't try to push me away.

She sighs heavily after the server leaves. She leans in. "Now *that* was sexy, Doctor."

"You think so?" I ask, withdrawing my finger. "Then you'll love this." I bring my finger to my mouth and lick it, tasting her juices as she watches with a slack jaw.

I follow the movement of her tongue as it traces her lower lip. My cock is engorged and pressing against my fly. I want to forget about dinner, drag her to the men's room, and have her against the wall. But that was the old Hudson. The new one is going to sit here and savor every second of my date with her as I tease every inch of her that I can touch under the table. The new one is going to hold off on selfish gratification until I've taken care of her thoroughly and completely. The new one is going to make her scream my name and declare her love for me before I sink deep inside her and seal our fate once more.

The new Hudson is going to fucking love her more than any man has ever loved any woman.

Chapter Thirty-six

Dakota

I toe off my shoes in his mud room. My belt comes off on our way through the kitchen, where Hudson stops to get a bottle of champagne from the refrigerator. My dress becomes a heap on the floor by the back door. By the time we make it outside, we're in our underwear. And mine are drenched.

The porch light is off, the only illumination coming from the moon and the kitchen light. Hudson uses his phone to turn on the hot tub, and the sound of bubbles is inviting.

He sets the bottle on the edge and pushes his skivvies to the ground. I stare at his impressive erection as I unhook my bra and slide my panties down my legs.

I glance over at the wall. "The last time I was out here you kissed me."

He strides forward. "The last time you were out here *you* were the one doing the kissing, Gator Girl."

"And your tongue just happened to fall into my mouth?"

He laughs, scoops me into his arms and carries me to the edge of the tub. When I slip down into the water, he hooks his hands under my arms, lifting me up and setting me on the side. "Huh uh. Here," he says.

Confused, I ask, "You don't want to go *in* the hot tub?"

"Have you ever tried to have sex under water, Dakota? There's no friction. It's awful." He opens my legs and settles between them. "And I plan on feeling every bit of you." He lightly pinches my clit. "Starting here."

My neck arches back when his tongue lashes out. I want to ask him just how many times he's had sex under water, because it seems like maybe it was a lot, but I don't. I know he has a past. I know what people in this town think of him. But I've only ever seen him as my thoughtful, caring neighbor. And it's only fair that I accept his past since he seems amenable to accepting mine.

Besides, with what he's doing to me with his fingers and his tongue, I'm not sure I could string two words together, let alone a serious conversation.

He stops the assault on my clit, rises on his knees, and looks me in the eye. "Relax, babe."

I cock my head and raise a brow.

He chuckles. "Yes, I realize what I just called you." He shakes his head like he can't believe it himself. "You're tense. I can feel it in your thighs." He massages my shoulders. "Everything is going to work out. I'm going to make sure of it."

I want to believe him. I *need* to believe him. There are so many things I want to tell him. Actually, there's *one* thing. But I can't. I can't say the words. Not until I have Travis back. How could I even consider allowing myself that kind of joy when I can't share it with my son?

Hudson pulls me against him. Our naked bodies press together. His erection is dancing against my thigh. "You're allowed to be happy, you know."

Tears threaten to fall. How does he know me this well? Well enough to read my mind. Know my thoughts.

He cups the sides of my face. "Do I make you happy, Dakota?"

I nod. "I never thought I'd feel this way again."

"Then let go. Just for tonight. Our problems will still be problems tomorrow." His lips caress my neck. "Let me kiss you." He palms a breast. "Let me touch you." He trails his tongue across my collar bone. Then he stops and looks directly at me. "Let me fucking love you, Gator Girl."

A tear falls. But it's not a tear of sadness. "Okay," I say, not breaking eye contact.

It was one word, not three. But it may as well have been. Because if I'm not mistaken, we just declared our love for each other. So, yes, in this moment I'm going to claim my happiness. I'm going to get lost in his eyes, his arms, his magical touch.

His lips crash into mine, resulting in a kiss so passionate and desperate it's as if our very souls have collided. My entire body is humming. My head spins. My toes curl. My heart thunders.

And as he enters me and we become one, all I can hear are his words. *Let me fucking love you.* So I do. I let him love me over and over until we both shout in ecstasy and sink down into the soothing water.

~ ~ ~

Twenty minutes and another orgasm later, he's practically pounding his chest.

"You're awfully proud of yourself," I say, rolling my eyes.

He pops the cork on the champagne and offers me a sip right from the bottle. "Most women will never experience female ejaculation. And the majority who do can only achieve it through the use of sex toys."

I shake my head and hand him the bottle. "Did you take a class on this in med school?"

"After it happened last time, I did more research."

"Research?"

"I'm a physician. I like to be thorough and up to speed on all things, especially when it pertains to the female body."

"Oh, so work stuff. Right," I say sarcastically.

He runs a hand up my thigh. "This is definitely not work stuff."

"Well, now that you've achieved the impossible, what's next, Doctor?"

"I was thinking we'd go for the length of your orgasm. Apparently, the average female orgasm only lasts from three to thirty seconds."

"Thirty? That sounds like a long time."

"But, studies have shown women are capable of having a two-minute orgasm."

"Studies?" I laugh. "As in women are clinically observed while they get off?"

"Yes and no. There have been studies centered around brain mapping during orgasm. But most information comes from self-reported data."

"How do you know they aren't lying?"

He shrugs. "I guess we don't. Which is why I'm determined to find out just how long we can extend yours."

I take the bottle from him. "I like your ambition, Doctor. I've also been wondering about something. I'm sure you've seen a lot as a gynecologist. Has a woman ever, you know… *come* during an exam?"

"You'd be surprised how often I get that question. The answer is no. Never. And I've never heard of it happening. Vaginal exams are clinical. Not to mention chaperoned. And unlike males, women require the use of their brain to orgasm. Those studies I was talking about, they show that female orgasm is more than just arousal, it requires a release of inhibitions and control, something that just doesn't happen when a woman is being examined by her doctor."

"That's good to know."

He laughs. "You're worried about women getting off on my exam table?"

"I'd be lying if I said I wasn't. I prefer to be the only woman getting off by your hands."

He traps me against the side of the spa. "And my tongue. My fingers. My cock."

I sigh. "Those too."

"You are," he declares. "The only one."

"So are you."

I lean up and peck him on the lips. "Speaking of your job, I want to know more. Like, what's the best part of what you do? It has to be babies, right? Everyone loves babies."

"Truthfully, my favorite part of the job is seeing Mom and Dad's faces when I put the baby on her chest. The world stops for a second. Everything pauses. It's just them and this beautiful human they created. Before delivery, the baby is a hope. A dream. But the second it's delivered and it becomes a reality and I see it on their faces—that's the best part."

I'm speechless. He's wrecked me with his confession. And if at all possible, I believe I just fell in love with him even more.

He places the empty bottle on the deck and stands in the water, carefully lifting me out of the hot tub. "I'm taking you to bed."

"Aren't you exhausted?"

"We're going to sleep, Dakota."

"You want me to spend the night?"

His lips caress my ear. "I want you to spend *every* night."

After a quick trip to the bathroom to dry off and finish an abbreviated bedtime routine, he crawls in behind me on his bed and spoons me. His minty breath flows over my ear. I feel safe in his arms. It's a place I know I always want to be. And I drift off peacefully to sleep, forgetting about my problems that will still be problems when I wake. But maybe, just maybe, those problems won't be so bad with him loving me.

Chapter Thirty-seven

Hudson

I'm feeling especially good this morning. Not just because of who's in my bed, but because it's Saturday. And for the first time, I'm not worrying about who Dakota is rushing off to see in the city.

She turns over in bed and sleepily puts her arm across my chest as if it's a habit. I trap her hand underneath mine, and she opens her eyes and smiles. "Good morning."

"It is indeed. Are you excited about seeing Travis today?"

She nods. "I am. Not as excited as when I got to have him here, but I'll take anything I can get."

"Do you want me to go with you?"

"You can't. It's supervised visitation at the Daniels' house."

I scoff. "Supervised?"

"I'm a drug dealer and an unfit mother, didn't you know?"

"Sweetheart, I've known a lot of people, and you are by far the most genuine and inherently good person I have ever met."

She snuggles into my shoulder. "That might be the nicest thing anyone has ever said to me."

"Why did you get him for the weekend if they insist on supervised visitation?"

She sighs. "Don't even get me started. My lawyer thinks it's because they're scared we're getting closer to the truth. Patty made me think it's to taunt me."

"How is allowing him to visit you at your house taunting you?"

"Giving me a taste of what I can't have I suppose. They're twisted like that."

"When all this is over, and you have him back, you're the one who'll be cutting ties with them. Blood relatives or not, nobody has the right to treat you this way."

"They aren't…"

It looks like she wants to say more. But then she just smiles and gets out of bed, pulling on one of my button-down shirts.

"They aren't what, Dakota?"

"Nothing. They're just selfish is all."

That was most definitely not what she was going to say.

"Can I make you some eggs before I go?"

My eyes rake over her shapely legs. The hint of cleavage showing from the undone top buttons. Her sexy messy hair. "I'd eat dirt if you made it looking like that."

She grins. "Go take a shower. I'll have breakfast ready in fifteen."

Naked, I make my way to the bathroom, baffled by how much I love this. I woke up with a woman in my bed who's wearing my shirt and making my breakfast. It's so goddamn domestic. So unusually normal. So extraordinarily sensational.

When I'm dressed and walking to the kitchen, I stop and look in each of the other rooms, wondering which would be the best for Travis. Then I wonder what the hell happened to the old Hudson McQuaid. The one who wouldn't give a single mom the time of day let alone invite her and her kid to live with him. Yet that's exactly what I want to do. In some ways, I feel there is still so much I don't know about her. In others, I think we're connected on an existential level. And her kid? I don't know the first thing about him. So why do I feel compelled to invite him into my home? My life?

I hear voices in the kitchen and turn the corner to see Dakota having coffee with my sister.

"Holland, what are you doing here?"

I look between the two women. Dakota has buttoned up the shirt and is plating food.

Hol kisses my cheek. "Am I not allowed to check in on my big brother?"

"Of course you are. But you rarely do. Did Katarina give you the day off?"

She holds up her phone. "I never get a day off. But she's overseas for the next week, so I'm not at her beck and call until she comes back."

Dakota puts three plates of bacon and eggs on the table. "Who's Katarina?"

"I work for Katarina Bellasandré."

"The clothing designer?" Dakota asks, impressed.

"The one and only."

"That's incredible."

"One would think," I say. "She's basically her servant. Tell her, Hol."

Holland shrugs. "It's true. But in this business, you have to pay your dues. I've been with her for close to two years now. She hates everyone. I've made it my mission to get her to warm up to me."

"I don't know why you bother. You could open your own clothing line if you wanted."

"I'm not going to use Pappy's money to buy my way into something, Hud. I'm learning so much working for her. And just look at the clothes I get to wear." She turns to Dakota. "Do you like her designs? I could get you some clothes. Perks of the job."

Dakota looks excited. "Are you kidding? I *love* her stuff, but I could never dream of affording it. I'd seriously take anything. I'd wear her throwaways."

I recall last night when I was looking through her closet. Why would someone like her—a CPA for my grandfather—not be able to afford high-end clothing? She should be able to buy just about anything.

Holland holds out her phone. "Put your contact info in. Text me your size. I'll bring you some the next time I'm here. Or we could meet in the city. Do you ever go?"

"I'm going today, in fact. To see my son."

Holland's mouth hangs open and she looks between Dakota and me. "A *son?*"

"He's four. Five in September. Cute kid. He's staying with his grandparents for now."

I hope my explanation is good enough so Holland doesn't ask for details.

"Do you have a picture?" she asks Dakota.

Dakota smiles, gets her phone, and pulls one up. "This is Travis." Her face beams when she looks at the photo.

"He's gorgeous," Holland says. She looks up at me. "I think he has your nose."

"Ha ha. Very funny." I shovel eggs into my mouth. "What are your plans for the day, Hol?"

"I thought I'd have lunch with my brothers. Then Addy and I are going out. What time will you be back, Dakota? You should join us. Do you know Hawk's fiancée Addison?"

"We met when they all came for dinner last month."

Hol chuckles. "She's a badass one-legged chick, isn't she?"

"What happened to her?" Dakota asks.

"Lost her leg in a car crash. She was drunk and ran smack into an underpass. It happened after her brother's funeral."

Dakota's hand covers her mouth. "Oh, that's awful."

"That's not the half of it. You should hear how Chaz died. He was with his twin brother hiking at the top of a mountain. They got trapped and only one lived. It wrecked the entire family. It was Addy's accident that kept them strong. Rallying around her saved them in some strange way."

"For a small town, there sure have been a lot of tragedies."

"Oh my God, I know," Holland says sorrowfully. "What happened to Dallas's family is so heartbreaking. I'm friends with his sister, Allie. She said he's gone crazy and is living off the grid."

"Blake told us last night," I say.

Dakota finishes her breakfast and puts her plate in the sink. "I should get going."

"Leave the dishes for me," I tell her, earning me a strange look from Holland.

My sister and I eat in silence the whole time Dakota gets dressed. I just know Hol's going to give me the third degree the moment Dakota leaves.

A minute later, she appears wearing last night's dress. "It was very nice meeting you, Holland."

"You too. I'll text you and let you know where Addy and I will be. Donovan's most likely. Please join us if you can."

"I think I'd like that."

"I'll walk you to the door." I follow her down the hallway, take her hand, and trap her against the wall. "Have a good day with Travis. Then have a good time with Addy and Hol." I kiss her neck. "Then come back here. I don't care how late it is. I'll leave the door unlocked. Bring a toothbrush because you're staying over again."

Her eyebrows rise. "Oh, I am, am I?"

"Damn right you are. Tonight and every other night if I have my way."

An emotion crosses her face. Fear? Have I scared her? *Fuck.* I've gone too far, too fast. But there's no way to backpedal. It's out there. And it's the truth. And to be honest, I don't want to take it back.

"Hudson—"

I put a finger to her lips. "Just come tonight, Gator Girl. We'll take it one day at a time."

Her expression softens. "One day at a time, eh?"

I lean in and put my lips against her ear. "One minute at a time if we have to. But rest assured, I'm going to get my way."

She snorts. "Why do I get the feeling you always do?"

I kiss her. I kiss her hard. Then I send her off, missing her before she's even down my front porch steps.

A hand lands on my shoulder. "I never thought I'd see the day."

I turn to Holland. "What day?"

"The day you were in love. And with a single mom no less—kudos to you. Wow—three for three. Pappy must be ecstatic. And he didn't even have to threaten you with disinheritance."

I put an arm around her neck and fake strangle her like I used to when we were kids. "Guess that means you're next, Hol."

"Me?" She laughs. "I'm married to my career. I barely have time to see my own friends and family let alone have a relationship." She pulls me back to the kitchen. "Come on, I'll help clean up, then you can go with me to Mom's house to say hi to Dani."

Ordinarily, I'd refuse the invitation. After all, Mom's husband isn't exactly my favorite person in the world. But I figure it's better than sitting around here all morning thinking about what a lovesick idiot I've become. "Sure, I can do that."

She stops cold and studies me. "I didn't even have to convince you. That's new." She glances back at the door. "I think I'm going to like the new Hudson. So you'd better not fuck this up and force Dakota to spray paint your garage."

I laugh. "Don't worry, I'm not about to screw this one up."

Inside, though, I'm wondering if I'm the one who'll end up screwed. Hurt by a woman I've fallen too hard for. Fucked over by karma getting back at me for all the wrongs I've done. I try to put the thought out of my mind, but it stays on the outskirts of my brain all day, niggling away at me, making me feel something I've never felt before. Insecure.

Chapter Thirty-eight

Dakota

I stretch my arms as I wake up in Hudson's bed. The entire weekend was amazing. Seeing Travis. Going out with Holland and Addy. Sleeping here—three nights in a row. I graze a hand across the empty side of the bed, vaguely remembering him leaving early this morning. And the best part of all of it is that Travis said nothing about a puppy. Patty's trying to intimidate me. But I'm not going to let her.

I put on one of Hudson's button-downs, something that is quickly becoming a habit, and go to the kitchen, smiling when I see coffee in the brewer and a giant blueberry muffin on a plate next to it. He's taking care of me. After being the only one to do the taking care of for years now, I think I quite like being the recipient.

Not yet done with my muffin, the phone rings. At a glance I see it's my lawyer.

"Hello, Karl."

"Good morning, Dakota."

"Do you have good news I hope?"

"We're making progress, but since the Daniels are refusing blood tests, we have to rely more on the private investigator, and that does tend to get costly."

I sigh, having a feeling I know where this is going.

"The initial retainer has been exhausted. My office should have emailed an invoice requesting payment. I can't express how important it is that it be paid promptly to avoid any delay in the progress."

I put him on speaker and find the email. My eyes bug out at the bottom line. "Oh, my gosh. I didn't know it would cost so much."

"Yes. Well, we do have an impeccable track record. We're going to get your son back, Dakota."

I open my banking app. I'm making good money now, but most of it has gone to paying off the myriad of credit cards I'd maxed out with the previous lawyer. Accounts I've since closed. Stupid. I should have kept the lines of credit open, but I wanted it to look good should the Daniels have someone run my credit report again. I didn't want them to have any more ammunition against me. I only have two thousand dollars right now—more than I could have dreamed of having several months ago, but not nearly what they're asking for. "Can I make payments?"

"I'm sorry, no. I can delay the motions we were going to file this week."

"No. Don't. I'll get you the money."

"Good. We certainly don't want to lose momentum."

"I'll pay it as soon as possible."

"Great. Have a good day."

"You too."

I put down the phone and stare into my coffee, wondering how I'm going to come up with an additional eight thousand. I go online and apply for a credit card. I get instant approval on a new account, but it only has a two-thousand-dollar limit. Should I apply for more? For as many as it takes to get them the money? What choice do I have? I fill out a second application, submit it, and get denied. I close my eyes, feeling defeated.

I look at my surroundings. I'm sitting in the house of a doctor. A millionaire trust-fund kid. Ten thousand dollars to him would probably be nothing. He'd hand it over without a second thought if I asked. I sink back into the chair. I can't ask my new boyfriend for money. It would change everything.

But what is more important here? This relationship or Travis? The answer is clear. And I know I need to swallow my pride and deal with the consequences.

The front door opens. Did Hudson's morning surgery get canceled? It's as if fate is giving me the push I need to just get this over with. But it's not Hudson who walks into the kitchen, it's Tucker.

Mortified to be caught with bare legs and tousled hair, I quickly button up the shirt. "Tucker, what a surprise. I, uh… Hudson is at work. I was just… um…" I cover my face with my hands. "I'm sorry, I'm at a loss for words right now, and I'm completely embarrassed."

"You don't think I know you've been taking up with my grandson?"

I swallow. "He mentioned you had warned him to stay away."

He laughs. "And when has that boy ever listened to a damn word I've said?"

I cock my head. "You're not mad?"

He pours himself a cup of coffee and sits opposite me. "Dakota, I've never seen my grandson happier. Since the day you moved in, he's been a different person. So no, I'm not mad. Just keep doing what you're doing."

I blush. Because my state of undress is evidence of what I've *been doing.*

"Well, I'm happy too. Which is something I never thought I'd say with Travis not being here." I sigh. "Or at least I was happy until this morning."

He grimaces. "Did Hudson do something?"

"No, no. He's wonderful. It's nothing."

"Dakota, I like to think I'm not just your employer, but your friend. If something is bothering you, you can feel free to tell me."

Tell him. Ask *him* for the money. He may be the only one who truly understands. He was there the day Travis was ripped from my very arms. "You've done so much already."

"Something is tearing you up inside. Spit it out, Dakota. You'll get no judgment from me."

"It's my lawyer. He called just before you arrived."

Concern flashes across his face. "Is something happening with the boy?"

I shake my head. "The appeal is going well. But it's… costly."

"Tell me how much you need."

"You've been more than generous already."

"Dakota, do you know why I'm here? I wasn't looking for Hudson. I was looking for you. Went to your house first, figured at this hour there was only one other place you'd be."

"Why were you looking for me at eight-thirty in the morning?"

"To give you the good news. Your probationary period has ended. You've proven to be a valuable employee of McQuaid Motor Corporation, and if I can be so blunt as to say you've surpassed my expectations."

"So I *was* a pity hire. I'd suspected as much."

"I prefer the term empathy over pity. And what does it matter when you've blown us all away with your impeccable skill?"

"I'm very happy to hear it. Thank you."

"The end of your probationary period comes with a fifteen percent raise. So tell me how much the lawyers are asking for and we'll consider it another advance."

My jaw is on the table. "You're giving me a raise? But you pay me so much already."

"Did you not hear the blowing us away part? Dakota, believe me, you're worth every penny. And you're still only costing me half of what I paid Percy. Someday not too long in the future, I suspect you'll be able to command that as well."

"I… I don't know what to say. Thank you just doesn't seem enough."

He stands. "Will ten thousand be enough?"

I blink twice. This man truly has been my fairy godfather.

"I'll take that as a yes. It'll be wired to your account by the end of the day. Now I'll be off so you can get ready for work."

I follow him to the door. "I appreciate you so much more than you know."

He pulls a business card from his wallet. "Give this to your lawyer. Ethan Stone is a private investigator. I've used him for years. He may have information that will help seal the deal and make sure your son is placed back in his rightful spot—with you. But let's just keep all this between us, agreed?"

"Yes, of course. And please say hello to Rose."

"That I can do. Goodbye now."

"Bye."

I shut the door and lean against it wondering just what information this Stone guy has. Wondering how all the pieces of my life seem to be coming together so nicely.

Wondering if and when this good luck will run out.

Chapter Thirty-nine

Dakota has seemed happier this week. More at ease. Neither of us has mentioned the fact that I all but asked her to move in with me last weekend. She's spent the night more often than not. Still, I'm treading lightly. She's in a better mood, but she's fragile. This situation with Travis is always at the forefront. And I know it's the one thing that will make or break her.

On my way out the door Friday morning, she bounds across our yards, still in her sleep shorts and shirt, and jumps into my arms. I laugh at her enthusiasm. "Miss me?"

"He's coming this weekend!"

I smile as I set her on the pavement, happy she's going to have him again. "I thought it was a one-time thing."

"So did I. But he's coming. And there's more. A hearing has been set for the week after next. Karl believes they have enough evidence and testimony to restore custody to me."

She looks like the weight of the world has been lifted off her shoulders. Her eyes are brighter. Her smile is bigger. She's even more gorgeous than before. The way she loves her kid is… amazing.

"I'm so happy for you."

"Say you'll come. I know you have to work and it's a big ask, but I could really use some support there with the Daniels and all their family and team of lawyers."

"It's done. Just let me know when."

"Tuesday." She squeals. "Oh my God, Hudson. In eleven days I could have my son back. Can you believe it?"

"I can. I've only seen you together once, but I can tell what an incredible mom you are. The way you've fought for him." I think of Travis coming to live with her permanently. The new start they'll both have together. "We should go shopping. Get him new toys and stuff."

"We?" She raises her brow and bites her lip.

I pull her beautiful pink lip from between her teeth. "That's what I said."

She looks between our houses. "Things will change, Hudson. When I'm a fulltime mom again."

I tug her against me. "If you think I'm going to change my mind about wanting to wake up with you every day, you'd better think again."

"I'm a package deal, you know."

"I have a medical degree, Gator Girl. I figured that one out all on my own."

She smiles. She smiles big. Then she kisses my cheek. "Speaking of your medical degree, you'd better go or you'll be late." She hesitates.

"What is it?"

She shrugs. "I was hoping maybe you could join us for lunch tomorrow. Get to know Trav. Hudson, you'll love him. He's the sweetest. He rarely whines. He's an easy kid. He—"

I put a finger to her lips to shut her up. "Babe, you don't have to sell me on him. I only need to know one thing." I lean close to her ear. "How light of a sleeper is he?"

She chuckles. "A freight train couldn't wake him."

I laugh out loud. It feels amazing to laugh with her. "Good. Because I'm going to have you screaming my name more often than not."

She backs away. "I'm counting on it, Doctor."

I don't get in my car. I follow her every move with my eyes as she dances across our lawns and goes back into her house. I swear I'm going to tell that woman I love her. The words are rooting around inside me, percolating, getting ready to explode out of me like lava from a volcano. It's getting harder and harder to contain them. I just need to know the same is happening with her. What if once she gets Travis back, her life will be fulfilled and she won't have time for obsessed neighbors? What if all along I've just been a distraction?

I can't say it. She needs to say it first. And she needs to say it after her life gets back to normal.

~ ~ ~

Lyle Richards comes into my office during lunch and sit in the chair opposite my desk.

I look up from my laptop. "What's up?"

"Hmm." He rubs his chin between two fingers. "I'd have to say your satisfaction rating among the office staff."

"Come again?"

"The nurses. The techs. Even reception. There hasn't been a complaint about you in weeks. Even the gossip has subsided. Care to fill me in on why this might be happening?"

I raise an innocent shoulder. "Just getting my act together I suppose."

"It's more than that, Hudson. I could swear I heard you whistling the other day when you were doing paperwork."

"That's ridiculous. I don't whistle."

"So who is she?"

I don't answer. We're not friends outside of work so I don't feel the need to bring up my private life.

"Oh, come on, McQuaid. I know firsthand the only thing that makes a man whistle is the love of a good woman. I whistled for months when Grace and I started dating. So who is she?"

I roll my eyes. "My neighbor."

His head bobs. "Ah, neighbors to lovers. My wife reads a lot of romance novels. She likes those kinds." He stands. "Keep up the good work. And, Hudson, take a vacation. Peterman and I were just saying the other day that we don't think you've ever taken one. Nothing more than a long weekend anyway. And you've been here how many years? Four?"

"Almost five."

"Five years and no vacation. That's dedication."

I chuckle. "That's having nothing else to do with my life, Lyle. Oh, and hey, I do plan to take the day off a week from Tuesday."

"Tell Nicole. She'll reschedule your morning surgery and have the rest of us cover your dailies."

"One more thing."

He turns. "What is it?"

"How old were you when you became a partner?"

"Thirty-five I believe."

"And Peterman?"

"Maybe a little older."

"Anyone ever become a partner under thirty?"

"Not likely."

"So I'll be the first?"

He snickers. "Pretty sure of yourself, aren't you, McQuaid?"

"Damn straight. And getting surer every day."

He lifts his chin and leaves.

I finish my lunch thinking about how my life has changed so dramatically. How everything is fitting together so well. How fucking perfect everything seems to be.

I pull up a photo of Dakota on my phone. It's one I took of her after a night together. She's wearing one of my button-down shirts. Her hair is tousled. Her face clean and fresh. I trace the curve of her seductive smile with a finger. Yes—everything is falling into place.

I'm paged by the hospital. One of my expectant moms has been admitted. So to top off my great day, I get to go deliver a baby. Could my life be any better?

Chapter Forty

I'm not sure why I'm so nervous. Hudson and I have shared dozens of meals together. But this one is different. This one includes Travis. My two worlds are coming together. And I really really want them to fit in the same space.

But what if they can't? What if Travis doesn't accept Hudson in my life? What if Hudson decides my having a child is too much baggage? What if, for some other reason, the dynamic just isn't right.

"Mommy, the beeper."

I snap out of it and turn off the oven timer, getting out the mac-and-cheese casserole. I place it on a hotplate and then get the salad, the deviled eggs, and the finger sandwiches.

Travis looks over the spread. "Who is going to eat all this?"

"Remember what I told you on the train? Hudson from next door is coming over."

"Who else?"

"Just him." I gaze at all the food on the counter. "Okay, so I might have overdone it a little."

"You're acting funny."

"I know. I just want today to go okay."

"You don't think lunch will be good?"

I ruffle his hair. "I'm sure the food will be fine. I just want you and Hudson to get along. You know, be friends."

"He's too old to be my friend, Mommy."

I laugh. "Well, he's my friend, so I want you to like him."

My heart leaps out of my chest when the doorbell rings. I'm more nervous than when we slept together the first time. I straighten my top, check my appearance in the hallway mirror and answer the door. Hudson is standing on the porch with flowers in one hand and a gift bag in the other. He holds it out. "I had no idea what to get a four-year-old, so I just asked someone at the store."

I crack a smile. "You got him a gift?"

He hands me the flowers. "My mother said to never show up to a meal empty handed."

"I think I'm going to like your mother."

"You'll get to meet her. Today if you want to. I was going to ask you later, but Hawk is having a get together at his house tonight. You're welcome to come."

"I have Travis."

He leans in. "Sweetheart, you can assume whenever an invitation is extended, it's for the both of you. Package deal, right?"

My heart does a little dance. "Right. But we should see how lunch goes first."

"Fair enough." He looks over my shoulder. "Hey, champ. I got you a little something. I hope it's not something you already have."

Travis takes the bag, which looks heavy, and carries it to the living room. He looks up before opening it. "It's not my birthday yet."

"That's okay," I tell him. "You can open it anyway."

He pulls out the tissue paper and reaches in, coming out with a brand-new game console. My mouth falls open. I know how expensive these are. I could never afford one, and he wanted one so badly when his friends started getting them.

Travis looks up excitedly. "You got me an Xbox? Mommy! It's an Xbox!" He digs deeper into the bag. "And games. This is the Sonic one. And look, Minecraft. Oh my gosh, and a Hot Wheels one. Is all this for me? Grammy says Xbox and Playstation make brains mushy. The only games I can play are the boardest ones with Laura."

I nudge Hudson with my elbow. "That's four-year-old-speak for board games."

"Ahh." Hudson steps forward and sits on the chair next to him. "It's all for you, champ. We'll hook it up after lunch, okay?"

Trav looks at me. "Can we eat now?"

I laugh. "Yes. We can eat now. But, Travis, what do you say?"

He races over to Hudson and hugs him. *Hugs him.* "Thank you."

Hudson is taken by surprise. I get the idea he hasn't had many kids hug him before. He's stiff at first. Then he pats Travis on the back. "You're welcome, champ. You'll have to teach me this Minecraft thing. I've heard a lot about it."

"Yes!" He pulls my shorts. "Mommy… lunch."

While he trots into the kitchen in front of us, I hold back from chasing after him and grab Hudson's elbow. "You shouldn't have spent so much."

"Don't even start." He stares me down. "If this is going to happen for us, you need to get one thing straight; I have money. Money I've never wanted to spend on anyone until now."

"Just don't go too overboard okay? I don't want him thinking he can have anything he wants."

"He can, though." He grazes my ear with his lips. "And so can you."

"Mommy!" Travis calls from the kitchen.

"We'd better feed him before he goes ballistic."

Travis eats faster than any child has ever eaten, inhaling his macaroni and cheese as if he's a human vacuum cleaner. I make him wait until we're finished, but I can tell Hudson shovels his food down quicker than he should just to please him. I roll my eyes. "Go, you two play your games. I'll clean up."

For the next half hour, I listen to them talk as they get it set up. Then from the doorway, I watch my son and my boyfriend bond over a building blocks game I can't even begin to understand. Hearing them laugh together is everything. Seeing Travis happy warms my heart more than I thought possible. This is what I want. I thought all I needed was to have Travis back. But now, as I watch them together, I know that would never be enough. I want more. I want it all. And, hopefully, ten days from now, I'll have it.

~ ~ ~

"They're getting along great," Willow says. "I wasn't sure they would with their age difference."

Willow and Hunter's daughter, Izzy, is eight. Eight going on thirty apparently. The girl can have a conversation with her uncle, the MD, and still hold her own.

"I'm glad. I don't think he gets much interaction with other kids when he's with his grandparents."

"Hudson says he'll be coming to live with you soon now that you're settled in your new job?"

I'm relieved that he hasn't told his family all the details of my complicated situation.

"That's the plan. We can't wait."

"Look at them," Heather says, joining us. "Playing together like bonafide cousins."

I blush knowing she's putting the cart before the horse, but I'd be lying if I said the same thought hadn't crossed my mind.

Hudson's mom is great. From the second we met a few hours ago, she's treated me like she treats her daughter-in-law, Willow, and her soon to be daughter-in-law, Addy—who also happens to be her niece by marriage. It seems everyone in this town is loosely related to one another. Hudson tried to explain it once, but I told him he'd have to make me a family tree. He laughed and said there wasn't a tree big enough to fit everyone.

He's lucky. They all are. My family tree is nothing but a twig.

I look around. Hawk's daughter, Rivi, is running after Travis. She's not quite two so she can't keep up with him, but he's drunk on the attention. Hunter is bouncing seven-month-old Myles on his knee. Dani, Hudson's teenaged half-sister, is playing babysitter to all of the kids, keeping them busy with games and puzzles so the adults can eat and talk.

Heather pulls me aside. "I don't know what you've done to my son, but please don't stop. I've never seen him like this."

Hudson stares at me from across the room as if he can hear the conversation. "It's the same for me, Heather. He's amazing."

She laughs, shaking her head. "Never in my life has a woman described him that way to me. You are definitely the one for him."

"I hope so. Travis seems to like him."

"I know you must have been worried about that." She motions to her husband. "When Jonah and I got together, we had seven children between us. It wasn't as easy. My boys hated him. He's a Calloway. And back then, all McQuaids hated all Calloways and vice versa."

"But you didn't."

"I was only a McQuaid by marriage."

I sigh. "Oh, right. You were married to Robert."

She studies me. "By that reaction, I'd say you've had the displeasure of meeting my infamous ex."

I nod.

She puts an arm around me. "Sweetie, if he treated you poorly, I'll have him strung up by his balls."

I chuckle. "No need. Hudson took care of it."

"That's my boy," she says proudly, as if it's the first time she's ever gotten to say those words.

"What was Hudson like before? I've heard stories. And I had a run in with Lynda Graves. But I'd like to hear it from you."

She gazes at him from across the room as he converses with his brothers. "He was… lost, I think. Part of it was his job. Part of it was his father. Part of it was that he just hadn't found the right woman to love."

I swallow as I absorb her words. "You think he loves me?"

"Oh dear, he hasn't said it yet?" She shakes her head. "My stubborn, stubborn boys. Dakota, anyone at this gathering can see the way he watches you. They can see the way he leans in as he talks to you. How he tucks your hair behind your ear. How he smiles when you enter a room. And I never thought I'd see the day, but he even looks happy when he's with your son."

"Hudson!" Travis calls. "Come look at this cool bug outside the window."

"See that?" Heather says. "Did you see the smile on my son's face when Travis called out to him?"

"It all seems too good to be true."

"It's not. Just ask Willow. Ask Addison. Ask *me*. It is possible to go through hell and then get everything you ever wanted."

"Mommy! Come see. Hudson says it's a grasshopper."

"Excuse me, Heather."

I go to the large window where all the kids are taking turns touching the glass where the critter landed on the other side.

"Ewww," I say.

"It's not gross. It's cool. Isn't it cool, Hudson?"

"It sure is, champ."

Travis smiles up at Hudson. He sure likes all the attention he's getting today. It makes me wonder just what his days are like at the Daniels' mansion. Does Laura simply keep him busy and out of Patty's hair? Does he have other children to play with? He doesn't talk about it much when I ask, which is a huge area of concern.

Hudson corners me in the kitchen where we finally get a minute alone. "Are you having a good time?"

"This is amazing. Thank you for inviting us. Travis is so happy."

He traces my lower lip with his finger. *"You're* happy."

I smile. "I am. When he's with me and I'm with you…" I gaze into his eyes. "How could I not be?"

He looks left and right then kisses me. It's a quick kiss, but it still makes my knees go weak.

Travis appears in the doorway. Simultaneously, Hudson and I step apart, unaware if we've been caught or not. The question is answered when Travis comes over, looks up at Hudson, and asks, "Are you going to be my new dad?"

Hudson's eyes go wide. "I… uh…"

"Izzy and Rivi and Myles have dads. Dani, too. Everyone has a dad." His gaze falls to the floor. "I know my real dad is in heaven is why he's not here. But it's not fair. Mommy, I want a daddy like everyone else. Can Hudson be my daddy? He likes Minecraft and he can play soccer."

Heather swoops in, collecting Travis in her arms. "You don't want to miss cake, do you? Or ice cream? You'd better get out there before it's all gone." She puts him down in the doorway and we watch him scurry out before she turns back to us. "I didn't mean to eavesdrop. I was on my way to fetch a cake knife when I heard the compromising position you were in."

Hudson dramatically wipes his brow. "Phew. Dodged that bullet."

I laugh. But deep down, I wonder if he wasn't joking. Hudson is a certified bachelor. A man who does whatever he wants, whenever he wants. It makes no sense that he'd suddenly decide to settle down with a woman he barely knows and a kid he's seen only twice.

I try to remember what Heather told me earlier. She seems dead set on him having monumentally changed from the man he used to be—the man I never knew. But he was clearly spooked a moment ago. He didn't realize the gravity of the situation until it stared him in the face and tried to call him *Dad*.

I look between Heather and her son. Then I grab the knife off the counter. "I'll take this out there."

When I glance back, Hudson sinks into a chair looking like he just got kicked in the gut.

I'm pretty sure I have my answer.

Chapter Forty-one

I stare at my uneaten lunch thinking about how surreal yesterday was. Never in my wildest dreams could I see myself as someone's father. But the moment he said it, it was like a switch was flipped. It's completely bizarre thinking what I'm thinking after only seeing the boy a few times. The whole rest of the night, I sat and watched Hawk with Rivington. And Hunter with Izzy and Myles. And I became envious. No, I became downright jealous.

I want what they have. I want it more than I've ever wanted anything. More than I wanted med school. More than I want to make partner. More than I want my twenty-million-dollar trust fund.

Fuck all that stuff I was thinking about her saying it first. This weekend was amazing. I have to tell her. And I have to tell her in a way that she knows I'm inviting both of them into my house and my life.

Travis needs a father. Someone to keep him safe and show him how to grow into a man.

Dakota needs a partner. Someone she can trust, rely on, and grow old with.

And apparently I need both of them like I need my right arm.

Fuck me with a prickly cactus stalk. I sit, head slumped between my legs as I see my entire future play out in my mind: a big house; Travis chasing a dog in the back yard; us sipping lemonade on the back porch, my hand resting on her pregnant belly; Dakota looking over at me like I'm her entire goddamn world.

I dart out of my chair and get on my biking gear. I need to think this through. Every major decision I've made in my life has been made on a bike. There's something about fresh air and punishing exercise that brings clarity to every situation.

I ride to the park and then beyond, through the miles of trails along the creek before coming back into town and biking down McQuaid Circle. Pausing to rest my legs and catch my breath for a minute, my eyes land on the jewelry store. Glass cases line the front of the shop. Cases that contain rings. Engagement rings. And I swear to God if it wasn't Sunday and the store was open right now, I'd go inside and buy the biggest one.

Someone comes out of the door to my right. It's Maddie Calloway—owner of Gigi's flower shop—and she's carrying a large arrangement of roses. The shop used to be owned by my grandfather's girlfriend, Rose Gianogi, Maddie's grandmother.

"Oh, good," Maddie says, looking relieved. "I was hoping it was you I saw through the window. Hudson, you'd be a real lifesaver if you could deliver these to my grandmother. Tucker ordered them for her. It's the anniversary of their first date. My delivery boy called in sick, and I have a large order of wedding flowers that have to be done by three."

"I'm on a bike, Maddie."

She holds up some sort of backpack contraption. "That's what this is for. My delivery people use this for bike deliveries. Please? You'd be doing me a huge favor, and your next purchase and delivery will be on me—anything you want."

I laugh. "Maddie, when have I ever ordered flowers from you or anyone else in this town?"

I don't bother telling her I bought some yesterday from Truman's Grocery. For the first time ever, I bought flowers for a woman. For *the* woman.

"Okay, you have a point. But I hear things, Hudson. And you were just looking in a jewelry store like a man on a mission." She shrugs. "I'm just saying, you look like a guy who might be needing flowers soon."

I hold out a hand. "Give me the damn backpack."

I strap it on, and she secures the bundle of flowers inside. "Have her put them in water straight away."

"Sure. No problem. Want me to serenade her as well?"

"Would you mind?" she says, sarcastically.

I ride off. "Goodbye, Maddie."

"Thank you!"

It's only a mile to their house in the retirement village. Still, I must be a sight. Hudson McQuaid, a delivery boy for a Calloway. It's ludicrous. I wouldn't be surprised if my picture showed up on the front page of *The Calloway Creek Courier*.

I turn onto their street in the retirement community where they met. Rose once lived in the apartments on the grounds. And after my grandmother passed, my grandfather moved into, and expanded, the largest house on the property. He and Rose would go for walks, separately at first, then they began walking together. The rest, they say, is history.

Neighbors to lovers. Lyle Richards' voice echoes in my head.

Like grandfather like grandson, I guess.

I park my bike in the expansive driveway, take the flowers out of the backpack and hook it on my handlebars, then go up the walk and ring the bell.

There's no butler to answer the door—Rose got rid of all the help when they shacked up, short of the housekeeper who comes once a week—so my grandfather's girlfriend opens the door herself and her face beams. "Hudson! So nice to see you." She leans in and kisses my cheek. "Your grandfather is out, I'm afraid."

"I'm not here to see him." I hold out the flowers. "These are for you. They aren't from me. I'm just the one who got stuck delivering them." I turn to leave, but she stops me.

"Hudson, do come inside. You came all this way. At least stay for a cup of tea."

I think of all the things I could be doing. Shopping for rings. Shopping for kids' furniture. Looking at houses. My head is spinning and loud with all the voices in my mind. Maybe tea is exactly what I need to quell the chatter. "Sure. I can stay for a minute."

She holds the door open and smells the flowers. "Tucker sure is sentimental."

I chuckle on my way by, because that's the last word I'd use to describe him. Gruff. Steadfast. Driven. But sentimental?

"Don't let his harsh exterior fool you, Hudson. Your grandfather is a bleeding-heart romantic. In fact, he tells me you may be feeling the same yourself lately about your lady friend next door. She sure is a sweetheart, that one."

I silently stare at the roses as she trims them and puts them in a vase. Then she makes tea.

She puts two cups on the table and sits across from me. "Your quiet contemplative look is all the confirmation I need. So it's true. You've fallen in love."

Rose Gianogi must be approaching eighty years old. We've barely had a dozen conversations. Yet I'm about to spill my soul to her. The world has surely shifted on its axis.

"I'm not sure how this happened. Three months ago I wasn't even thinking about having a girlfriend. In fact, I was thinking how I was happy *not* to have one. And now…" I look down into my tea. "Now I'm looking through the window of fucking jewelry stores." I close my eyes. "Ah shit. I'm sorry for cussing. Twice."

She laughs. "I'm used to it, Hudson. Your grandfather may be a romantic, but he's got the mouth of a drunken sailor." She pats my hand. "Jewelry stores, eh?"

I nod. "It's too soon, isn't it? Of course it is. This is ridiculous. How can I even be thinking it? She's got so much going on."

"I don't know why you kids think everything has to be done on a certain timeline. You have to date for six months before declaring your love, and then another year before deciding to marry, and then another year to plan the wedding. Then you think you have to time your children so they arrive precisely in the proper intervals. Ridiculous," she scoffs. "Well, let me tell you this. God laughs when you make plans, Hudson. There is no timeline. And I wish someone would tell this old lady why people can't just say what they feel when they feel it. If you love the girl, tell her. If you want to put a ring on her finger, do it. If you want to whisk her off to Las Vegas and marry her on a Tuesday, nothing should stop you. As long as she feels the same way, why do you feel the need to wait?"

"What if she doesn't feel the same way?"

"In my opinion, a woman does not take so many overnights at a gentleman's home unless she's utterly smitten with him."

I raise my eyebrows.

"What? You think I don't hear the gossip in this town like everyone else? And it's not just what I hear at my ladies' luncheons. Your grandfather gives me an earful as well. He couldn't be happier with how the two of you are getting on."

"I thought he was pissed—er, mad—that I was dating Dakota."

She sips her tea, appraising me thoughtfully. "On the contrary. I've never seen the man so pleased."

I'm confused. What she's saying goes against everything Tucker has told me.

"Hudson, dear, you need to live for the day. Believe me, I know. You don't want to be my age and still searching for what makes you smile."

"You say I should live for the day. Then why haven't you and Pappy married? You've been together long enough."

She shrugs. "Maybe because we were both married once and neither ended happily." She gazes out the window. "Perhaps it's also because he hasn't asked."

My phone vibrates with a text. It's from Dakota. She's taking Travis back to the city and wants to see me after. Maybe I'll take Maddie up on that offer after all.

I go to text her back, but my phone runs out of battery. Damn, I haven't charged it in days. I hold it up. "My phone died. Would you mind if I borrowed your house phone?"

"Go right ahead. Use Tucker's study for privacy. I hope you're calling that lovely neighbor of yours."

I snort a puff of air out of my nose. "I heard you liked to play matchmaker."

"In this case, there's no need. Seems the match has already been made. Take all the time you need. I'll be out in the garden."

I put my teacup in the sink and round the corner, going down the hallway to his home office. Along the walls hang a slew of family pictures. Hawk's family. Hunter's family. Heck, even Mom's family even though Mom is no longer my grandfather's daughter-in-law.

Few photos are of me. There's one of us as kids. Another from Mom's birthday. But as I gaze over the ones of my brothers, a longing I've never known pangs away at my insides. I want to be on this wall. I want to be on it with *my* family. With Dakota. With Travis. With anyone else fate allows.

Once again, I wonder what the hell is happening to me.

In Pappy's study, I go behind his desk that I'm fairly sure used to belong to a member of Congress. I sit in his large leather chair and wonder if he sits here—the head of the family, the king of the castle, the CEO with more zeros behind his name than most people can count—and reflects upon his life. A sole picture of Rose sits on the corner of the desk.

I go for the phone when something catches my eye. It's a file folder. And it's got Dakota's name on it.

I'm not sure why it surprises me. She is his employee. But he has hundreds of employees. Why is hers the only folder on the desk? I open it. I mean, it's sitting right here, and she is my girlfriend.

But what I find has me feeling sick. And not in a *I'm about to ask a girl to marry me* kind of way. More like in a *I've been conned* kind of way.

Because what I see has nothing to do with McQuaid Motor Corporation. It's all personal. Photos of her and Travis—both looking much younger than when I met them. A background check dated far before she ever became an employee. Court records of Dakota's custody proceedings. But what guts me the most—what has my stomach turning, my blood boiling, and my eyes seeing red—are the wire transfer forms. Two of them for ten thousand dollars each. One is dated just last week. The other, before her first day at MMC.

I put down the file, unable to page through the rest. I know exactly what this means. It means my grandfather got to me after all. The bastard. He knew he couldn't use my trust fund against me after what he did to my brothers. So he hired someone. He hired Dakota to what, be my girlfriend? Make me fall in fucking love?

Jesus, it all makes sense. I'm so goddamn stupid. Of course he did. He said it himself, that I've never followed an order from him. He knew I'd go against his wishes if he made her forbidden. That was the draw he was counting on. He planted her next door. Told her to seem uninterested.

He found a poor woman desperate for money and hired her to fucking seduce me.

I throw the folder across the room and storm out, not even bothering to say goodbye to Rose. I bike home in a fury, change clothes, and then throw every goddamn thing I can find of Dakota's in a box and plant myself on her doorstep, my anger increasing with every tick of the clock.

Chapter Forty-two

Dakota

I have the biggest smile on my face as I walk up to the house and see Hudson waiting. Truth be told, I haven't stopped smiling all weekend. It's been perfect. Well, if you don't count the super awkward moment when Travis blurted out how he wanted a father.

My smile fades quickly, however, when Hudson stands and sneers at me in disgust. He picks up a box, walks down the front steps with determination and shoves the box at me. "Here's all your shit."

"I, uh… Hudson, is this because of what Travis said? He's four. Kids have no filter. Please don't take his words to mean anything needs to change between us. I like how things are. I thought you did too."

"Yeah, I'll bet you do. Had me exactly where you wanted me, didn't you?"

"What's that supposed to mean?"

"You know exactly what it means. Don't stand there and play dumb."

I look around as if someone will pop out of the bushes and explain what I'm missing. "Hudson, I'm sorry if this weekend was too much for you—"

"How can you look me in the eye and keep pretending? Keep lying to me? I know everything, Dakota. I know how you got the job. I know about the wire transfers."

My heart sinks. I was hoping he'd never learn how pathetic I was to have to ask for money. I'm sure my face says it all.

"You've been his little pawn all along. And I fell for it." He paces the sidewalk. "Stupid, idiotic me. Of course he'd be smarter than to straight out manipulate me by using my trust fund."

"You've lost me now."

He scoffs. "Yeah, keep playing dumb. Because that's probably what you are. Are you even a CPA? Or is that just another lie you both came up with to make you seem like some strong independent woman who didn't need a man? I always wondered how someone as young as you would be hired for such a powerful position. Now I know. You weren't hired for that at all, were you?"

"That's not fair, Hudson. Of course I'm a CPA. I get that maybe Tucker took pity on me, but I've proven myself to be a valuable employee."

His laugh is maniacal. "You most certainly have. You've worked your way right into my bed, just as planned."

"I have absolutely no idea what you're talking about."

He starts ticking items off on his fingers, his voice growing angrier with each observation. "You have no nice clothes. You're poor. You're desperate. And you would do anything to get your kid back. Including taking the bribe of an old man looking for a girl for his grandson."

My jaw drops. And now I'm the one who's pissed. All his accusations. He's gone completely mad.

"What's wrong with you? Are you really so freaked out about Travis that you'd go ruin what we have?"

"What we have?" He laughs and holds his arms out. "What we have is a fucking joke. You conned me. Sitting over at your house pretending you didn't like me. Making me want the forbidden girl next door. Oh, that's good. Which one of you came up with that one? And flooding your house so you could crash with me—whose idea was that? Is your name even Dakota? And how in the hell did he pick you? I saw the file on you. The background checks."

"Of course he would have done a background check on an employee. Hudson, you're scaring me. What's really going on here?"

"Stop playing stupid. Are you even a mom? Maybe Travis isn't your son at all. Maybe he's an actor playing a part and you're just some whore with a sob story Tucker picked up off the street."

My God, who is this man and what is he talking about? I throw down the box. "Did you just call me a whore?"

"Well let's see, you took money from an old man to fuck his grandson. I'd say that's the very definition. Tell me, how much more did he promise you? Were you going to get a bonus if I'd proposed? Another if we'd married?" He shakes his head in disgust "And to think how goddamn close I came."

Tears clog my throat. Five minutes ago I thought my whole world was going to change in a good way. Now it seems to be imploding. "Hudson, you should leave. Go cool down. Sober up or whatever."

"You think I'm drunk?" He steps forward and gets in my face. "I've never been able to see things more clearly. I'm leaving all right. And if I don't ever see you again, it'll be too soon."

He stomps away without looking back. Tears stream down my face as I pick up the spilled contents of the box and sit on my porch wondering what the hell just happened. He went off the rails.

Was he really so freaked out by Travis's statement that he conjured up a scenario in his head that makes me the bad guy so he could break this off?

Not even five minutes go by when I see him exit his house with a suitcase. He doesn't look over at me. He throws it in his trunk, gets in the car, and sideswipes his mailbox as he backs out of the driveway. Then, without even so much as a glance in my direction, he peels off and races down the street.

I replay the last ten minutes in my head. It's like we were in an alternate universe. What he said was just… confusing. Why would he be that upset about my job and the advances Tucker gave me? Was he mad that I hadn't told him about it? And what did he mean about Tucker hiring me to sleep with him. According to Hudson, Tucker forbade a relationship between us. It makes no sense at all.

I contemplate calling Tucker. But that would be embarrassing. I'm his employee. And I'm dating his grandson. I sigh and look down the street—or, I was.

Staring at my phone, I wonder if I should text him. But then I replay his words in my head. He called me poor. Desperate. A whore. He said he never wants to see me again. If anyone should be texting, it's him—with an apology.

I go inside and pack my own suitcase, refusing to sit here and wait for him like the poor desperate girl he believes me to be. His words were harsh, reminding me of the way Wayne and Patty speak to me. They all have one thing in common: money.

Maybe it's true, the things people say about Hudson. Maybe they were right all along, that he's not one to settle down, that he'd hurt me, that he'd eventually move on. That nobody could change him. He's proven to be the guy everyone told me he was, no matter how I refused to believe it.

The whole way to the city, I sit on the train and brood over this. I never set out to change him. I never set out to do anything at all. It just happened. *We* just happened. If anything, *he* was the one lying and pretending and conning. I've done nothing wrong.

No, I have nothing to apologize for. He's the one in the wrong. And at this point, I'm not even sure I'd accept an apology after the hateful words he said.

But, oh my God, what he said—was he really coming close to proposing? How could that even be? And then to go from that to this in less than a day. What happened?

I close my eyes wondering how I can still love a man who so clearly is incapable of loving anything or anyone but himself. I was so sure. I was sure he loved me.

An hour later I show up on Heidi's doorstep. She opens the door, sees what a mess I am, and invites me inside.

Chapter Forty-three

I don't even know where I'm going. Just away. Away from her. Away from my house and the yard that shares a border with hers. Away from having to see her face. Hear her voice. Listen to her empty pleas.

I press a button on my steering wheel and call the office to leave a message on my way out of the city. "Nicole, this is Dr. McQuaid, something's come up and I'll be out of the office for a while. Tell Dr. Richards I'm taking him up on his advice to take time off. Please handle my schedule accordingly."

I reach over and turn my phone off. I don't need Dakota calling me to try and lie her way back into my good graces. She knows what she did. Fuck her. Fuck her and her kid and my grandfather.

At a stoplight, I pound my fists on the steering wheel. How could I have fallen for it? I should have known something was up. All the clues were there. The young attractive woman moving in next door. His warnings to stay away. The broken pipe and the 'perfect solution' of her moving in with me while it was fixed. I let my guard down, but I should have seen it coming. I knew Pappy would do something. I was just so sure it would have to do with my trust fund.

I should drive back to his house and call him out on it. But right now I'm so pissed, I'm afraid I'd break his old body in two. I need time to cool off. Time to get away. Away from her.

Fuck.

I can't keep her face from appearing in my mind. The look when I called her out on the money she got from Tucker. She didn't even deny it. And damn it, I feel sorry for her kid. Regardless of what I said to her, no way was that part of the ruse. He was real. And I'm one hundred percent sure he's the reason she agreed to all of it. I can't blame her for wanting to protect her son. But I sure as shit can blame her for agreeing to lie to me about everything.

This. This right here is why I don't do relationships. Who the hell needs them when all they do is come with complications? I was stupid to fall into their trap. And what the hell were they expecting? Was she thinking I'd marry her? Support her and her kid and live happily ever after? All on the basis of a lie? Would she ever have told me the real reason we met? About the manipulation that had me slowly falling for her, and the seductive tactics she pretended weren't meant for seduction at all?

But, dammit, I was sure her feelings were real. Nobody is that good an actor. Still, even if they were real, even if she ended up falling for the guy she was hired to reel in, that doesn't excuse her lies. I could never forgive her for agreeing to be a part of it. Hell, I almost expect this kind of shit from my grandfather. He's built his empire by manipulating situations to get what he wants. But I never anticipated this kind of trickery from the seemingly gentle, kind, empathetic girl next door.

I pull into a parking lot, my chest tight as if it's being squeezed by a carnival strongman. Am I having a heart attack? Breathe, Hudson. It's stress. I get out of the car and shout at the top of my lungs into the forest at the back of the empty lot. I yell at her. At Pappy. At the whole fucking world.

I thought it would make me feel better. But my chest still hurts. I put a hand to it and close my eyes, finally grasping what it is. It's my heart. It's fucking broken. She broke it. Shattered it to pieces. It might as well fall out of my body so I can stomp it into the pavement. Because one thing's for sure: I won't be needing it anymore. I'm done. With women. With love. With feelings.

Scrubbing a hand across my face, I sit on the curb, cursing repeatedly, wondering how I can both hate and love a person at the very same time.

And I vow never to be put in such a position again. Not for the rest of my miserable life.

Chapter Forty-four

Dakota

I've been crashing in Heidi's spare bedroom for two days. And the entire time, I've been waiting for Hudson to call. I was sure he would once he realized he'd gone too far. That what happened was him panicking at the thought of becoming a family. But I still can't get his words out of my head. Even if he got spooked, that's no excuse to put me down. Call me names. Label me a liar.

My phone rings and my heart pounds. It starts racing every time I hear the noise. And every time, I'm disappointed that it's not him calling to grovel and beg for my forgiveness. Forgiveness I'm not sure I'd be able to offer him.

My boss's picture appears on the screen.

"Hello, Tucker."

There is clear hesitation on his end. "Dakota. Is everything okay?"

"Sure. Why wouldn't it be?"

"Rose went by your house last night. Said all the lights were off and it was locked up tighter than a vault."

"That's because I'm staying with a friend in the city for a few days. I don't have any in-person meetings this week so I didn't think it would be a problem."

"It's not. Of course you're free to stay where you please."

"Is there something you needed?"

"No. I was just calling to make sure you and the boy were alright. I know your hearing is coming up shortly."

"Next week in fact."

"And did you provide the lawyer with the name of the private investigator I gave you?"

"I did."

"Good. I expect that will help your case."

"Thank you for everything you've done." I blow out a long breath. "Tucker…"

I almost tell him. I almost blurt out that Hudson went crazy for no reason on Sunday. That I've been sick to my stomach ever since. That I've had a hard time doing my job because my heart has been broken into a million pieces and I'm not sure all the glue in the world could put it back together. That his grandson is the bastard I'd been warned about. That he was right to warn Hudson to keep away. That I wish he'd issued *me* the same warning.

But I stay quiet. Because I need this job. I'm so close to getting Travis back. I can't do anything to jeopardize that. I thought I was close to getting even more. I thought I was close to the happily ever after that only happens in fairy tales. But fairy tales are just that—fantasies of things that don't truly happen.

"What is it, Dakota? Is there something you're not telling me? You can confide in me."

"Thank you. But I'm fine. Everything is fine."

"I'm here if you need anything. Anything. I mean that."

"You've already done so much that I could never repay."

"Nonsense. You're deserving of everything. Don't forget it."

"Thank you, Tucker. Goodbye."

"Goodbye."

I put the phone on the table, lean over and let my head slump into my hands. Then I cry. And I can't stop. I literally can't stop sobbing. It's like a spigot has opened and it won't close. I've never been much of a crier. Especially when it comes to things other than my son. I cried when Brian died, for sure. But this… this soul-crushing emptiness I feel, it's even worse than when I lost Brian. How can it be? I'd known Brian for years. Hudson was barely a blip on the radar.

Heidi puts a hand on my shoulder and I look up.

"Sorry to startle you. I knocked but you didn't hear me."

I shake my head. "I'm the one who's sorry. I've disrupted your life. I'm a sniveling idiot sitting here feeling sorry for myself. I'm not even sure why. I despise the man for what he said to me."

"There's a fine line between love and hate, Dakota. Sometimes both have to exist in order for you to know exactly how you feel."

I can't even begin to digest her words, because the sandwich she's brought with her has my stomach turning. She shoves it at me. "You have to eat."

I push it away. "Not hungry."

"When was the last time you had anything?"

"I had some fruit yesterday."

"Fruit." She looks at me like a mother scolding a child. "Fruit can't sustain a body. You need to keep up your strength. You have a pretty big deal coming up next week with the Travis hearing."

"I do. So I really need to concentrate on work so I won't feel guilty taking the day off next Tuesday. I'll eat at dinner. Promise."

"Good. Because I'm making your favorite. Turkey meatballs in red sauce with lots and lots of garlic."

"You don't have to go through the trouble, Heidi."

"Dan and I have to eat. It's no trouble. Six thirty?"

"Six thirty sounds great. Thank you."

She kisses the top of my head. "Anything for you, chica."

I spend the rest of the afternoon doing my best to concentrate on work. I have to double check my numbers constantly because my mind is anywhere but here. When five thirty rolls around, I pull up an apartment rental website. All the places in the city are expensive. And I know it's ridiculous to try and get into anything now with my court case looming. If I entered into a lease and put down a security deposit, it would drain the rest of my savings. I close the window, knowing I can't move until after things with Travis have been settled. Who knows if that will be next week, next month, or next year.

Will I have to go back to being his neighbor? Could I live in a house knowing the man I both love and hate is next door? Maybe I'll talk to Tucker eventually. Surely they have other properties in town. Yes—that's the solution. I get to keep my job, live in Calloway Creek which I love, and not have to see him.

It's a small town.

You'll see him.

You'll see him and want him and miss him and think of how things shoulda coulda woulda been.

I lie on the bed and stare at the ceiling until I hear Heidi calling me for dinner. At least I have my favorite meal to look forward to. That's something.

I make my way to the kitchen and do what I always do when my favorite dinner is percolating on the stove. I lift the lid and take a huge whiff, inhaling the overpowering smell I love so much—garlic.

I'm caught completely off guard when my mouth waters and my stomach heaves. Suddenly, I feel like I'm going to vomit. I race back to the bedroom and into the connecting bath, positioning myself right over the toilet just in time to throw up coffee and Diet Coke.

I sink down onto the floor and wipe my chin as Heidi comes up behind me. "Dakota! What's wrong?"

"The universe hates me. That's what's wrong. Oh, my God. The irony."

"What do you mean?"

"It's the garlic," I say with a heavy shake of my head. "The last time I showed such a strong aversion to it, I was pregnant with Travis."

Chapter Forty-five

The sound of kids running down the hotel hallway wakes me. I stretch my arms over my head and work the kinks out of my back. I should ask for a better mattress. You'd think the Presidential Suite would come with the Mercedes of mattresses. But no such luck.

I roll over and get my phone. Another missed call from Pappy. He's been calling all week. Fortunately, nobody knows where I am so he can't just show up on my doorstep.

My brothers keep calling as well. And my mother. I've been avoiding all of them. I responded to a text from Hunter just so they wouldn't call in the National Guard.

One person's calls I haven't had to avoid are hers. Because she hasn't called. She hasn't called, texted, or even emailed. Not one time.

And I know why. Because everything I said was true. Because she was lying. Because even if somewhere along the way her feelings became real, she knows there's no chance for a future with me, not after what she's done.

It's been six days since I took off. Six days of doing mindless shit to keep me occupied. I've gone to every Nighthawk's home game. Visited The Met. Rented a bike a few times and trekked through Central Park. I even did some stupid touristy shit. I'm running out of things to do to keep busy. I miss home. I miss my job. I miss… *her.*

But I only miss the her I thought she was. Not the her she proved to be. Not the grifter who was in it for the money.

I get up and pour coffee, scolding myself again for being so goddamn gullible.

My phone vibrates with a text. I contemplate throwing it against the wall but check the message instead.

Hunter: You should come home. Dude, half the town thinks you two eloped. The other half is convinced you dumped her.

Hawk, Holland, and Mom have sent similar texts over the past week.

Hunter: Listen, if you didn't elope and you're not with Dakota, nobody has seen her in a week. She's not here anymore.

I sit on the bed and close my eyes trying to decide if this news makes me happy or sad. I suppose it's both. It's her I've been avoiding. The thought of seeing her every day. Of watching her drink wine on her back porch. Of hearing her phone conversations with Travis. The thought of her just being a hundred feet away. It was why I couldn't be there. How could I live next to the woman I hate to the depths of my soul?

Now is when I throw something, but it's the coffee cup, not my phone. It smashes against the wall and a liquid brown trail stains its way to the floor. Because I know I also love her. My fucking heart is betraying me. It's going against all my wishes. It has me dreaming of her every night and thinking of her every day.

How can I have two opposite emotions for the same person?

Me: We didn't elope. I haven't seen her.

Hunter: That's what I thought. Whatever happened, she's obviously moved on, bro. Don't you think it's time you did too?

Me: Has Pappy moved out of Cal Creek too? Because I swear if I see his face I won't be responsible for my actions. I'm sure he hasn't bothered mentioning that he's the asshole behind all this.

Hunter: I've been where you are, Hud. Just ignore him. Eventually this whole thing will blow over.

Me: Highly doubtful. But I'm sick of living out of a hotel room. If I come back, don't tell anyone. I don't want to deal with Pappy's shit. Don't tell Mom either. I know whose side she'll take, and it won't be mine.

Hunter: Listen, I don't know what happened, but you do realize you'll have some explaining to do. The whole town will think you ran her off.

Me: I didn't. And you can take that fact to the fucking bank.

Hunter: So you'll come back?

I look out the window at the city, wondering if she's out there somewhere. And if she is, is she as broken as I am? Or is she just pissed that she couldn't get more money out of my grandfather?

I sigh long and hard.

Me: Yeah, I'll come back.

Hunter: Come over tomorrow night. We'll do drinks. Guys only.

Me: Sure. Whatever.

I set the phone down, take a shower, and pack the new clothes I accumulated over the course of the week.

~ ~ ~

Driving into Calloway Creek is different now. It doesn't feel like home anymore. Maybe it's time to move on. Find another practice to work for. Upstate maybe. It's nice up there. Then again, I'm not exactly keen on moving to another small town where everyone knows the business of everyone else. Maybe Boston would be the better option. Not the city. Definitely not the city.

I pull into my driveway. Not looking at her house is hard. It's like my eyes are drawn to it and I have to physically keep them from glancing over. From seeing if she's looking out the window like she always used to do in the mornings. Or if she's getting the mail in her pajamas as she sometimes did.

"Don't fucking look," I tell myself. "She's nothing to you." I hold steadfast and drive into the garage. Entering my house, I'm considering calling the office to tell them I'll be in later, when movement in the living room scares the shit out of me. For a second, I wonder if it's her. And for a fraction of that second, I hope it is. I hope it's her coming to explain how the whole thing was some big misunderstanding.

But on further investigation, it's not. I shake my head in disgust. "Pappy, what the hell are you doing here." Then I see he's not alone. There's a guy sitting on the couch. "And who the hell is he?"

The stranger rises and holds out a hand. "Ethan Stone."

I shake. "Well, Ethan Stone. I'm not sure why you're here with my grandfather, but as you're both trespassing, I'm going to ask you to leave."

"There are things I need to tell you, grandson."

"What?" I bite. "What more could you possibly have to tell me? I saw the file. Obviously, you know I did. And how did you know I'd be here? Hunter sold me out, didn't he?"

"Your brother did no such thing. Boy, don't you realize I know things. I knew where you were all along."

I get out my wallet and toss it on the table. "Are you tracking my credit cards?"

"It doesn't matter how I know. You need to sit down. It's evident you don't know the whole story."

"You mean the one that had you planting a woman next door to seduce me so I would fit into some mold you think all your grandkids need to fit into?"

"You're not wrong that I had a plan, Hudson. But if you kick us out, you'll never know the other half of it. You'll never know Dakota had nothing to do with it."

I laugh. "You expect me to believe that? I saw the wire transfers. You *paid* her. And you're a liar and a cheat if you think you can convince me otherwise."

"Those wire transfers were not payments. They were advances against her salary so she could pay her legal bills to get her son back."

"Sure they were." I look at this Ethan guy. "And you still haven't told me why *he's* here. You thought you needed a witness in case I tried to kill you?"

"I thought you might not believe me when I tell you what I have to tell you. Ethan's my proof. He's a private investigator. He's been working for me for many years."

"Working for you?" I scoff. "Or spying for you?"

"Hudson, sit down."

"You can't tell me what to do in my own house, Pappy."

"Fine. Stand. But believe me, when you hear what he has to say, you'll wish you were sitting."

"I'll be the judge of that."

"Did Dakota ever tell you how the two of us happened to meet?"

"I assumed when she applied for the job. But now I know that isn't true."

"You're right. It isn't. We met on the steps of the courthouse right after Travis was taken away from her. I'd never seen a woman more distraught. You could literally see her heart breaking. I took her to lunch."

"Why would you do that?"

"Well, grandson, it wasn't a coincidence that I ran into her there. I knew she was going to be there."

"You've lost me."

He motions to Ethan. "Mr. Stone, maybe you should take it from here. I'm not sure Hudson will believe it unless it comes from the horse's mouth."

Ethan stands and leans against the back of the couch. "Like your grandfather said, we've worked together for quite some time. And as a private investigator, not all cases come to a quick and easy conclusion. Some of them go cold. One of those cases happened to be one I was working on with Tucker. But I don't only work for him. I've had thousands of clients over the years. And sometimes when working a case for one client, you fall upon information that can help with another. About a year ago, that very thing happened."

Ethan looks at my grandfather. Pappy nods. "Go on, tell him."

"Last year, I was hired by an eighteen-year-old to track down her biological father. It's not the first time I've been hired to do that. I've worked on many cases involving both adoption and anonymous sperm donation." He nods to Pappy. "Ten years ago, your grandfather hired me to track down every vial of sperm you donated."

My jaw goes slack as I eye my grandfather. "You knew about that?"

"Do we need to go over this again?"

"Okay, fine." I scoff. "So you know fucking everything. And I suppose you didn't want a bunch of biological descendants out there who could come after your money."

Pappy laughs. "Actually, you're right about that. Back then, I wasn't the same man I am today. And I wasn't about to have a grandson helping populate the tri-state area."

"So they just let you walk in and buy all my jizz?"

"It's not as simple as that," Ethan says.

"Oh, I get it. You bribed them into giving it to you."

"It doesn't matter how I got my hands on them. The point is," Pappy scoffs, "you made so many donations, we weren't able to get all of them."

"Every sperm donor is assigned a number," Ethan explains. "And every vial of sperm is labeled with that number so it's traceable. There were two vials that were not accounted for. One of them I tracked to a fertility clinic in New Jersey, but the insemination failed and did not result in a child. The other one vanished."

"Vanished?"

"It's not a perfect system. The vials go from the donation center to any number of local storage facilities and then on to one of the myriad of fertility doctors in practice. So it's not uncommon for mistakes to be made. Vials get broken in transport. They fail to get scanned. Any number of things can happen. After months of investigation, I came up with nothing and the case went cold. Until a year ago. I was working for the aforementioned teen when I recognized a file with a sperm donor ID that matched your number."

I swallow hard as my brain catches up to his words. I think I know what he's going to say next, but until he says it, it's not real.

Until he says it, I can stand here in denial that some idiotic thing I did ten years ago got me into a hell of a situation today.

The room is eerily silent.

I pace the floor and Holland's words float through my head. *He's got your nose.* I scrub a hand across my jaw. "Just fucking say it."

"Five and a half years ago, Brian Daniels and his wife, Dakota, purchased the sole remaining vial of your sperm which resulted in the live birth of one Travis Daniels."

I want to throw up. I bend over, hands on my knees.

"I did mention you should be sitting down for this," Pappy says.

I stumble to the couch, drunk on information overload. I have a son. And he's Dakota's kid. And I met him. Almost hyperventilating, I try and calm my breathing as the two other men whisper to each other.

"So that's why she agreed to all this?"

Pappy sits on the chair across from me. "I told you, grandson, Dakota wasn't aware of any part of my plan. All she knows is that an empathetic old man saw her breakdown on the courthouse steps and subsequently offered her a job."

My head is spinning. "She… doesn't know?"

His head shakes from side to side. "Not a bit of it. She's not to blame, Hudson. She's just a scared single mother trying to win her son back from unscrupulous people who don't think a poor girl from rural Florida belongs in their family."

"But she knows the kid wasn't her husband's, right? She has to."

"She knows."

"She never told me."

"She never told anyone," Pappy says. "It was a sworn promise she made to her late husband, who never wanted anyone to know the child wasn't biologically his. The truth didn't come out until after Travis was taken away and she felt she had no choice. That's what's fueling her appeal. Well, that and the Daniels' lies about her extracurricular activities."

I turn to the PI. "Are you helping with her case?"

"As of last week, yes. I'm scheduled to appear as a witness at the Tuesday hearing."

"But…" I look at Pappy. "Why the elaborate scheme?"

"You needed someone to ground you. She needed a father for her son. And who better for the job than the boy's own flesh and blood?"

"You forbade me to go out with her."

"I did. I know you well, grandson."

"She knew nothing about any of this? You swear?"

"On Rose's life, I swear it."

"Have you spoken to her about this?" My heart races. "Oh, Jesus, does she know about Travis?"

"I called her the morning after I found the file folder strewn across the floor of my study. She admitted to nothing when it came to leaving. She said she was staying in the city helping a friend and working from there. But Hudson, she was clearly devastated. I can only imagine what was said after you saw the wire transfers. I'm afraid you may have your work cut out for you if you want to salvage your relationship."

"She was just a pawn in your grand scheme. Who the fuck do you think you are playing with people's lives like this? And why the hell didn't you do anything earlier? You've known for a year? Brian has been dead for *two* years. Why didn't you swoop in and help her as soon as you found out?"

"I don't like to meddle. I just kept tabs. But it came to a head when the boy was taken away. I was going to intervene then. Put my own lawyers on it. Take care of everything. But I thought of another plan. One that could benefit everyone involved. And rest assured, we've been keeping tabs on the boy and the Daniels. If it came down to it and we thought he was being mistreated, I'd have immediately come clean."

I belt out a sarcastic laugh. "You don't like to meddle? Are you fucking serious?"

"Boy, I'm a tolerant man, but it'd do you good to remember who you're talking to. Show some goddamn respect."

The unimaginable shock of the full situation slams into me but quickly becomes overshadowed by another emotion: guilt. I remember the words I said to Dakota. Horrible words. Accusations. Holy shit—I slump my head into my hands—I called her a whore.

Pulling my phone from my pocket, I look from Ethan to my grandfather. "I have to find her."

Pappy hands me a slip of paper. "Here's where she's staying."

"She gave you the address?" When he doesn't say anything, I add, "Right, you know *everything.*"

"What are you going to do when you find her?"

I shake my head, because, honestly, I don't have a damn clue. This whole thing is unbelievable. Will she even buy it? Or will she think I'm even crazier than she thought I was Sunday night on her porch?

I turn to Ethan. "Whatever your hourly rate, I'll double it if you come with me."

Out of the corner of my eye, I see Pappy smile.

"Text me the address," Ethan says. "I'll meet you there in an hour."

Chapter Forty-six

Dakota

Just after lunch, there's a knock on my bedroom door. Heidi peeks in. "You have visitors."

I glance down at what I'm wearing. I haven't gotten out of my pajamas for days. Not since I peed on the stick and read the one word that will forever change my life.

Work is the only thing keeping me sane. And luckily, it doesn't matter what I wear for that.

But I'm certainly not up for guests. Not to mention, nobody knows where I'm staying. "Who is it?"

When she doesn't answer, I know exactly who it is. "It's him isn't it? Send him away."

"I can't do that."

"Heidi, we've been best friends for years. If you want to keep that distinction, you'll get rid of him."

"Hate me if you want, Dakota, but the man was seriously begging me to let him see you. The man you've been crying about and hating on all week. The one you've told me about—he doesn't seem like a man who would beg. Yet he's refusing to leave until he sees you. Says he'll camp out in the hallway."

"He brought reinforcements? Is it Tucker?"

"I don't think so. He didn't introduce us, but the well-dressed guy with him is definitely not the old guy who called me for a reference."

"So he brought one of his brothers. As a character witness, no doubt." I close my eyes and sigh. "It doesn't matter. He could bring the Pope to vouch for him, it still won't excuse all the things he said. Things like he never wanted to see me again."

"Well, he obviously wants to see you now." She walks to the dresser and pulls out a pair of shorts and a shirt. "Get dressed. Brush your hair. I'll make coffee and then go hide in my bedroom where I'll be if you need me."

I touch my stomach. "I'm not sure I can do this, Heidi."

"Don't you at least want to hear what he has to say?"

"I think I'm going to throw up."

"Well, then be sure to brush your teeth too."

I scold her with my biting stare. "You think this is funny?"

"I think you've been devastated by this breakup, and now the very guy who you clearly love, after you never thought you'd love again, is out there demanding to see you. He looks determined. And sad. And even a little scared. And oh—news flash—this same guy is your baby daddy. And if you ask me, he's here to beg for forgiveness." She points to the hallway. "There's a billionaire out there who literally wants to sweep you off your feet. Girl, if you don't at least hear him out, you'll never forgive yourself."

"What'll I tell him about..." I look down at my belly.

"You don't have to tell him anything yet. I promise I'll be right down the hall. If things get out of hand, I'll kick them out. I'll call the police if I have to. But somehow, I think I won't have to."

"I can't believe I'm going to do this. I really thought I'd seen the last of him."

"Girl, get ready." She's practically bouncing with anticipation. I'm not sure why. After I spilled my guts to her all week, you'd think she'd be on my side, not his.

She leaves, but I don't move. I breathe deeply. I'm about to see him again—the man I both love and hate. And I'm wondering which emotion will win the war when I look at him. I vow it will be the latter one. He doesn't deserve my love, not after the things he said. There isn't anything he could say to me that would excuse his behavior.

Determined to show him he didn't break me, I change clothes and brush my hair. I even put a little blush on my cheeks so I don't look pale and washed out. Then I put on mascara so it doesn't look like I've been crying. Then I dab on a bit of eye shadow. Then lip gloss.

I stare at the stupid girl in the mirror wondering who she's trying to impress. Surely not the entitled asshole in the other room. I get it now, why Lynda painted such epithets on his garage. And I wonder if in eight months, I'll want to do the same. Only mine will be more along the lines of *Deadbeat Dad*. Because I can only imagine the words he'll have when I tell him about the baby. He'll assume it was all part of the plan to trap him.

I put a hand on the doorknob, take some deep breaths, and shore myself up. Then I walk out into the living room, determined not to let him further break me.

Before he notices me, I see him pacing the floor. Hudson McQuaid is pacing. I'm not sure I've ever seen him so unsure of himself. The man sitting on the couch is a stranger, not one of his brothers. He's dressed in business attire. Who is this guy, a lawyer? And why would Hudson bring a lawyer?

My heart stops. Is he here to sue me or something? Get back at me for the things he claimed I did? Oh, my God. Hudson is a doctor. Does he somehow know I'm pregnant? Could he tell just by looking at me? Is he here to stake his claim on the McQuaid heir and take the baby away once it's born? I try to hold down my breakfast at the thought of losing another child to a rich narcissistic millionaire.

"Why are you here?" I spit out contentiously.

Both men turn in my direction.

"Dakota." Hudson takes two steps in my direction, almost like he's going to hug me, then he thinks better of it and stops. His eyes graze over me from head to toe. "You look good. I mean, great. Beautiful as always."

Heidi puts a pot of coffee and coffee cups on the table. She winks at me on her way by. Her bedroom door shuts behind me.

"Nobody knew I was staying here. How did you find me?"

"Tucker."

"I didn't tell him where I was, just that I was staying in the city for a while."

"My grandfather has his ways."

I roll my eyes. "Clearly. Now how about you say what you came to say so I can get back to work."

"You might want to sit down."

I lean against the wall, far away from him. "I'm fine here."

He said I was beautiful. And he's looking at me differently. Certainly not the way he was looking at me on Sunday, like I was the devil reincarnate. What changed?

"We have to talk."

"I'm not sure what there is to talk about. You can't just walk in here and expect me to forget all the hurtful words and accusations."

"I can explain all that."

"I doubt it."

"No, I can. And this man is going to help me. This is Ethan Stone."

I look at the man in surprise. "Ethan Stone? As in the private investigator Tucker had me put in touch with my lawyer?"

The man stands, walks over, and offers his hand. "The very same. It's nice to meet you, Dakota."

"I guess I should thank you for helping me."

"No need. Just doing my job."

"I'm confused. Why are you here, and what do you have to do with the fight I had with Hudson?"

"It was all a huge misunderstanding," Hudson says. "My grandfather orchestrated this entire thing."

I scoff. "You're blaming Tucker for how you treated me?"

Hudson goes to the table, pours three cups of coffee and offers me one. I shake my head, refusing it.

"We were both played by my grandfather."

"Played how?"

He sits near Ethan and puts a file folder on the coffee table. "When I found this in Tucker's study, I admit I jumped to conclusions. I saw the wire transfers and assumed he was paying you to seduce me. Settle me down. Whatever. I watched him manipulate Hawk and Hunter, and I knew this was his way of doing the same to me. And the money going into your account convinced me you were in on it. But now I know you were just as much in the dark as I was. And you'll never know how sorry I am that I accused you of those things."

"What was I in the dark about?"

"He set us up. It was his plan all along to get us together."

"His plan?" I shake my head, confused.

"He hired you because of me. He moved you in next door because he wanted us to meet. He forbade me to date you because he knew in doing so, that's exactly what I would do."

I walk around the back of the couch and lean against the kitchen table, still not wanting to be any closer to him. "What you're saying makes no sense at all. I don't think you know the whole story. I didn't apply for the job, Hudson. I had no intention of leaving my old job. Tucker saw me on the steps of the courthouse after Travis was taken away. He was sympathetic. He took me for lunch. I told him my story. He felt sorry for me and later called my boss to get a reference. He hired me out of pity. He didn't hire me to find his grandson a 'girl'."

"Don't you find it suspicious? A random stranger finds you in a bad way, takes you for a meal, and suddenly you're the CPA for a Fortune 500 company? A job you didn't even apply for?"

"I was hesitant at first, but he was rich and I was poor, and what he was offering made it possible for me to file the court appeal. Of course I accepted the job."

"Show her the pictures," he says to Ethan.

Ethan pages through the folder, pulls something out, and gets off the couch to give me some photos.

I stare at pictures of Travis and me. At the park when he must have been only three. Walking down the street. Laughing in a café. The creepiness of it sends uneasy feelings crawling up my spine.

"How did you get these?" I ask Hudson.

"I took them," Ethan says. "Or rather an employee of mine did."

"You? Why? Somebody better tell me what's going on before I call the police and report you for stalking."

"My grandfather didn't just happen to see you at the courthouse that day. He knew you were going to be there. He'd been keeping tabs on you for a while."

"Keeping tabs? Is he…" I turn to Ethan. "Are you working for the Daniels?"

"Quite the opposite," Hudson says. "Tell her, Ethan."

Ethan shakes his head. "Somehow I think you should be the one, Hudson."

"Well, *someone* tell me!" I shout, more than frustrated.

Hudson's eyes soften. "Dakota, please sit down."

"You can't tell me what to do."

Hudson approaches. Part of me doesn't want him within a few feet of me. The other part, the part deep down in my soul, hopes what he's going to tell me will absolve him and he can take me in his arms and we can live happily ever after. But things like that don't happen outside of books.

"I promise you'll need to be sitting down to hear what I have to tell you." He holds out a chair for me. He leans in closer. I can't help but breathe him in. "Sweetheart, please." His desperate words flow over my ear. "This will all make sense in about two minutes."

He called me sweetheart. None of what is happening makes any sense. But I sit, anyway. Following his command like an obedient puppy.

Hudson retrieves the file folder from Ethan and sits in the chair next to me. "This is going to shock you. I just found out about it an hour ago and haven't quite wrapped my mind around it myself. It's unbelievable in the oddest of ways."

He looks from Ethan to me and swallows. He's nervous. And almost vulnerable. I can't remember a time when I saw him like this other than maybe the day his patient lost a baby.

"Ethan stumbled across something last year when he was investigating a case totally unrelated to me or you. He found…" His eyes close and open again. "He, uh…"

"What did he find, Hudson?"

He opens the folder and pulls out a piece of paper, handing it to me. I don't recognize it right away, but the more I read, I begin to understand. I look up. "This is the agreement Brian and I signed at the fertility clinic."

"You never told me Travis wasn't Brian's biological child."

"What difference would that have made?"

"No difference really, until I saw this." He pushes another piece of paper across the table.

This one has Hudson's name on it. It's dated ten years ago. Highlighted in yellow is a number. When I look closely, it's labeled 'Sperm Donor ID.'

My heart begins to race as my consciousness spins to catch up with what my brain is digesting.

Hudson points back at the first paper Brian and I signed. "Look."

My eyes go back and forth between the papers, going over the numbers once, twice, ten times. I look up at Hudson, barely able to get words out. "*You* were our sperm donor?" My hand flies up to cover my mouth. "*You're* Travis's biological father?"

Chapter Forty-seven

Dakota's hands are shaking. She looks like she might get sick. I scoot my chair closer. "Yes. It's unbelievable, I know."

"How? I mean these things are supposed to be anonymous."

I nod to Ethan. "That's where the private investigator comes in. When I was eighteen, my grandfather and I had a falling out about what college I would go to, and I sort of separated myself from the family money for a while. I donated sperm to make ends meet. What I didn't know until today is that when Tucker found out, he hired Ethan to track down every vial. He didn't want any of them being used. But some slipped through the cracks. Yours was the only one that resulted in a child."

Her breathing is ragged and unsteady as she absorbs this information. Then suddenly, she turns to Ethan. "You're testifying before the judge next week. This proves Travis isn't related to Wayne and Patty."

"And along with the sworn testimony of the witnesses interviewed by your lawyer and their PI, I'm fairly sure you'll have no problem regaining custody."

She's on the verge of tears. "I'm going to get him back."

I reach out to her. "*We're* going to get him back."

She pulls away. "Is that why you're here? To claim your son? The heir to your fortune?" She stands and moves away from me. "You're helping me get him back just so you can take him away? That makes you no better than they are."

"Jesus, no. I'm here for *you*, Dakota."

"Bullshit. You wouldn't have come if you hadn't found out this information."

"As soon as I knew you had no part in Tucker's scheme I wanted to come. I'd have come no matter who Travis's father was. I'd have come because…" I close my eyes.

"Because *what*, Hudson?"

I open my eyes and stare right into hers. "Because I fucking love you, Gator Girl. Because I love your strength and your resilience. I love that you dove right into a job you didn't think you deserved and proved to everyone you *did* belong there. I love that you took the chance because it was the only way you knew to get your kid back. I love that you love him enough to do anything for him. I love that you never saw me as a guy with money, but as a neighbor who had to earn your respect. And I swear to God, even though I've only met him twice, I knew in my soul that Travis and I had some connection. And I promise, if you'll let me, I'll love him too. I'll love both of you. I'll love you as hard as I fucking can for as long as you'll fucking let me."

Tears stream down her face. I'm just not sure if they're happy or sad ones.

Ethan clears his throat. "I'm going to take off now." He slips out the door without either of us looking his way.

We're left staring at each other. She feels it. She feels it too. *Say it. Say it back to me.*

I've never wished so hard for anything in my life.

"I thought you got spooked when Travis asked if you were going to be his dad."

My heart slows with a thud. She didn't say the words I wanted to hear. "If anything, hearing him say it showed me what I was missing in life." I take her hand, grateful she lets me. "Sweetheart, is that all you have to say after I just put it all out there?"

She sighs. Big. I don't like that sound. And I've never been so goddamn scared about what words are going to follow.

"Would you be spooked if you found out Travis was going to have a sibling?"

"I told you, all the donations were accounted for. Travis was the only one."

"That's not what I mean." She bites her lip and looks down at her stomach.

My heart races. Hell, it thunders. It all but explodes. "Are you saying…?"

"I'm pregnant. I didn't know until a few days ago. Hudson, I swear I didn't do it to trap you. I was on the pill. If anyone is at fault it's you for prescribing me one that didn't work."

I slip out of the chair and fall to my knees. I put both hands on her flat belly. I choke back tears like a blubbering idiot. "I'm going to be a father." I look up at her. "I mean… again?"

"If you want to be. I'm not expecting anything from you."

"Not expecting anything? Dakota, I want to give you the fucking world. You and Travis and this baby. I told you on Sunday that I was thinking about asking you to marry me. Look at me, I'm already on my knees. I don't have a ring, but I'm going to ask anyway. Be my wife. Together we'll get Travis back and give him the life he deserves. And this baby, I'm going to be the one to deliver him or her. I'm going to be there when she takes her first steps. When he throws his first baseball. When she walks down the aisle."

I don't know if I've stunned her into silence or scared the shit out of her.

I wipe a tear from under her eye. "Sweetheart? You okay?"

She nods and clears her throat. "I never thought it was possible."

"What? A guy like me groveling to get the woman he loves?"

"No. I never thought it was possible for a girl like me to end up living a fairy tale."

I laugh. "Well that depends on the fairy tale. *Beauty and the Beast?*"

"Hmm, maybe that fits, too, but I was thinking more like *Cinderella.*"

"Cinderella needed someone to rescue her. You, sweetheart, don't need rescuing. It's *me* who needed it."

"Tucker rescued me. If it weren't for him, none of this would have happened. So while you see him as a manipulator, I can only see him as my fairy godfather—so you see… *Cinderella.*"

"On that we can agree to disagree." I press my hand to her lower back and draw her closer. "But there is one thing you have yet to agree to. Are you going to be my fucking wife or what?"

A smile brightens her face, making her look more radiant than I've ever seen her. "On one condition."

"Anything."

"You stop cussing so much."

I laugh. "Done. I'll never utter another curse word again."

She leans in. "I didn't say ever. You can be as naughty as you want when we're alone."

For the first time in six days, my dick springs to life. "Pack your things. We're going to a hotel." I nip at her earlobe. "Right fucking now."

She squeals when I scoop her into my arms and carry her back to find her bedroom.

Heidi peeks out of her door. "Well done," she says as we pass, tears heavy in her eyes.

I put Dakota down on the bed and hover over her. "You haven't said it yet." I stare at her, my love for her burning into her eyes. She knows exactly what I want to hear. What I need to hear. What I've never wanted anyone else to say to me. "Tell me you love me, Gator Girl."

"I love you."

She doesn't taint it by using my nickname. The words are pure. They're honest.

They're fucking everything.

Chapter Forty-eight

Dakota

Hudson pulls my suitcase behind him down the street until we reach a hotel. With his other hand, he holds my hand. The smile on my face is so big it hurts.

He walks us to the front desk. "Do you have a honeymoon suite or whatever?"

"Of course. How many nights?"

"One."

"Yes, sir. That'll be—"

"I don't care how much it is." Hudson hands over a credit card. "And send up your finest bottle of champagne." He looks down at my stomach. "Make that sparkling water."

"Yes, sir. Right away."

The desk clerk hands over the key card and Hudson steers us away from the counter. He can't get to the room quick enough. He's like an impatient little boy going to his first baseball game.

The whole way up in the ornate elevator (with an actual elevator operator), I try to absorb what's happening. How my life has changed in the past hour. How staying in hotels like this will become normal. Honeymoon suites. Maseratis. Bank accounts with more money than I can imagine.

I can only hope Mr. Stone and my lawyer are right and Travis will be back with me soon. Because none of this will mean anything without him. We need to be together as a family—all four of us. Only then will I truly get my happily ever after.

The elevator doors open and Hudson steps out. But I stand there, still in a trance. "Dakota? Sweetheart?"

I blink once, twice, then hurry out behind him. "Sorry. I guess I'm having a hard time believing this is real."

"Believe it, Gator Girl. You're stuck with me."

He opens the door to our suite and I enter, walk straight into the middle, and spin around slowly. How is this my life? Before I can explore it further, he sweeps me into his arms and carries me to the bedroom.

Gently placing me on the bed, he climbs over me and hovers above my lips. "Tell me again."

I trace his stubbled jaw with my thumb. "I love you."

His eyes close. I'm amazed by how those words affect him. Surely other women have said them.

When his eyes open, they are ablaze with passion. "I love you. I swear I'm going to spend the rest of my life making you understand just how much. Do you even know what you do to me? Do you have any idea how being near you affects me? And I'm not just talking about my cock." He touches his chest. "Here. When I look at you. When I hear your voice. When I just smell you after you've left a room. It's changed me. *You've* changed me. I want to be a better person. A better man. For you. For Travis. For whoever is growing in your belly." He nuzzles into the crook of my neck. "Say you're mine. Say you'll be mine until the day we die."

Tears flow down the sides of my head. Never in my life has anyone made such declarations. This man—he's my knight in shining armor. My beacon of hope. "Until the day we die," I say, as our salty lips collide.

This kiss, it's unlike any others we've shared. It's like the seal on a promise. The window into our souls. The kiss all other kisses strive to be.

I begin to understand why I'm feeling the way I do with him right now. So… free. It's because for the first time in my life, I can be my true self. Even when I was with Brian, there was always something tainting our happiness. I had to be someone I wasn't around his family. I had to fit in. Conform to what they thought a Daniels should be. But with Hudson, he knows everything. His grandfather knows everything. The acceptance I feel. The sheer love he has for my true and genuine self; it's all amazing.

Through our clothes, his erection is pressing against my thigh, and I squirm beneath him, wanting him so badly. I put a hand between us, slip it beneath the waistband of his pants, and stroke him. He groans into my shoulder. Then he sits up, strips me naked, and stares at my stomach.

His hand comes to rest on it as he looks in complete awe. "I never truly understood it until just now. We *made* something. In there is a bundle of cells that are growing every second into our baby." He leans down and kisses my belly button. "Our fucking baby." He looks up with misty eyes. "I can't wait to see you grow bigger. To share every detail about what is happening every day of your pregnancy. To see him or her on an ultrasound. To feel my son or daughter move inside you. How did I never understand what a gift this is?"

I smile through my tears because the love he's exuding is palpable. It fills the room. I can see it. I can touch it. It surrounds me like a warm blanket. A protective bubble. I pull him to me until his lips are inches from mine. "You're the gift. And I promise to treasure you every day."

"Say that in your vows. When you marry me, say that."

"I'll say it. I'll say so much more."

"God I want you."

I arch my hips into him. "You have me."

He sheds his clothes. He tongues my nipples. Kisses my belly. Runs his fingers over my clit. All of it has me begging for more. I push him onto his back and climb over him. I trap his arms on either side of his head as he's done to me so many times. And as I sink myself down onto him, I whisper, "Mine."

Our gazes collide. We stare into each other as I slide up and down. He works his hands free and palms my breasts. They've become more sensitive, and it heightens my pleasure when he toys with my nipples. My unabashed sounds please him. It's everything I want to do—please this man. Honor him. Be with him. Because with him, anything is possible. *Everything* is possible.

I'm holding my breath at my impending climax. But at the same time, it feels as if this is the first time in my life I've really been able to breathe. It's the most incredible feeling. And as his fingers go lower and rub across my clit, I explode into waves of altered consciousness. He grunts heavily, coming right along with me as we solidify our promises. Our souls. Our future.

I collapse down next to him, and he wraps me in his arms. "Tonight is just the beginning. It's going to be like this always."

I chuckle. "You say that now, but when there are two kids in the house, we may have to control ourselves."

"Hmmm. I guess we'll have to buy a bigger house. And soundproof our bedroom."

I laugh. "I like the way you think, Doctor."

He turns me toward him. "Now I know why I've stayed in my house so long. It was you—you were the reason I stayed. If I had moved into some mansion with a huge privacy fence, this never would have worked out. I wouldn't have been able to look out my windows and see you. Hear you. Admire you. It's crazy. I'm not religious. Not even spiritual. But I swear the universe had plans."

I poke him playfully. "The universe or Tucker McQuaid?"

He laughs boisterously. "I suppose one day I'll have to thank the old bastard."

There's a knock on the door and Hudson hops out of bed, wraps a towel around his waist and answers. I roll my eyes at his boldness. But at the same time, I hope he never changes. I love the man he is. I love how protective he's become. I love how accepting he is of our situation.

He comes back in with two glasses of sparkling water, shimmies his hips until the towel drops, and climbs onto the bed. He hands me one. "To us. To getting Travis back where he belongs very soon. And to the little one we have yet to meet."

"I'll drink to that."

"Speaking of Travis. Do you have him this weekend?"

I shake my head sadly. "No."

"Good."

I'm surprised. "Good?"

"Tomorrow morning, after you've been thoroughly bedded two or three more times, we're flying to Vegas and you're going to make good on those vows."

"W-what?"

"I want to marry you before you come to your senses and change your mind."

"I'm not going to change my mind, Hudson. I love you."

"Then prove it. Fly with me to Vegas. Marry me. Become my wife this weekend."

"I… uh…" I want to say no, that it's too soon. That we have other things to deal with first. That the promise of our future is enough. But my heart has other plans. "Yes!" I blurt and throw my glass down on the bed before climbing on top of him.

We laugh and kiss and revel in things to come.

"Are we crazy?" I ask.

"Probably."

"How do you know we can even get a flight at this short notice?"

He moves me off his lap, gets his phone off the nightstand, and taps out a text. I assume he's trying to book flights. "There, it's done."

My brows go up. "It's done? You booked us already? How?"

"We're taking my grandfather's jet."

I cover my mouth. "You just booked a private jet to fly us to Las Vegas for the weekend?"

His mouth turns up into a grin. "Face it, sweetheart, you're about to become a McQuaid." He pushes me down and climbs over me. "And I'm going to spoil the shit out of you." He touches my stomach. "All of you."

Epilogue

Hudson

I'm in the first row behind the barrier in the courtroom, sitting directly behind my wife.

Wife. It still amazes me every time I think about it. I can't believe she married me. I'm still wrapping my mind around having a wife. Having kids. Us becoming a family.

But part of me is worried that, despite what Ethan Stone and Dakota's lawyer have told us, the Daniels will do something underhanded simply out of spite. They don't strike me as people who take kindly to losing.

What they don't understand, however, is neither do McQuaids. And I'll fight like hell to win back what is rightfully mine.

I haven't seen Travis since I found out he's my son. They don't allow kids that young to sit in on court proceedings. I haven't even spoken to him. Dakota called him Sunday night when we returned from Las Vegas. He was so happy to learn we had gotten married. He said he would go to bed every night and tell Charlie, his stuffed frog, that he wished for a dad.

My nerves are on edge. As Dakota sneaks a peek back at me, I can tell hers are too.

Mom pats my hand. "Everything is going to work out. I know it is."

Pappy, Rose, and all my siblings also line the front row, everyone having been brought up to speed over the past few days. I've never seen my family come together like this and rally around one another so fiercely. It makes me proud to know my kids will grow up with such love and support.

My kids. Holy shit how my life has changed.

I glare across the aisle at the enemy. Wayne sits stoically, not bothering to look in our direction. Patty glances over, her eyes perusing the many people who've come to support Dakota. She whispers to her husband who has no reaction. Patty shakes her head. Does she know they're about to be roasted on a spit and served up for dinner?

I can only hope this judge is not a close personal friend. Karl has assured us she's not. But everyone in the legal system seems to know each other. It's difficult to anticipate exactly what will happen.

The judge enters the courtroom, and we all stand. Once seated, the judge asks if there are any opening statements before the proceedings.

The Daniels' lawyer goes first, reiterating all the reasons they filed for guardianship the first time.

It makes my stomach turn, seeing Dakota painted in such a bad light. Labeled as an unfit mother and a drug user.

When it's our turn, Karl rises, gives Dakota a reassuring smile, and confidently presents his opening words. "Your Honor, we have a half-dozen witnesses who will testify to Mrs. McQuaid's character as an exemplary mother who would never put her child in harm's way."

"Excuse me, Your Honor," opposing counsel interrupts, "would counsel care to explain who Mrs. McQuaid is?"

"Certainly," Karl says. "My client, formerly known as Dakota Daniels, was married to Dr. Hudson McQuaid over the weekend." He holds up our marriage certificate. "I'm happy to enter this into evidence if it pleases the court." He glances at the other lawyer. "So as I was saying, some of these witnesses were former neighbors of Mrs. McQuaid and her late husband, Brian Daniels, and will testify they never had occasion to witness Mrs. McQuaid selling, taking, or so much as handling drugs of any kind. In fact, they will testify that she went out of her way to shield her young son from Brian Daniels' addiction."

He picks up another piece of paper. "Furthermore, we have sworn testimony that Hudson McQuaid, who has been proven to be the donor of the sperm that resulted in Travis Daniels' birth, has filed paperwork to adopt Travis Daniels. As the court is surely aware, Mr. McQuaid is a respected physician as well as the grandson of Tucker McQuaid, making him an heir to the McQuaid fortune from which Mrs. McQuaid and her son will benefit.

"I also intend to present evidence that Wayne and Patricia Daniels used their position and stature to persuade the judge of record, who should have recused himself from the case due to the nature of his relationship with the Daniels, to rule in their favor. Further, I intend to present a reluctant witness from the Department of Child and Family Services who will testify to being approached by a representative of Wayne and Patricia Daniels to 'find' reasons to open an investigation against then Dakota Daniels in exchange for a substantial sum of money. I also intend to press—"

"Excuse me, Your Honor," opposing counsel says. "I'd like a moment to confer with my clients."

"Granted," the judge says.

Dakota looks back at me, neither of us knowing what to expect. Karl grins and pats Dakota's hand, a sign I take to mean things might be about to go our way.

"May we approach the bench?" the other attorney asks after several tension-filled minutes.

Karl and the other lawyer go close to the judge. She covers the microphone while they speak in hushed tones for several more minutes.

Karl's expression says it all when he turns and resumes his seat next to Dakota. The judge then confirms what's written all over Karl's face. "The complainants are withdrawing their petition for guardianship. The case is dismissed, and Travis Daniels will be returned immediately to the custody of Mrs. McQuaid who will retain sole and lawful custody of the boy."

Our side of the courtroom erupts in cheers. Dakota belts out the most relieved cry I've ever heard then turns and falls into my arms over the partition.

The judge leaves and, as things quiet down, Wayne and Patty storm out without a word.

"Wait," Dakota calls. "Where is he?"

They don't turn around. But their lawyer comes over and shakes Karl's hand. "Travis is waiting outside with the nanny."

I look at the courtroom door. "He's right out there?" My heart thunders. My son is out there—fifty feet away. And he's coming home with us. All I want to do is run to get him. But there are people to thank first.

"Karl, Ethan, we couldn't have done this without you."

"It's a glorious day when truth and justice prevail," Karl says. "Now go on, I know you're both dying to see your son."

Dakota and I look at each other, grab hands, and race toward the door.

Before we get there, I stop and pull her back. "What if I'm a terrible father? What if he hates me? What if I can't do right by all of you?"

Dakota cradles my chin in one hand. "Babe, you were a great father even before you knew you had a son. The way you were with him that day, it's all Travis has talked about ever since. He wants this. You want this. If love is there, the rest will come."

I take her left hand and touch her wedding ring. "Oh the love is there, all right. You can bet your life on it."

"Then come on, let's go greet your son."

My heart pounds through my chest. "My son. My fucking son." She raises a brow. "Sorry."

When we push through the doors, Travis is sitting on a bench next to a woman I've never seen before. I thought for sure Patty and Wayne would be saying their goodbyes. Are they really so cruel that once they knew he wasn't their flesh and blood, they could just ignore him? It doesn't matter. He'll never be ignored again. Never made to be raised by nannies or shipped off to boarding schools.

Every fiber of my being has me wanting to scoop him up and squeeze him tightly. But I don't want to scare him. Besides, this is Dakota's moment. The one she's been waiting for for months. I stand back and allow her to have it.

He sees her, hops off the bench, and runs into her arms as she falls to her knees. "Travis, you get to come home. Finally, you get to come home. And I promise we'll never be apart again."

"Mommy, you're squeezing too hard."

"I'm sorry, baby. I just love you so much. We have a lot of hugs to make up for."

The nanny says her goodbyes and walks away, looking back as if she's the only one who will actually miss him.

Travis finally notices me. "Did you really marry my mom?"

"You bet I did, champ." We show him our rings.

"Do I get to call you Daddy?"

I swallow the lump in my throat. "I'd be honored, Travis."

"Does that mean yes?"

I laugh, forgetting that I'm talking to a not-yet-five-year-old. "That means yes."

He grasps onto my legs. I can't help myself when I lean down and pick him up, finally giving him the hug I've desired since the moment I heard he was mine. I close my eyes and savor the moment, taking it all in, committing every second to memory.

When my eyes open, Dakota is staring at me, her face wet with tears. And her smile is huge. "I get it now."

My head tilts. "Get what?"

"The best part of your job. When you see a child with his parents for the very first time. I get it."

I pull her to us and we share our first hug as a family.

Others file out of the courtroom and come by to say hello. Few of them are strangers to Travis. He met almost everyone a few weeks ago. Mom is already planning a welcome home party in his honor. Me—I just want to go home and enjoy my family.

As I set Travis down, he takes Dakota's hand and then mine, settling happily between us. He looks up at me. "Daddy?"

My whole fucking heart melts upon hearing the word. I look over to see Dakota's eyes sparkle. "Yeah?"

"Can we get a dog?"

I smile. "It'll be the first thing we do."

He smiles back, and that's the moment I see it. I see my own face in him. He *does* have my nose. He has my smile. He has my *everything*.

"Daddy?"

I get the idea he's going to be using that word a lot. And I also get the feeling I'm going to love it.

"Mmm?"

"Can we go home now?"

I squeeze his hand. "Yes, son. Yes we can."

We walk out the courthouse doors, Dakota and I eyeing each other, both of us knowing we're leaving one world behind and entering another. The one we both dreamed of but never thought possible. The one I didn't even know I wanted until the girl with the flat bike tire moved in next door and turned mine upside down. The world I vow to cherish every goddamn day for the rest of my life.

Acknowledgements

I now have EIGHT complete series and three standalone novels. Twenty-seven books in all. If you'd told me back in 2014 when I started this journey that this was where I'd be today, I'd have called you crazy.

Thank you, dear readers, for loving my books so much and giving me the inspiration to continue.

I couldn't have done any of this without the help of my amazing support team.

Shauna Salley, Joelle Yates, Laura Conley, and Ann Peters—you are the best beta readers a writer could ask for. I'm forever grateful.

My sincere appreciation goes out to Kimberly Kernek, M.D. FACOG (fellow of the American college of obstetrics and gynecology). Kimberly is my go-to gal for all things OB/GYN.

Thank you to my editor, Michelle Fewer, who works her ass off to meet my (sometimes impossible) deadlines.

To my PA, Julie Collier, who is also my alpha reader, friend, and cheerleader. You take so much off my plate giving me more time to write, which is my happy place.

On to the next…

About the author

Samantha Christy's passion for writing started long before her first novel was published. Graduating from the University of Nebraska with a degree in Criminal Justice, she held the title of Computer Systems Analyst for The Supreme Court of Wisconsin and several major universities around the United States. Raised mainly in Indianapolis, she holds the Midwest and its homegrown values dear to her heart and upon the birth of her third child devoted herself to raising her family full time. While it took time to get from there to here, writing has remained her utmost passion and being a stay-at-home mom facilitated her ability to follow that dream. When she is not writing, she keeps busy cruising to every Caribbean island where ships sail. Samantha Christy currently resides in St. Augustine, Florida with her husband and four children.

You can reach Samantha Christy at any of these wonderful places:

Website: www.samanthachristy.com

Facebook: https://www.facebook.com/SamanthaChristyAuthor

Instagram: @authorsamanthachristy

E-mail: samanthachristy@comcast.net